"Cat is a great heroine with a lot of spirit that readers will enjoy solving the mystery (with)."
—*Parkersburg News & Sentinel*

## SCONED TO DEATH
"The most intriguing aspect of this story is the writers' retreat itself. Although the writers themselves are not suspect, they add freshness and new relationships to the series. Fans of Lucy Arlington's 'Novel Idea' mysteries may want to enter the writing world from another angle."
—*Library Journal*

## OF MURDER AND MEN
"A Colorado widow discovers that everything she knew about her husband's death is wrong... Interesting plot and quirky characters."
—*Kirkus Reviews*

## A STORY TO KILL
"Well-crafted... Cat and crew prove to be engaging characters and Cahoon does a stellar job of keeping them—and the reader—guessing."
—*Mystery Scene*

"Lynn Cahoon has hit the golden trifecta—Murder, intrigue, and a really hot handyman. Better get your flashlight handy, *A Story to Kill* will keep you reading all night."
—Laura Bradford, author of the Amish Mysteries

## TOURIST TRAP MYSTERIES
"Lynn Cahoon's popular Tourist Trap series is set all around the charming coastal town of South Cove, California, but the heroine Jill Gardner owns a delightful bookstore/coffee shop so a lot of the scenes take place there. This is one of my go-to cozy mystery series, bookish or not, and I'm always eager to get my hands on the next book!"
—*Hope By the Book*

# Books by Lynn Cahoon

## The Tourist Trap Mystery Series
Guidebook to Murder * Mission to Murder * If the Shoe Kills * Dressed to Kill * Killer Run * Murder on Wheels * Tea Cups and Carnage * Hospitality and Homicide * Killer Party * Memories and Murder * Murder in Waiting * Picture Perfect Frame * Wedding Bell Blues * A Vacation to Die For * Songs of Wine and Murder * Olive You to Death * Vows of Murder

## Novellas
Rockets' Dead Glare * A Deadly Brew * Santa Puppy * Corned Beef and Casualties * Mother's Day Mayhem * A Very Mummy Holiday * Murder in a Tourist Town

## The Kitchen Witch Mystery Series
One Poison Pie * Two Wicked Desserts * Three Tainted Teas * Four Charming Spells * Five Furry Familiars * Six Stunning Sirens * Seven Secret Spellcasters

## Novellas
Chili Cauldron Curse * Murder 101 * Have a Holly, Haunted Holiday * Two Christmas Mittens

## The Cat Latimer Mystery Series
A Story to Kill * Fatality by Firelight * Of Murder and Men * Slay in Character * Sconed to Death * A Field Guide to Homicide

## The Farm to Fork Mystery Series
Who Moved My Goat Cheese? * Killer Green Tomatoes * One Potato, Two Potato, Dead * Deep Fried Revenge * Killer Comfort Food * A Fatal Family Feast

**Novellas**
Have a Deadly New Year * Penned In * A Pumpkin Spice Killing * A
Basketful of Murder

**The Survivors' Book Club Mystery Series**
Tuesday Night Survivors' Club * Secrets in the Stacks * Death in the
Romance Aisle * Reading Between the Lies

# Vows of Murder

*A Tourist Trap Mystery*

## Lynn Cahoon

**Lyrical Press**
Kensington Publishing Corp.
www.kensingtonbooks.comLyrical Press

LYRICAL PRESS books are published by

Kensington Publishing Corp.
900 Third Avenue, 26th Floor
New York, NY 10022

Special book excerpts or customized printings can also be created to fit specific needs. For details, write or phone the office of the Kensington Sales Manager: Kensington Publishing Corp., 119 West 40th Street, New York, NY 10018. Attn. Sales Department. Phone: 1-800-221-2647.

Lyrical Press and Lyrical Press eBooks logo Reg. U.S. Pat. & TM Off.

First Electronic Edition: February 2025
ISBN: 978-1-5161-1174-9 (ebook)
First Print Edition: February 2025
ISBN: 978-1-5161-1175-6

150189379

*To my Eastern Tennessee mountain friends. Thanks for pulling me away from my desk now and then so I can see the sky.*

# Chapter 1

The January business-to-business meeting agenda for South Cove, California, was pretty light. I had volunteered to run the meeting since Darla Taylor, our chairman and owner of the South Cove Winery, was on vacation this week with her boyfriend. I looked down at the list of things we still needed to cover in the last thirty minutes before people would abandon the meeting to open their businesses. I didn't blame them. My staff members, Judith Dame and Deek Kerr, were both busy helping customers who were wandering through the bookstore and lining up for coffee to get them through a busy day of shopping. Everyone was looking for a magic bullet or perfect system to reframe their New Year's resolutions.

"The city council wants to let you know that next year, they're closing Main Street the weekend of Thanksgiving through New Year's Day. It's to protect Santa's workshop. There have been complaints that cars have been parking where Santa's sleigh and reindeer are supposed to park." I looked around the room. "They say it's a safety hazard. This isn't up for debate here. If you want to complain, call city hall."

My best friend, Amy Newman-Cross, gave me a dirty look. She would probably be the one fielding those calls. "Call your city council reps instead. I'm sure they'd love to hear from you. And besides, they'll probably forget to make the change before next Christmas."

"Closing Main Street makes it hard for people to carry big-ticket items from your store to their cars," Josh Thomas stated. He ran Antiques by Thomas next door to my bookstore. "I suppose *you* expect everyone to provide delivery service?"

"Not me. The council put this out. I'm just reading what they sent me. Besides, your customers can park behind your store and pick up large items in the alley," I pointed out. Josh always wanted to complain without looking for an alternative. "Anyway, there are a few more items, but they're related to the winter festival at the end of the month, so I'll have Darla send out an email next week. Don't ignore it, please. One more thing. If you haven't received your invitation yet, Greg King and I are getting married next Sunday at the La Purísima Mission at three p.m. sharp. Afterward, we'll have a reception on the grounds as well. Hopefully, the weather will hold out for as long as the band wants to play."

Yep, we were finally getting married. The ceremony had been scheduled for June, October, and now January. I just needed Greg's mom to feel well enough to make the trip this month. If not, we were still getting married. Come hell or high water, as my aunt always said. Maybe saying it aloud was tempting disaster.

"The mission site will be lovely," added Matty Leaven, the owner of the newest business to South Cove, a jewelry shop. "My husband and I went there just last week to walk around. Of course, we didn't see the ghost, but it was early. Hopefully, he'll show up for your festivities. His appearance is supposed to be a blessing."

"Hopefully not," Amy murmured.

Matty turned her head and glared at my friend.

Before she could say anything, I jumped in. "Unless there is anything else?"

Kane Matthews stood and held up a hand. Kane was another new arrival to town. His tall stature, dark hair, and piercing eyes made an impression. Even in a boring meeting. He scanned the room. "I'm sorry to delay closing, but I wanted to invite everyone to our open house at New Hope on Friday. We still have all our holiday decorations up and would love to have our neighbors come and see our new home."

The Central California Society for the Advancement of the Mind and Body was a new addition to our town. CCSAMB, or C-scam, as most locals called it, was a group of more than a hundred people who lived on a converted ranch outside of town. They also went by New Hope. Which was much easier to remember. The first thing the group had done when they'd purchased the property was put a stone wall all around the hundred acres. Then they'd added a black gate and guardhouse that was staffed twenty-four seven. Before they'd registered with the city as a religious organization, the townsfolk had assumed that a celebrity from Hollywood was moving onto the property.

Instead, now we had our own cult, New Hope. Greg hated it when I called Kane's organization a cult, but it seemed like the description fit. The women who visited town wore their hair long and in braids or pulled back in a bun. They were always in modest dresses, no pants. And the men wore jeans and button-down shirts. Some wore suits, and I'd seen gun harnesses underneath the expensive jackets. And they had earbuds connected to a wire that ran into their suit jackets. Kane did as well. No religious order I knew had that level of security on their leader. Except maybe the pope. And he didn't live in a small California coastal community.

The guards surrounded Kane every time he left the property. In fact, two men in suits sat outside the bookstore right now, waiting for their leader to appear. I suspected at least one of the guards was watching the back of the building.

I didn't know what Kane Matthews had done in the past, but clearly, he thought he was a target now. Which made me question his New Hope organization and its sunshiny *Make Your Life A Masterpiece* motto even more.

Today Kane wore an expensive black suit with a purple dress shirt and no tie. He wore a variation of that outfit every time I saw him in town. Or riding in his black Hummer.

The one good thing for me and the bookstore was that the residents of the compound bought a lot of books. Reading must be an approved activity.

I realized Kane had stopped talking while I thought about his cult. I faked a smile. "Oh, how fun. Will there be open house hours?"

He smiled at me, and I felt a chill running through my body. Maybe some women found him attractive, but I never had. He looked cold and mean. "Of course. The gates will be open from eight to eight. I do hope you all will come by. The rumor that we are some sort of cult has been circulating in our lovely town. We want to show you all that we're good neighbors."

I hoped I wasn't blushing since I'd just been thinking that. I scanned the table, but no one else seemed to want to make an announcement. "Okay then, let's call an end to the monthly meeting. You'll be getting an email from Darla regarding the winter festival. Please read and respond. And I'll see you all next month unless I see you before."

"I'm not sure 'winter festival' is an appropriate name based on the lack of snow," Kane said to the person next to him.

"Okay, we'll see you all later." I ignored the comment. I wasn't going to get into a discussion of Darla's favorite festival without her here to defend it. Besides, festivals brought in tourists who bought stuff. Kane's group wasn't even a business, so I didn't understand why he attended our meetings. The mayor originally had invited him just to meet the group. Of course, the mayor rarely attended the meetings. A fact that pleased me to no end. I banged the gavel and people started fleeing the store.

Kane Matthews looked around the now almost-empty table and smiled. "I guess I'll have to fight that battle next year."

After he'd left, Amy started helping me move tables back to the dining room setup. "He's so creepy. I can't believe you stood up to him. Now if you disappear, at least I'll know the first place to look. That ranch of theirs. But with so many acres, I'm not sure we'll ever find your body."

"Stop it. They're nice people. At least, the women who come into town to shop are nice. He's just a little off. Maybe it's the mantle of leadership that has him up in everyone's faces." I was trying to be welcoming.

"I heard Kane and Pastor Bill got into it Sunday after services at Diamond Lille's. The guy came over and challenged Pastor Bill's beliefs, if the story I heard was true." Amy moved to another table. "Did Sadie say anything?"

"No, but I haven't seen her this week. Since Aunt Jackie retired, I'm only working the morning shifts on Thursday through Sunday—a schedule Greg doesn't understand. He wants me to work Tuesday through Thursday. That way our weekends are free." We'd had the discussion again this morning before I'd come in for the meeting.

"Like Greg ever takes a weekend off," Amy said, supporting exactly what I'd told him during our last discussion. Amy and I had been friends for a long time.

"Being gone on the weekends makes it hard to plan for festivals and impossible to take out the food truck." I was pretty sure Greg was just grumpy about his mom and her health. She'd had a hard year. Hopefully, now she was in full remission and he could relax a little. When we put off the wedding in October, it was due to her inability to travel. The wedding was beginning to feel like something we had to do rather than something we wanted to do. Weddings could be stressful. One more delay and I was voting for a run to Vegas. "Anyway, I told him we could revisit my schedule after we got back from the honeymoon."

"A week in Hawaii on the beach. I'm jealous." Amy glanced around the dining room. Judith and Deek had jumped in to help as soon as the meeting adjourned, so we were already done.

"Don't be jealous yet. He's being cagey about where we're going. I'm thinking we're probably going to Alaska or Antarctica rather than Hawaii." I went over to the counter and refilled my coffee. "Is it too early for lunch?"

"Yes. It's only ten. I can't get away today anyway. Mayor Baylor has me working up a new PR campaign to bring more retreat groups to South Cove. He thinks that maybe Kane's group will allow the town to host a yoga retreat or something out at the compound."

"Is that what he's been working on?" That made a little more sense than inviting a group with religious tax exemptions to the area. "If they host a retreat, they'll have to pay taxes, right?"

"Or at least our tourist counts will increase in the off months." Amy grabbed her purse. "I think the mayor's in bed with the devil, but it wouldn't be the first time."

Amy was right about that. Our mayor had a habit of supporting big developments for the sake of lining his pockets. Whether or not the town wanted the new business. He'd tried to get me to sell my house and property for years. Almost since I moved here.

My phone buzzed with a calendar reminder. I had the final fittings on my dress in Santa Barbara at noon. It would take at least an hour to get there. I'd take a book and eat lunch at my favorite Mexican restaurant after the fitting. Or maybe I'd be on carrots and water until after the wedding. It all came down how the fitting went.

I grabbed my tote and said goodbye to my staff. Deek held up his hand, so I stopped by where he was stocking books. "Do you need me?"

"Your aura is a funky orange today. Did you and the dude fight?" Deek Kerr was the son of a fortune teller. He thought he read auras. Or maybe he did read auras and I was just a nonbeliever.

"We're fine. Greg's just a little freaked out about the upcoming wedding." Greg had been worried about something else. He hadn't talked about it, but Esmeralda had let it slip. He was being courted for a job by a state law enforcement agency. He'd always said he'd never leave South Cove, but I thought this position might be tempting him. I'd made him a resume last night and had planned on giving it to him this morning. Now, I'd just have to send it to him. He needed to review it and see if there was any work experience missing and if the dates were right. I'd heard that the agency was a stickler for absolute accuracy in the application process. "I'm hoping by the end of the month, he'll be back to normal."

Deek set down the book he'd been shelving. "Orange is a serious color for you. Maybe you should chat with my mom or Esmeralda. Sometimes having a professional's take on life helps."

Professional? Rory Kerr and Esmeralda DeClair were fortune tellers, not mental health counselors or even life coaches. I shook my head. "I'm not much into taking advice from the beyond. Anyway, I need to go."

When I moved to open the front door, a woman came inside, holding a stack of flyers.

"Excuse me, have you seen this girl?" The woman thrust a flyer into my hand. "It's her senior picture. She went to Cal Poly in September, just down the road. She didn't come home for Christmas, but she said she was skiing with friends. Then I went to her dorm last week and found out she's been gone since October. Following this Reverend Matthews. I hear they have a church here. A place called New Hope."

The picture was of a typical blond-haired, blue-eyed California girl. She grinned at the camera like she had her life in order and a plan to conquer the future.

I didn't recognize the girl, but only a few of Matthews's followers came into town. A few of the men drove a van into town once a week to pick up mail, deliver their crafts to the shops that let them sell on commission, and drop by the bookstore. I'd heard from others that they did their food and supply shopping in Bakerstown. I felt lucky that they came to South Cove to buy books, at least.

I tried to hand the flyer back, but the woman shook her head. "Keep it. Maybe you'll see her. Her name's Carolyn. But she likes going by Carlie. She was studying engineering. And she worked so hard to get admitted to the school. I don't understand what she's thinking."

"I haven't seen her, but Deek will put the flyer up on our community board." I handed my crumpled flyer to Deek, who looked up after seeing the picture and shook his head.

"Sorry, I haven't seen her either. I'll take another one for my writers' group. Maybe someone has seen her around." Deek held out his hand for a second flyer.

"Bless you. It's just the two of us after her dad died last year. I thought she just needed some time at school." The woman was sobbing now.

"Deek, why don't you get—" I turned to look at the woman. "Sorry, I didn't get your name."

"Molly. Molly Cordon." She sank into a chair at a table. "I'm so tired."

"What do you want to drink, on the house?" Deek listed off all the coffee drinks with a little flair.

I smiled at him and left Molly Cordon in good hands. Getting a free coffee and some friendly attention from Deek wouldn't bring back her daughter or solve the mystery of why she disappeared, but it might just brighten her day for a few minutes.

Walking home, I noticed the flyers in the windows of all the local businesses. If Carlie was living with Kane's cult, he wouldn't be too happy when he came back into town and saw them posted. But keeping him happy wasn't my problem. I felt for the woman sitting in my coffee shop right now. No one should be faced with losing a child and not knowing why.

Josh Thomas was sweeping the sidewalk in front of his antiques store. His wife, Mandy, now worked for him along with his longtime assistant, Kyle. I'd seen a softer touch in the store's decorations since their marriage. And if my unscientific count of increased customers was correct, adding her to the business had been a good thing. He picked up one of the flyers that someone must have dropped. "Did you see this?"

I nodded. "Her mom's in my bookstore right now. She looks like she needs a good month of sleep."

"I know the feeling." He glanced over at the bookstore windows. "I can't imagine having your child go missing."

I thought that out of everyone in town, Josh was the one person who *could* imagine it, since Mandy had disappeared before their wedding. I didn't bring up the past, as I knew it was still painful. "Hopefully, she'll be able to make contact with her. If Carlie's in the—" I almost slipped and said cult, "—at the New Hope compound, I hope someone will see this and have her call her mom."

"I hope it's that easy." Josh took the flyer and his broom back inside his shop.

"Me too," I muttered under my breath. I needed to get home and get the Jeep so I could get to my fitting. Then, maybe later this afternoon, I could take Emma for a run. As long as nothing else slowed me down.

As I hurried down the hill to my house, I saw a slight woman slowly walking up the hill. She had short salt-and-pepper hair and was wearing a pink T-shirt. When she saw me, her face filled with a large grin.

"Jill, I'm so glad to see you. I just got in a few minutes ago and left the rental car at the house. I thought I'd walk up and surprise Greg at work. If he's there." Amanda King, Greg's mom, had finally arrived for our wedding. A week earlier than we'd expected her.

I might not make my fitting today.

# Chapter 2

Amanda and I did make my fitting that day. I thought maybe she'd be tired from traveling, but we had a great drive and lunch at one of my favorite seafood restaurants while we were in Santa Barbara. I called Deek to cover my shifts for the rest of the week. I was on vacation. As much as any business owner could be on vacation. I still checked in, but things were calm.

On Friday, Amanda and I decided to drive to the New Hope compound and check out the open house. Amanda King hadn't been my biggest fan at first. She'd sided with Jim, Greg's brother, in the Sherry camp for the first few years of our relationship. Sherry King had been Greg's first wife and everything I wasn't. She was glamorous even on the days she stayed home. She loved fashion. I liked watching *Project Runway*, but I didn't shop at designer stores. Sherry had opened Vintage Duds, an upscale vintage clothing store, in South Cove with her best friend, Pat Williams. But Sherry moved away a few years ago to a condo on the beach near San Diego and married the guy who'd promised her the world. Pat still owned the store, and now that Sherry was gone, Pat and I had a friendly relationship. I'd heard rumors that Sherry wasn't happy with this new guy, but so far, she hadn't returned to South Cove.

Amanda was examining a map she'd brought with her, marking off places she'd seen and those she still wanted to visit. We'd already scratched off three must-see spots from her list, including the elephant seals and the road James Dean was killed on. With the wedding hanging over my head, I thought I was doing an amazing job as a tour guide.

As we drove toward the compound on Highway One, skirting the ocean, Amanda sighed. "I can't believe how beautiful it is here. Sherry always put me up in a hotel in Santa Barbara and we hung out there when I visited. We didn't come into South Cove at all. Of course, Greg was usually working, like he is now."

I couldn't tell if the comment was a dig at me for not having her stay in a nice hotel or at Greg for working all the time. "Greg takes his job seriously. He's in charge of the entire police station, including staffing and working with the town. And he's getting ready for the wedding, so he can't take time off now. The nice thing is he's just working his normal hours, so he's home for dinner with us. You should be here when he's in the middle of an investigation. Sometimes I don't see him for days."

"Oh dear." Amanda looked over at me. "I sounded like I was complaining. I know Greg has to work. That boy has always been the one to take care of everyone. I'm just glad I'm here for your big day next week. Where are we going this morning again?"

"The New Hope compound. They're having an open house for the town today." I explained their name and mission statement as I understood it. "I've heard the compound is beautiful."

"So they're a religious organization?" Amanda leaned forward as we pulled up to the gates. Men in suits were meeting each car before they sent them into the compound. "Seems like a lot of security for a church."

I didn't disagree. I couldn't be sure, but I thought I saw someone taking pictures of the license plates of each car that drove through. I pulled the Jeep up to the man with a clipboard. "We're here for the open house?"

"Can I see your driver's license, please?" the man asked, not looking at me. "Excuse me?"

"Your driver's license. The open house is limited to residents of South Cove and their guests. It's just a safeguard. We've had issues with nonbelievers trying to break in and cause problems." Now the man looked at me. He smiled, but the emotion didn't hit his eyes. He was cold as ice. "I'm sure you understand."

I dug out my driver's license and handed it to him. We weren't getting in without me agreeing to it. One more reason I didn't trust Matthews or his crew. He didn't trust anyone. "Here you go."

He looked at the name, then checked off something on his clipboard. "Thank you, Ms. Gardner. Is your significant other joining us today? Reverend Matthews would love to chat with him."

"Detective King is working, but he said he might try to break away from his desk later to visit." I glanced at Amanda, who was watching the exchange. "And your guest? Can I get her name?" He smiled that same cold smile at Amanda.

"I'm Amanda King. Detective King's mother." She narrowed her eyes. "Do you want a birth certificate or a vial of blood?"

The guard wrote her name down by mine. He handed me back my license. "That won't be necessary. Please enjoy your tour."

I glanced behind us as we went through the gates and saw another man checking his phone to see if the photo he'd just taken of my plates had turned out. A third man pointed the way to a parking lot. As we followed his directions, I saw another guard standing with Molly Cordon off to the side. She was pointing at the buildings and yelling something.

"Did that woman just climb the fence?" Amanda turned in her seat to watch as we drove past the argument. The guard realized people were watching, so he took Molly's arm and walked her back to the guardhouse. I kept an eye on them in my rearview mirror as they turned the corner and disappeared from view.

"I think she did." I pulled into a spot and turned off the engine. "That was weird."

"You all are very detailed in your security systems out here." Amanda got her purse off the floor and nodded to more men in suits near the walkway. "I've counted ten guards so far and we haven't even been near the silver."

I snorted as we got out of the Jeep. I locked it, glad I'd put the top back on last weekend before Amanda showed up. "Well, let's go see what they are hiding in Fort Knox."

"I don't think they're going to show us that part of the compound." Amanda took my arm as we walked up the pathway. We passed another guard, his arms folded and an earbud in his ear. "What a beautiful day to be outside. The landscaping is so well maintained. It takes a lot of love to have grounds like this."

The guard smirked as we walked by.

After we'd gotten out of earshot, Amanda looked at me. "I believe this is going to be a very entertaining and informative visit."

Up ahead, the pathway divided into three different directions. A paper sign that read OPEN HOUSE, THIS WAY had been taped over the permanent wooden sign. The wooden sign indicated that we were heading to the meetinghouse. The other two paths were to the women's dormitories to the left, and the men's to the right.

"Apparently there are no family units here. I wonder if they have more than one complex." Amanda slowed down a little and I glanced over to see if she was okay. She'd gone through two sessions of cancer treatment in the last two years. She was in remission, but her body was severely weakened from the poisonous treatments that hopefully killed the cancer. She nodded. "I'm fine, it's just a bit of a walk from the car."

I glanced around and saw a bench near where the path divided. "Let's sit a moment and enjoy the flowers."

She let me lead her over to the bench and sank onto it. "Sorry, I get tired easily. But I am determined to keep building my endurance. I want to dance all night at your reception."

"I'm glad you came out early." It had been a bit of a shock, but it had been nice to get to know Amanda a little more before I became part of the family.

"After you put off the wedding twice, I didn't want anything I was going through to affect this date. If I fall here, the hospital is nearby. I can get a day pass to attend the ceremony." She patted my arm. "You look like I just scared you. I'm joking."

Except I knew she wasn't. My phone rang as we were sitting. "Hold on a second, it's Greg."

When I answered the phone, he didn't even waste time on a greeting. "What are you doing?"

"Your mom and I are at the open house for New Hope. I'm sure I told you about it last night." I could hear the anger in his voice. Had he expected us to be home? "What's wrong?"

"No, not where are you. Why did you send me this resume?" He was talking about the email I'd sent over that morning.

I had been going to give it to him last night, but I'd forgotten. "Oh, sorry, I misunderstood. That's for the state position you've been talking about. I think I have all the dates and jobs right, but you need to review it. Especially since they are such sticklers for accuracy."

"I never asked you to do this." He didn't sound happy.

From the tone of his voice, I was missing something big. "I know. I was just being helpful. I know this is a big step."

Amanda was looking at emails on her phone, trying not to listen to the conversation. And failing.

"Stay out of my career. If I wanted your help, I would have asked for it. Besides, your dates are wrong on the South Cove job," he muttered, clearly reading the resume.

"I just wanted to help." I tried to explain, but he cut me off.

"Jill, this is important. Don't mess with my career. You have your bookstore to look after. I'm a big boy and can make my own decisions."

I started to tell him that I knew that, but the line had gone dead. He'd terminated the call. I put the phone back into my purse.

"Everything okay?" Amanda asked from beside me.

I stood and smiled, probably looking like those guards had when they'd smiled at us. "I'm fine. Greg's fine." I added to myself, *We're fine*. I just hoped that was true. I hadn't heard Greg that mad for a long time. Something I'd done had triggered this reaction and I still didn't know what or why. Maybe this was the orange that Deek had seen in my aura on Tuesday.

The meetinghouse was a log structure. It had tall ceilings and tons of windows. One wall looked out over the ocean. The building had been built on a hill, so you could see for miles. I would bet you could even see whales in the distance. The large foyer had handouts on a table and a large library on one side of the room. I wandered over to the library as Amanda went to find a restroom. Now that I was alone, I thought about calling Greg back, but I decided to let him cool down a bit before I delved deeper. We could talk later.

The library had a variety of books, from philosophy to memoirs to current fiction titles. The lower shelf on each bookcase was filled with children's books. It was mostly secular, but there were a few shelves of books on world religions. There were more versions of the Bible than I even knew existed. King James, NIV, and others focused on women's studies or teens or even kids.

"My favorite is the Bible comparing Greek to the King James version. It brings us much closer to the original meaning that the authors had for the books as they were written. It's huge, but so worth the read." Kane Matthews stopped beside me, then pulled out a book and opened it to a random page to show me. He'd come up behind me without me noticing. "It's all about the context, where an author's coming from, don't you think?"

I didn't look at the book. Instead, I turned to meet Kane's gaze directly. "I think it's always about context. Words can mean so many different things. You have to have the context to be able to correctly interpret any work."

He smiled and nodded, reshelving the book as he did. "Now, there's something you and I agree on. I didn't think it was possible."

"You have a lovely library." He somehow looked softer today. Maybe it was the shared affiliation to books that was helping. I nodded to the shelves. "I'm surprised your flock even needs to buy new books from my shop."

"There's always room for another book." His eyes twinkled for a second. "To read a story that someone created out of thin air? Now that's a blessing. You must feel that way about books. You sell them for a living."

"Authors do have a type of magic. Some call it the muse, others inspiration. The good ones, anyway. They can spin a tale with just a few starting points." She nodded to the great room they were in. "This building is beautiful. Do you only use it for services?"

He pointed to a door hidden between two shelves of books. "That's the way to my office and the restrooms. I spend most of my time there during the day. Preparing my sermons, what I like to call my talks. Reading spiritual texts."

"Oh, so it's an administrative building?" It definitely would be amazing to work here.

"No, this building is where we live, most days. There are a few offices, like mine, carved out of the space here. On normal days, people are here studying, working, and, of course, eating. The dorms are for sleeping or when you need some time to yourself." He pulled out another book and pressed it into my hands. "I want to give you something. I feel like we aren't communicating well. This book explains a lot of our beliefs."

I glanced down at the book, titled *The Four Agreements*. "You don't have to give this to me. I can order a copy for myself. If I don't have it currently in stock."

"I've made notes in this one. I think you'll find it most interesting." He glanced over at the door, then tucked the book into my tote. "I won't let you leave without it."

"Okay, then." I tried to follow his gaze, but he turned me away from the door. This was getting weird. I was beginning to regret coming. "I'll read it and let you know what I think at the next business-to-business meeting."

"That would be lovely. I look forward to talking with you about the contents." He took me by the arm and led me over to where a table had been set up for refreshments. "Have you tried any of our delectables? The goat cheese is made on-site. And of course, all our breads and sweets are made here in our bakery."

"I'll have to try some." I glanced around the room to see if I could find Amanda. I wanted an excuse to end this conversation.

"You sell bakery items in your shop. Maybe you'd be interested in talking about switching your supplier." He stepped closer and handed me a business card. "I'm sure we can beat the prices you're paying."

"I have a relationship with Pies on the Fly. I probably won't be needing another supplier." To be truthful, even if the New Hope product was cheaper, I wasn't going to switch. Sadie Michaels, the owner of Pies on the Fly, was one of my best friends. The only way I'd need a new supplier was if Sadie closed her bakery.

"That's unfortunate. I know Diamond Lille's is considering taking on our business." He smiled and tapped the card. "Keep that handy. You may find you need our products sooner or later."

He walked away and greeted someone else. It had all been a sales job. I should have known. I bet the book talked about their bakery products too. I felt a hand touch my arm and I jumped. Amanda stood next to me, her eyes wide. "Are you okay?"

"Sorry, just a little edgy. Let's continue our tour." We moved past the treats. Women were standing with trays, waiting for people to take a cookie or other sample. They didn't say anything, just smiled. I scanned the group to see if the missing girl, Carlie, was part of the welcoming committee, but she wasn't there. I wondered if Reverend Matthews had seen the missing person posters all over town.

I didn't take anything, even though the chocolate mini pie looked so good. It was the principle. I didn't want Kane to see me eating one. We walked into the chapel and stood to the side. The stage in front was huge and had a television screen to match. They could watch movies here. Instead of pews, there were couches lined up in the room. The first two rows were all recliner chairs. Apparently, these were available for the most important worshippers.

There was a video running on the large screen. People singing in what appeared to be a choir, but the songs, though uplifting, weren't hymns. They were pop standards from the oldies station. The pictures showed parishioners working in the meetinghouse. Chatting, and talking over dinners, and some were praying, eyes closed in their place on the couches.

On the screen, Kane took the stage and started talking. The sermon was on personal responsibility. Being true to your word. He was magnetic. The camera panned over the audience, their eyes closed and heads lifted up.

I could see that other visitors were listening to Kane's words and nodding along. I wondered if they even knew they were doing it. The man could sell ice cream to Alaskans.

An elbow dug into my side and Amanda leaned close. "Do you think they're praying or sleeping?"

I swallowed a giggle and we moved on. When we walked through the next door, we found ourselves outside in a backyard, surrounded by buildings. A playground was to the side, by what appeared to be the women's dormitories. Although there were several women members standing and helping with water or sodas, there were no children out there. Guards stood around the yard watching as people came and went from the area.

A man greeted the group that had just left the meetinghouse. "This is our communal yard. Our members enjoy being outside and we spend a lot of time here when we're relaxing. We eat out here as often as the weather allows." He went on to point out the dorms, the bakery, the laundry, and the schoolhouse.

Wherever the kids that attended the school were, they weren't on display today. I scanned the buildings and saw a young woman standing in the window of the women's dorm. She was watching the tour. She looked like the picture of the missing girl. Our gazes met and she waved at me. I started to raise a hand, but then she was gone, pulled away from the window.

When the guide, Maxwell, asked if we had any questions, I raised my hand. "How many people live here?"

"We're up to five hundred souls as of our last meeting." He smiled as he held out his arms. "We've been welcoming so many new members, we're starting work on another set of dormitories. Who else has questions?"

I pushed on. "How many kids attend school here? And where are they? I haven't seen a child since we arrived."

Maxwell's mouth tightened into a line, and the guards who were near the doors stepped closer to me. I figured three questions were too many. He took a breath and I saw him shake his head. The guards behind me stepped back in place. "We feel that the children are here in our care. Adults choose this life. The kids aren't old enough to choose, so we are keeping them out of the limelight, so to speak. But to try to answer your question, our schoolhouse can accommodate up to a hundred students."

Amanda met my gaze. He'd skirted the question, but the warning in her eyes made me rethink my usual persistent nature. I let go of the next twenty questions that had popped into my head.

Maxwell nodded, and when there were no more questions, he smiled. "Feel free to hang out here in the sunshine. When you're ready to leave, the path to your left will take you past our vegetable garden and back to the parking lot and your cars. Thank you so much for visiting our home today."

We wandered around the yard, but everywhere we went, guards were close by, watching us. I'd made us a target. There would be no sneaking off-tour today. If Carlie was here, she was hidden away with the children and most of the women.

I took Amanda's arm. "Are we ready to head back to the house? Or maybe we should stop and grab lunch on the way. I know a perfect little seafood restaurant that overlooks the ocean."

"This was lovely, but I'm feeling a little worn out. I'd love to go get some clam chowder." Amanda smiled as we passed by another guard. "And maybe a glass of wine. Do you think the members here drink wine?"

When we got into the car, she leaned back against the headrest. "Greg told me that you can be a little direct when things don't add up. I think you just found another mystery."

"Remember the woman we saw arguing with the guard, who you thought climbed the fence?" I told her about talking to Molly Cordon the other day about her missing daughter. "I wanted to see if we could spot her, but they didn't have many women out to meet the community. Most of those women who were serving food and drinks, I've seen in my bookstore."

I would talk to Greg when he got home. The girl I'd seen in the window may not have been Carlie, but she'd had the same long blond hair. It was worth mentioning.

# Chapter 3

The next morning, Greg and I decided to take his mom to see the wedding venue. It was an outing where Emma could come along. There were only a few cars in the dirt parking lot when we arrived, even though it was a beautiful day. As we wandered the mission grounds with Emma, Amanda was quiet. I was worried that she didn't approve. The weather was cooperating for our outing. The temperature was in the seventies, so we were in short sleeves. Except for Amanda, who wore a hoodie as well. Several of the walkers we ran into wore shorts. We paused at the fountain. The mission's groundkeepers had kept it running for the winter and cleared some of the vegetation from around it. There was a bench nearby and Amanda sank onto it, pulling out her water bottle. Emma sat by my leg, watching her. She looked up at me and whined.

"Mom, are you okay? Are we doing too much?" Greg sat next to her, holding the water bottle as she dug in her purse.

She didn't look up as she shook her head. She pulled out a ChapStick and applied it to her lips. "Don't be silly. I just get a little tired now and then. It's so dry here. I have to put lotion on right after my shower."

"What do you think of the venue?" Greg decided to take her at her word. But I could see the concern in his eyes. "The arch will be covered with flowers and the chairs will be set up over there. The reception will be held back by the main building. Our friend Sadie Michaels is baking the cake and we brought in a caterer for the reception. As long as it doesn't rain next Saturday, we'll be good."

She surveyed the area. "Make sure the chairs are on either side of that stone pathway. You don't want Jill's dress to get dirty."

I glanced at the pathway to the arch. I'd assumed that the chairs would be set up that way, but maybe Amanda was right, we should check with the venue to make sure. They'd offered the old chapel as an alternative site for the wedding in case of rain. It would work as an option, especially since it would keep me from having to call everyone on the day of the wedding to let them know of a venue change. This wedding had been a pain to pull together, three times already. I was done changing the date. If we didn't get married next Saturday, I would chalk it up to the will of the gods. Even though I knew in my heart that Greg was the one, I just didn't have the energy to try again.

Greg must have heard my thoughts because he winked at me. Sometimes that man knew exactly what I was thinking. More likely it showed on my face. I just wished I had the same insight into his head. Like that bump we'd had when I'd made him a resume. I'd thought I'd done something nice. He, on the other hand, thought I was meddling.

We still needed to clear the air about that, but not until after our house was just the two of us again. I refused to fight with his mom staying with us. We had the rest of our lives to do that. I smiled as Amanda stood. "So, do you like it?"

"It's beautiful. I hope that it's warm like this next weekend." Amanda pointed to the old buildings near the foothills. "Can we see the rest of the buildings?"

"Of course." I started telling her about the Spanish missionaries who had built the original mission with the help of the local tribe, the Chumash people. The Spanish priests who ran the missions were more worried about claiming the area for their crown than taking care of the natives. This mission had been wiped out in an earthquake, then rebuilt as part of the Civilian Conservation Corps program during the Depression. "There's even a ghost story about a Catholic priest who died here during the earthquake."

"Well, let's hope he doesn't like attending weddings." Amanda stepped closer to me. "Are you sure you wouldn't rather get married in a church nearby?"

"We love this site, Mom," Greg interrupted. "And with so many changes, our options have been limited. But when we found this, it was like it was meant to be."

I appreciated his support. I'd been searching for wedding venues for months. Especially after our first choice had been snatched from our grasp due to the location's rules. "We love it, and Emma will be able to attend, as long as it doesn't rain. She's not allowed in the chapel."

"Well, as long as the two of you are happy with the venue," Amanda said, but from her tone, I didn't think she meant it. Greg's first marriage had been in a huge, historic church. Mine had been at the justice of the peace's office. This was right in the middle. The place was perfect for us. We were outdoor people who appreciated the history of the area where we lived.

I paused at the chapel entrance. I'd been inside several times. "You guys go ahead. I'll stay out here with Emma."

The chapel had two entrances, one you could see from where we were standing at the back, and the one Greg and his mother had used, closer to the edge of the building where the cemetery was located behind the mission walls. Most of the graves were unmarked, but there was a large stone cross that marked the cemetery boundary by the walls. My phone rang, making me jump. I answered the call. "This is Jill."

"Are you coming to the author event tonight?" It was Deek Kerr, my barista and bookstore author-event wrangler. He'd invited a children's author for an appearance, hoping it would bring in the kids with their Christmas money.

"Probably not." I didn't want Greg to think I was working just to get away from his mom. "Unless you need me."

"Nope. I just wanted to make the offer. We're all ready. How's the in-law visit going?" It sounded like the shop was busy behind him.

"As well as can be expected, I guess." Emma was watching the side of the wall where the adobe had been broken. Anyone could step into the cemetery from the back near the foothills. Of course, there wasn't much here to protect. I heard Greg talking behind me. "I've got to go. They're coming."

"Have fun," Deek said before I hung up.

I'd thought we were going to have a nice walk and show off where we were going to be married. Now, Amanda had me rethinking all my decisions. The good news was it was too late to change anything. All I needed to do was breathe.

When they walked into the courtyard, I saw Amanda frown. I turned around to see what she'd seen, but we were the only people there.

Greg's phone buzzed, and he held up his hand. "Sorry, I've got to take this."

He left the cemetery area, and it was just me and Amanda. She nodded to the benches outside the walled courtyard. "Can we sit out here? I'm still a little sensitive to all this."

I realized she meant the graveyard. We moved to the benches, which were warmed by the sun along with the wall behind us. We could see the sheep's pen from where we sat. "I'm sorry. We should have skipped this part of the tour."

"Death is a part of life, my dear." Amanda reached out and tapped my leg with her hand. "I've just been thinking about that part of life a little more than normal this past year. I'm a little superstitious, so I've been trying to keep it all light and focused as I went through treatment."

"I'm sorry we weren't there for you." I'd offered to stay with her, especially when she was going through chemotherapy, but she'd rejected my offer. Instead, Jim's new girlfriend had moved into Amanda's house with her since they lived in the same town. Beth was a sweet woman whom Jim had met at church. And even though he'd thought he'd never remarry after losing his wife, I'd heard they were starting to talk about wedding plans. Life was too short not to enjoy every day. Especially if you found love a second time.

"Beth was perfect for me. She was born to be a caretaker. Jim's a lucky man. I didn't think he'd ever find love again." Amanda closed her eyes and tipped her face up to the sun. "Life is funny, isn't it?"

Now that I could agree with. Life had a way of throwing you unexpected presents, even if you didn't want them. "I would have come, though."

"I know. And I appreciate it. I just didn't want to interrupt your life here. But with both my boys now in serious relationships, maybe it's time for me to think about who I want to come into my life."

"You know both of the guys are going to throw a fit when you start dating." I could see Greg agonizing over whether to run a background check on any man who dared to date his mom.

As we laughed about his overprotective nature, he returned to where we sat. "Sorry, we need to cut this short. I've been called out to the New Hope complex. They caught someone trying to break in. I'm glad you're here with me. I've got one less suspect."

"That's so unfair." I stood and shortened Emma's lead. "I'm not always involved when bad things happen."

Amanda looked between the two of us. "I hope you're kidding."

"Of course I am." Greg held out his arm to his mom. "Are you ready to go? Should I drop you girls off at Diamond Lille's for lunch? I might be able to meet you if this call out doesn't go long."

"Sounds like a plan." I started walking toward the Jeep. "We'll need to take Emma home first, though."

\* \* \* \*

Greg didn't make it back to join us for lunch, so we walked home after we ate. When we got there, Amanda excused herself to take a nap. "I need to stay with you two for a while. As much as you all walk, I'll be back to normal sooner rather than later."

I worried about how active we were being, but Amanda had asked us to keep to our normal routine, especially since we were going to be leaving for our honeymoon a few weeks after the wedding. We'd decided to wait until we'd gotten Amanda back home and a few things handled here before taking off. I still didn't know where we were going, but I was hoping for someplace warm. I wasn't much of a skier.

As I cleaned up the kitchen, I found one of the flyers for Carlie Cordon. I'd mentioned what we'd seen at the compound to Greg last night when we were getting ready for bed. He'd acknowledged what I'd said, but not much more. Then he'd said the one thing that burned me. "She's an adult. We have to assume she knows what she's doing, being part of that group."

I still disagreed with that statement. If your friend was jumping off an unsafe cliff, you'd tell them. And try to stop them. And eighteen wasn't much of an adult.

When the kitchen was cleaned and Amanda was still sleeping, I grabbed a book out of my tote. Deek expected a review from me, even if I was getting married and hosting my mother-in-law for the month. The good news was the book sucked me in quickly.

I was checking on the roast I'd put into the Crock-Pot that morning for dinner when Amanda came downstairs. She grabbed a soda out of the fridge and sat down to watch me work. "I feel bad not helping. I'm just so tired. I wonder if it's all the fresh air I'm getting here."

"You're probably overdoing it." I was turned away from her so I didn't see the anger at my statement, but I felt it with her next words.

"I know what I can do, and contrary to my sons' beliefs, I can take care of myself." She opened her soda.

Emma looked up from her bed, clearly expecting an argument. She was watching both of us to see where this would go.

I called uncle first. "Sorry, I'll try not to smother you."

"I'd appreciate it." The smile shined through Amanda's words.

The front door opened. Greg came into the house and went straight to the den to get rid of his gun, then came into the kitchen. "That cult is going to be the death of me. That mom, Molly Cordon? She tried to climb the back wall to find her daughter."

"I told you I thought I'd seen her daughter hidden away in the dorms at the open house. Molly tried to sneak in that day too." I felt bad for Molly. All she wanted was to talk to her daughter. To understand her decisions.

"Well, so did a few others. Molly got no fewer than five calls saying Carlie was at the event." Greg sank into a chair next to his mother. "Kane swears he's never met her. He suggested that maybe the girl hooked up with some guy and left school on her own."

"What a nice thing to say to her mom." I was beginning to dislike Kane Matthews even more. And I wasn't sure that was possible. I decided I'd give his book back unread at the next meeting.

"Well, I had to drive Mrs. Cordon back to town and listen to her cry all the way. The good news is that Matthews didn't file charges since he felt bad for the woman." He closed his eyes. "This is getting hard to manage."

"Do you think the girl is there?" Amanda asked her son.

Greg shrugged. "Honestly, I don't know. Everything Mrs. Cordon has provided seems to indicate that Carlie's on the grounds. But Matthews is adamant that he's never met her. Anyway, I'm starving. When's dinner?"

\* \* \* \*

The next morning, I was downstairs at the stove. Greg was making pancakes. Amanda came down to the kitchen and started looking around. "Have you seen my purse?"

"You had it at the mission. Did you leave it in the Jeep?" I grabbed my keys and went out to check my car. No purse. When I came back, I shook my head. "Sorry, it's not there. I know you didn't have it at Diamond Lille's because you said you'd left it at the house."

"I know, I thought I'd left it here. Now I think I left it in the chapel when I sat down. I took a pill there." Amanda poured herself a cup of coffee. "I'll have to go home to get my pills if I don't have them."

"Greg, can you finish the bacon? I'll run over to the mission and see if I can find your mom's purse." I grabbed Emma's leash. "And I'll take the girl, so she gets out this morning."

"Oh, Jill, I can go. I feel like such a burden." Amanda stood and looked down at the slippers she wore. "I'll need to change first."

"Just stay here and chat with your son. Emma and I will be back soon." I grabbed my keys and wallet. Emma followed me to the door and we headed out to the mission. When we arrived, a light fog covered the parking lot. I didn't worry about paying since the mission had a fifteen-minute grace period. I parked next to a gray car. Someone else must be on the trails, since employees parked behind the visitor center. I clipped Emma's leash on and we headed toward the chapel building. The fog was thicker as I made my way down the trail. Emma was quiet as she walked as well. I couldn't be sure, but I thought my dog was a little freaked out.

We went into what I thought was a doorway, but I realized we were in the graveyard. I saw a dark blob in the corner, but as I watched, it disappeared. Probably a trick of the light.

I went back outside the wall and moved to my right. I passed the first entrance, which was the priest's quarters. The next entrance took us into the chapel. Three benches lined the wall and I saw something under one. I pulled out a purse and dug for the wallet to check to see if this was Amanda's. Her driver's license was in a plastic sleeve in her wallet, giving me my proof.

As I tucked the wallet back away, a letter fell out. It was to Greg. And not in Amanda's writing. I read the first paragraph and realized it was from Sherry, Greg's ex-wife. She was trying to convince him to take her back. Amanda had agreed to bring the letter to him. She was still Team Sherry. I'd hoped we'd gotten past that.

Emma nudged my leg and I realized I'd brought her with me into the chapel, one of the two places in the park she wasn't welcome. I tucked the purse under my arm and headed out to the trail. As I did, I saw a priest dressed in robes go into the graveyard. Did they still have Sunday services here? I needed to apologize for taking Emma into the chapel. I followed him, and Emma growled softly under her breath.

As we went into the graveyard, the blob I'd seen before was visible again. But now, it was closer and looked like something on the ground. The priest I'd followed into the cemetery had disappeared.

I walked over and realized a man was lying on the ground. He was face up and his eyes were fixed. Kane Matthews looked arrogant even dead. I dialed Greg as Emma and I stepped away and out of the graveyard. I could barely see Kane's body, but he was still there. When Greg answered, I told him what I'd found.

"Kane Matthews is dead in the graveyard at the mission. I'll meet you in the parking lot." I hung up and took Emma back to the car. The gray car was gone. My Jeep was the only vehicle sitting in the fog.

# Chapter 4

As soon as Greg arrived at the mission, Emma and I were on our way home. "Don't you want me to show you where I found the body?" I sat in the driver's seat with the Jeep running and the heat on high. I was still freezing. "I'm sure I'll find it. I just want you out of here before the rest of the emergency vehicles get here. Besides, Mom needs her purse—well, the pills in her purse. Did you find it?" Greg looked around me and saw it on the floor at Emma's feet. "Good. At least we don't have to worry about that."

"Nope, there's no worrying there." I thought about the letter. Sooner or later, I would blurt out my knowledge of what Sherry was trying to do. But right now, there was a murder, and he had enough on his mind without me complaining about a stupid letter from his ex. We were getting married, no matter what.

I was already on the road when I realized I hadn't told him about seeing a priest at the mission or the gray car. That letter from Sherry had rattled me more than I'd realized. I used the Bluetooth setting to call Greg. As I expected, I got his voice mail. I left the information and added, "Don't worry about entertaining your mom. We'll work through her list of tourist sites to visit."

Emma looked at me, probably hoping for a hint that she would be going along. But I knew I'd be leaving her home when we went out sightseeing.

When I arrived home, I handed Amanda her purse. "Here you go. So, what do you want to do today? Greg won't be home until late."

Amanda rummaged through the purse and paused before pulling out a bottle of pills. She tucked the opening closed and stood. "After I take this, I'd love to go visit the Castle. Is it open on Sundays?"

"Let me check." I moved to the office. It wasn't lost on me that Amanda took her purse with her as she went to the kitchen for water to take her pill. I thought that my soon-to-be mother-in-law knew that I'd seen the letter. She just didn't want to ask me directly. I was going to have to be the bigger person here. Not one of my strongest characteristics.

I turned on the computer and looked up the Castle's website. If we left soon, we'd be able to stop at the bookstore too. I needed caffeine and a lot of it to be able to keep up this cheery attitude all day.

When I came back out, I decided to put the problem in the safe in my head. I wouldn't think about it until after the wedding or after Amanda had left. I didn't know if I could get past her part of the Sherry caper, but I wasn't giving anyone the satisfaction of getting upset over something that wasn't an issue. Greg loved me. We were getting married. No matter what anyone else thought.

I smiled at Amanda as she stepped out of the kitchen, still clutching her purse. "It opens at eleven. I need to make a stop first, if you're ready to go."

She nodded. "I'm ready when you are."

Maybe she thought she'd gotten away with it. Whatever she thought, didn't matter. Greg was investigating who had killed Kane Matthews. I wanted in on this investigation. The killer needed to be given a medal before Greg arrested him.

Maybe I wasn't in the best of moods.

We drove to the bookstore, and I parked in front. It was busy for a Sunday morning in January. Several months ago, when she'd lived above the shop, Evie had suggested that we open for a few hours on Sundays. She'd watched a lot of people pause at the doorway, checking the hours listed. Now that Deek was living above the shop in the apartment, they switched out working on Sundays. Today, Evie was behind the counter, making coffee drinks for a couple.

I pointed Amanda to the stools and the menu. "What can Evie make for you?"

Amanda studied the menu carefully. "A double shot mocha with caramel?"

"Sounds good." I waited for Evie to finish with the customer before stepping up to the register. "Have you been busy all morning?"

"It's been steady since I opened. The best news is that I've sold a book with every coffee." She smiled at Amanda. "You must be Greg's mom. You have the same eyes."

"I've never heard that before." Amanda smiled at Evie. "But yes, guilty as charged. Maybe I should grab a book while we're here. I finished the one I brought on the plane."

"What do you like to read?" I asked. I had sent her books during her treatment, but I'd been working off a list she'd sent me. And the list had been all over the place. Women's fiction, fantasy, mystery, nonfiction, and even some lawyer mysteries.

"I think I need some fantasy. Where's your young adult section? I'll go grab a couple while you're getting our coffee."

Evie pointed out the section to Amanda and reached for travel mugs. "You want your coffee to go?"

I nodded. "And put this and the books on my account. What's in the back? Any good advance reader copies?"

The publishers sent out advance copies of books to bookstores to entice them to order the titles. The staff and I tried to make sure every book was read and reviewed for Deek's newsletter, but we also wrote Staff Pick cards on one new release a month that we fell in love with when we were reading. We all had different favorite genres so we had a lot of variety in the books we recommended.

"There's a new women's fiction from that author who came here last January. The one that writes books set in New Orleans. And a mystery. I think everyone's been leaving those for you." She handed over the cups and held up a finger. "Hold on, I'll go get them."

"See if there's any new fantasy back there too," I called after her.

Deek had set up a table in the back that held all the advance copies when they came in. They each had a sheet. If you took one, you wrote down your name and made a check if you wrote a review. That way, not everyone reviewed the same book. Although a lot of the popular books got several reads on the sheet before Deek rotated the book off the table.

When Evie came back, she had four books in hand. She tucked them into the bag along with the books that Amanda had brought to the counter. Then she handed the bag over to me. "Do you want any treats to go with the coffee?"

"None for me." I held out my hands to ward off the sugar. "My final fitting is done. I don't want to gain an ounce between now and next Saturday."

"I don't think it works that way." Amanda gave me a sideways hug. "But I'll have one of those snowflakes if you don't mind."

"Bag up two, just in case you get hungry on the drive." I turned toward the door and saw Molly Cordon hurry into the shop. She came up to me and grabbed my arm. "Molly, what's wrong?"

"You need to help me. The other guy, Deek, told me that you are married to the head cop. That you could help me." She glanced at Amanda and Evie, who were watching the exchange. "I need to talk to you alone."

"Come over and sit down. Evie, would you get Molly a cup of coffee? Or would you like cocoa?" I put my arm around her and led her to a table near the wall.

"Do you have tea? I'm a little chilled. I've been waiting outside for you to show up." She sank into a chair. "I parked my car behind the bed-and-breakfast where I'm staying and walked into town."

"Okay." I still wasn't sure what she was saying. I turned back to the counter and told Evie to make a hot tea instead. I sat down and waited for Molly's breathing to slow a little. When Evie brought the teapot and cup, I pushed the basket of tea bags toward Molly. "You pick what you want."

Molly grabbed a cranberry herbal tea out of the pile and took it out of the package, letting it steep in the hot water. She pressed her lips together and looked up at me. "I think someone's trying to frame me for murder."

\* \* \* \*

I called Greg, and he sent Toby over to take Molly's statement since Greg and the crew were still out at the mission. She had told me the story before Toby arrived and kept the same points when she talked to him as I sat there and listened.

"When they kicked me out of the open house on Friday, I left a note for the head guy, Kane Matthews. I told him that I was Carlie's mother and I just wanted to talk to her. To make sure she was all right. This morning, I got a call from a man. I don't think it was Kane. He said Mr. Matthews would meet me at the old mission and gave me an address. I asked if Carlie would be there, and the man said that Mr. Matthews wanted to talk with me first. To see if my heart was pure. If it was, he'd let me on the compound to see my daughter." Molly was on her second cup of tea and her hands had stopped shaking.

"So you drove to the old mission. What time did you get there?" Toby's voice was calm and warm. Like all he wanted was to hear her story. No worries.

She nodded. "I arrived a few minutes before nine. He said he'd be in the old graveyard. That there was a bench inside the walls where we could sit and talk."

"The graveyard. Did you consider that you were being pranked?" Toby had a sweet smile.

This time Molly laughed. "I did a little. But on the off chance that he would let me talk to Carlie? I was going to take the chance. She's been gone since October."

"Okay, so then what happened?" Toby asked.

"I ignored the sign to pay for parking. I want to be completely honest, even if it costs me a fine for not paying the charge. I parked and found a map of the trails. I followed a wooden sign and went over a tiny bridge, then headed to the large building. The graveyard was in a courtyard at the end of the building." She closed her eyes for a minute. "It was foggy and I could barely see the trail in front of me. I just followed the map. Soon, the adobe wall came into view, and I headed to the far left side and the first opening in the wall."

This time, Toby didn't encourage her to continue. He let the silence do that.

"I went into the courtyard and saw someone by a large stone. I thought he was kneeling in prayer. When I walked over, I called out hello, and when I touched his shoulder, he fell over. It was Kane Matthews. I'd seen a picture of him on their website. He was dead."

I held up a finger and Toby nodded. "Molly, what color is your car?"

"The rental? Gray or silver, I guess." She looked confused at my question.

"One more question. When you left, did you see a vehicle parked next to your car?"

She hesitated. I could see the thoughts running through her head. "To the right of my car, yes, there was a Jeep. I'd forgotten about that. I don't think it was there when I arrived."

"I take it you saw Molly's car in the parking lot?" Toby looked over at me.

"Yes. I went to see if I could find Amanda's purse. She left it there yesterday when we went to tour the site. I took Emma with me so she'd get a walk today even if we got busy. I saw a gray car when I parked, but it was gone when I left."

Toby stood and grabbed his phone. "I need to call Greg. Where are you going to be?"

"Amanda and I are heading to the Castle. Call us if you need anything else. Can Molly go now? I can drop her off at her bed-and-breakfast." I smiled at Molly, who looked a little less shaken than she had when she came into the bookstore.

"I'm staying at South Cove Bed-and-breakfast. It's not far, I can walk." Molly stood and looked at Toby. "If we're done? I need to buy a book to try to relax. It's been a crazy day."

"You can go. Please stay in town until we figure out what's going on." Toby met her gaze.

"Don't worry about that. My daughter is at that compound. I'm not leaving here until I talk to her. If she's happy there, I'll go home. But I need to hear it from her." Molly stood and went over to the bookshelves.

Toby smiled at me. "At least Greg can't say you intended to get mixed up with this one. It found you."

"He'll say it anyway." I grabbed the bag with the books and looked at Amanda. "Ready to go?"

"Are you still up to going? I mean, you find a dead body. Then you chat with a woman who claims she had nothing to do with it, yet she was there. Maybe we should just go home and wait for Greg." Amanda watched Toby walk away, already on the line with her son.

"If I stayed home and waited for Greg when things like this happened, I'd never leave the house. Let's go put another check mark on your vacation to-do list. Besides, I need a distraction." I took Amanda's arm and we headed to the Jeep.

I thought this might be her first investigation that she'd been close to. Man, she had a lot to learn.

# Chapter 5

I kept my phone turned on as we went on the Castle's museum tour. The company that had bought the historic home had done a great job restoring the main house's first floor and one of the guesthouses into a museum, showing off the large number of priceless antiques that the former owner had collected, many from his trips to Europe. The large dining room had a long medieval-era table and church pews around the walls of the room. Tapestries hung everywhere.

Amanda was in heaven. She must have photographed each room a hundred times from every different angle. I was sure she'd need to spend some quality time sorting through her pictures between now and the wedding. Which would give me time to do other things.

Like, figure out who killed Kane Matthews. I was pretty sure that Molly Cordon would be off Greg's suspect list sooner rather than later. The woman was too open about what had happened this morning.

Oh, and we had a wedding on Saturday. Not to mention a rehearsal and dinner on Friday. The dinner was set for The Wooden Bench, an upscale seafood restaurant. Aunt Jackie had taken on the planning, helping out Amanda, but the cost was coming out of the Miss Emily fund. It's what I called my unexpected inheritance from my friend I met when I moved to South Cove. I used the money sparingly, mostly to support local charities or help with college costs for staff members of Coffee, Books, and More. It also supplemented the bookstore's retirement payments for my aunt.

Greg and I had talked about the money when we attended Pastor Bill's finances for couples class. He agreed with me that it should be used for extras, not everyday living expenses. At least we both agreed about that. As I wandered behind Amanda as she toured the Castle, I realized that Greg and I had never talked about the tense phone call regarding his resume. I decided to put off the discussion until either the wedding was done, Amanda had left for home, or the investigation was over.

Having some sort of emotional argument on top of all three of those life factors was just too much. Even for me.

My thoughts went back to Kane. From our short conversation on Friday, I knew he was an intellectual, at least in the spiritual lane. The books in the meetinghouse seemed to portray a group that prized learning and thought, if not free thought. The group seemed very patriarchal, with women in a servant role. It was like Kane had turned the clock back to 1950 and turned all the women who followed him into Stepford wives.

I wondered if *that* book was on his communal bookshelf. I imagined not.

"Jill, isn't the pool beautiful?" Amanda asked as we ended the tour at the Grecian-style outdoor pool in front of a bar. The Castle bar offered cool drinks and sweets and, according to the tour host who'd just left the group, we were welcome to sit and enjoy a drink or two before exiting the property.

"Greg's college buddy, Levi, had his bachelor party here at the Castle." I flinched at the memory. Levi had also died here, poolside, during that weekend. Sometimes I put my foot in my mouth, and sometimes, my entire leg. This was one of those times.

"Greg told me about Levi's passing." Amanda pulled out her wallet. "Can I buy you a drink? Or is being here too painful?"

Now Amanda was being thoughtful. I smiled and nodded to the board. "I'll have an iced tea, unsweetened. I'll go grab us a table."

The one thing about spending time on the patio was you had both an ocean and a mountain view, depending on how you turned your chair. The designers had spent a lot of time making sure of it. Back in the day, the owner had a private zoo on the property. There were still zebra and deer running around, but most of the animals had been rehomed. Maybe we'd be lucky today and see part of the remaining herd.

I wasn't getting too far in thinking about Kane and his death, except for the way he treated women in his cult, I mean, group. But with all that security around on the day of the open house, Kane had to be hiding more than just a few people who didn't want to talk to their families. Like Carlie.

Amanda set two plastic cups on the table, my iced tea, and something that looked like a milkshake. She saw me looking at the cup. "It's a strawberry smoothie with a protein boost. I guess it's popular with the weightlifting and over-fifty crowds. We both want more protein in our lives, according to the twelve-year-old who was making our drinks."

I snorted at her description of the young woman who was manning the outdoor bar. "Everyone looks so young anymore. I went to my doctor the other day and there was an intern following him around. I asked if he was in an advanced placement high school class. I was off by about ten years."

"That must have been embarrassing. But I know how you feel. Every time I went to get a scan or a biopsy last year, I always had students watching. I go to a teaching hospital, I get it, but I didn't realize that diagnosing breast cancer was a community event. Everybody wants to see my boobs." Amanda took a sip and sank back into the chair. "I love the sun out here. The air just feels soft on my face."

"I'm glad you like it here. You should visit more often." I sipped my tea and scanned the hills for zebras.

"I think you mean that," Amanda said.

I turned and saw she was watching me. "Of course I do. The upstairs guest room is always open. I know Emma can be a handful, though."

"Oh, I love Emma. She's perfect." Amanda stirred her pink smoothie. "I just, well, when I'd visit before, Sherry always said the right things, but I could tell I was intruding."

"I'm not Sherry." I turned back to watching the hills. I wanted to say so much more. Like, why do you have a letter from Sherry to Greg in your purse? But that wasn't my battle.

"I'm beginning to understand how completely different from Sherry you are. Greg made a better decision choosing you." Amanda reached out and squeezed my hand. When I turned back this time, I saw tears in her eyes. "All I've ever wanted is for my boys to be happy. Thank you for being Greg's path."

Thinking about the resume fight, I smiled. Maybe I wasn't perfect for her son in Amanda's eyes. And we still argued. But I knew Greg was my path to happiness as well. "I love him."

She let my hand go and pulled out a tissue from her purse. "I know that."

We sat in silence for a bit. I was watching for zebras. Amanda was watching the ocean in the opposite direction. The air was cooling down and I could see the sun dropping in the sky. I finished my drink. "Are we ready to head back to the house? We can stop at Lille's and pick up fried chicken for dinner."

"That sounds wonderful. Do you think Greg will be able to join us?" Amanda stood and threw away her protein smoothie.

I glanced at my phone. I hadn't received a text message from him, so I sent my own. "I just told him that we'll have Tiny's chicken at the house in an hour. If he's hungry and available, I'm sure he'll be there."

As we walked back to the Jeep, Amanda said, "It must be lonely sometimes. Being with Greg, I mean. Especially when he's in the middle of an investigation."

"He's threatened to move into a hotel when he's investigating, just to keep me out of his hair," I said as I remotely unlocked the Jeep. "I see him enough. Besides, I have the bookstore. And Emma. And friends."

I called in our dinner order, then thought about my answer as we drove to Diamond Lille's. I did have a good life. Even when Greg was busy with his job. It wasn't like we lived separate lives, but we both knew how to keep busy if the other one wasn't available. I hadn't even mentioned my reading habit, but I guess she'd already figured that one out.

Greg didn't come home until ten—not even for Tiny's fried chicken. Emma and I were curled on the couch with a book and a cooking show on the television. She was watching the show, I was reading.

He went to the office and stored his gun in the safe, then came and gave me a kiss. "Mom in bed already?"

"Yeah, I think being out in the open air is wearing her out. But she had a blast at the Castle. I got her some books from the shop to keep her busy." I reached up and touched his cheek. "You look tired."

"I am. But I'm starving. Any of that chicken left over?" He kissed the top of my head and went into the kitchen.

"Nope, we ate it all ourselves." I got up and followed him. I saw the pained look on his face. "Just kidding. There's a lot left over. You know I always buy too much."

"Leftovers are a vital part of a cop's food source." Greg pulled out the chicken. "Turn on the oven and I'll heat this up. Do you want a piece?"

"Sure." I turned on the oven to 400 degrees and got out a sheet pan. We had nailed the specifics of keeping Tiny's chicken perfect during the leftover stage. I got out a pot for the gravy while Greg put the chicken into the oven, keeping out a leg to snack on.

We moved around the kitchen like we'd been doing it for years. Of course, it had been a while since Greg had moved in with me. We had a rhythm together. As we waited for the food to reheat, I got out two sodas and sat down at the table.

"Your mom asked me if I was lonely when you were on a case."

He sat down after throwing the bones from the chicken leg into a sack in the sink. We always took the chicken bones to the outside trash because of Emma's magical ability to get into any indoor trash can she wanted to raid. "That's an oddly specific question. What was the answer? Are you lonely?"

"I hadn't thought about it before she asked. I mean, you've always been on the job since I met you that first time I visited South Cove." I sipped my soda.

"I was married to Sherry back then." He leaned back in his chair. "I hope Mom's not trying to play that card again. Being married to Sherry was like trying to serve two masters. She didn't care what I was doing, as long as I was at her beck and call and made enough money to support her in the way she was accustomed to being cared for. Mom was like Jim. She thought Sherry and I were perfect together. But she didn't have to live with her, I did."

I smiled at that image. "She said that you put her in a hotel in Santa Barbara when she'd visit back then. Maybe she's missing the upgrade. The house is cozy, not upscale."

"She's fine in the guest room. And if she's not, she can pay for the high-end hotel herself." He rubbed the back of his neck, a sure sign he was tired. "One investigation-related question, please. Do you think Molly Cordon is telling the truth?"

"I've only met her twice. But the story she told me before Toby got there was the same as what she told him. I don't have a reason to doubt her. She's admitted to being at the mission and going to meet up with Kane. She was pretty freaked out when she came into the bookstore." I watched Emma curl back into her kitchen bed. All was right in my dog's world since her daddy was home and she'd had dinner. I turned back to Greg. "Please tell me that Kane's murder isn't going to change the wedding venue."

"There's my sensitive fiancée. Always worried about others," Greg teased as he stood to stir the gravy. "But no worries. We cleared the mission site tonight. That's why I was late. I wanted all traces of Kane's killing to be gone before we had our rehearsal on Friday. I'm clearing my schedule from five p.m. on Friday to nine on Sunday evening. We might not be able to leave on our honeymoon when we've planned, but we've already put that off for a few days."

"I don't want to look for another venue, so thank you for your assistance." I stood and got us plates. I was going to eat not only a piece of chicken but mashed potatoes as well. The dress had a little stretch in the seams. And I'd run tomorrow morning with Emma before starting my sightseeing day with Amanda.

"Anything for my girl." He got the chicken out of the oven. "Don't let Mom freak you out. This wedding, this marriage, is ours. No one else gets to have an opinion on what we're going to do with the rest of our lives. Except maybe Emma. But she's our immediate family."

I leaned over and kissed him. "Thank you for that. I needed to hear it."

"It's just pre-wedding jitters. And all the juggling we have to do to get our friends and family all in the same place for a day. Jim and Beth are coming in on Wednesday, but they're staying at the Castle. He called me and left a message. I called him back on my way home. They're looking forward to seeing us." Greg must have seen my face. "I thought you liked Beth."

"I do. But I'm glad I've had some time alone with your mom before she gets here. I think those two are as thick as thieves since Beth helped her this last year." I grabbed my food and sat down. "Now I sound like a jealous outsider."

"You offered to go. Beth was just able to work remotely. You have the shop," Greg reminded me.

"I know. But I still feel—" I paused as I saw the look on his face. "Don't worry about it. You've got enough on your plate. I'm glad they're coming in on Wednesday. We'll have dinner here, grill steaks or something. And hopefully, you can even be here."

"That's my girl. Always the optimist."

\* \* \* \*

Monday morning, I was back from my run before Amanda came downstairs. She saw me in my running sweats and headed for the coffee. "You have way too much energy for me. I'm still in my morning slow speed."

"Emma likes to run, and if we go early, it's off my list. Otherwise, I always feel guilty about doing something else. Since the restructuring of the bookstore schedule, I have a few mornings at the beginning of the week where we can make sure getting her out of the house happens first. Although this week, all bets are off." I went over and poured my own cup. "Well, don't worry about me being up and wanting to go anywhere before ten. Unless we need to. I like this sleeping-in idea." Amanda rubbed Emma's head. "Do you have wedding stuff that needs to be done or can we go exploring again today?"

"I need to check in with the florist this morning, but other than that, it's all done." I sat at the table. I needed to run upstairs and get in the shower before we took off for the day. "Oh, and I need to pick up my dress tomorrow."

"What about the mission site? Are you decorating?"

I stood and grabbed my planner, just to make sure I hadn't missed anything. "My friends Amy, Darla, and Esmeralda are doing the decorating on Saturday morning. Then everyone's coming here to get ready. The mission staff will have the chairs set out on Friday so we can rehearse."

"That's nice of them." Amanda sipped her coffee.

"I just added Jim and Beth coming on Wednesday. So we'll do dinner here that night. Maybe Beth would want to go wandering with us on Thursday." I'd taken the week off from the store, but maybe I should think about taking some shifts. My week didn't seem that busy.

"I'd love to show her Santa Barbara. I'm always talking about the Mexican restaurant there." Amanda looked up at me, hopeful. "After the visit to the Castle, I'd love to do some antique shopping. Maybe at that little store next to your bookstore?"

"Sure. We have to go there on Tuesday, but we can go back on Thursday, it's not that far of a drive. Do you want to go to the beach one day?"

Amanda nodded. "I'd love that. And this town named Solvang? It seems fun."

"Then let's go to Solvang today." Greg would appreciate me being out of town. That way I couldn't get involved in his investigation. Solvang's bookstore had just gotten a new owner. I needed to stop by and say hello anyway. "I'll run up and get ready and we can eat lunch there."

Amanda pulled a notebook out of her purse. "There's a Danish Pancake House there that Jim says is amazing. Can we go there?"

"Sure." I'd find something there to eat that wasn't pancakes. At least I hoped. At the Mexican restaurant, I'd call designated driver status and avoid the margaritas. Maybe I'd find a salad at both places. There was no way that dress wasn't fitting on Saturday. My Friday rehearsal dress was a little less formfitting. Thank goodness.

My phone rang. It was my aunt. "Good morning."

"Don't forget my hairdresser is coming to the house on Saturday morning." My aunt didn't say hello. She just got right to the point.

I glanced at my planner. I hadn't written this down. "That will work fine. Amanda and Beth might need a stylist. Do you think they could be part of the schedule?"

"Who are Amanda and Beth?" My aunt's sigh said it all.

"Greg's mother and his brother's girlfriend? I know I mentioned them." I smiled at Amanda, who was pretending not to listen. She was pretty good at it.

"I'll tell the shop there will be two more." Aunt Jackie paused. "I know you're not working this week. Do I need to go in and check on anything? Make deposits?"

"Evie's handling anything that comes up. I told her that if it gets crazy and she doesn't know what to do, she could call me, or you if she can't reach me." Since my aunt's retirement this last year, I'd been trying to keep her out of the day-to-day business. When she was in town. Which wasn't often due to her love of travel.

# Chapter 6

We'd already taken three windmill statues back to the car and Amanda was still shopping. We were near the bookstore, so I aimed her that direction. "I need to chat with the owner here for a few minutes. See if there's anything you need."

"You just got me three books. I'm going to have to ship back books along with all these cute souvenirs I'm getting today," Amanda gushed.

I thought maybe she was on a shopping high. Maybe that was what she'd had in common with the first Mrs. King—they both loved shopping. I liked it up to a point, then I was done. Most of my friends were that way as well. My aunt had insisted on a designer dress for my engagement party, then the designer had moved out of South Cove and down to LA. So a friend of mine had offered to make my dress but ended up going to work for a designer in Europe. She recommended this bridal shop in Santa Barbara instead.

I was happy with my dress. My aunt thought I should have found a new designer and gotten a one-of-a-kind creation. I didn't want the one-of-a-kind price tag. I had a feeling that Amanda would have sided with my aunt. Luckily, all of the wedding decisions were already made. Again. For a third time. If Amanda complained about something not being good enough, I could use that excuse. But so far, she hadn't complained.

I paused at the entrance and found the cashier's desk. Walking over, I introduced myself and asked if the owner or manager was available. The clerk shook her head. "Sorry, it's Monday. Alisha works weekends and takes off the first two days of the week. She's the owner and manager."

I pulled out a card and handed it to her. "If you'd give her this, I'd appreciate it. I'd love to come and chat about possible joint ventures we could do together."

The woman glanced at the card. "I've been to your shop. I'm part of the writer group that meets there on Thursday nights. It's a nice place."

"Thanks. This is nice as well." The shop had floor-to-ceiling bookshelves surrounding the small first floor with an additional two rows of shelving down the middle.

"I like your seating area. When we have events, they're held upstairs in the children's section. That's the only place we have for people to sit. Then we have to drag chairs in and put them away after the event." The woman, Faith per her name tag, pointed upstairs. "We usually have two people on staff at all times. One for each floor. This morning, it's just me."

A woman was standing behind me, waiting to buy a book. I stepped out of her way. "Well, I'll let you get busy, then. Please ask Alisha to call me. I'd love to talk."

"Sounds good," Faith responded, turning to the customer. "Did you find everything you needed?"

I wandered through the stacks and found Amanda looking at the self-help books. "Finding anything?"

"I need something on turning your life around when you've been challenged. But I don't see anything with that subject. If I needed a twelve-step program or was codependent, there are a ton of choices." Amanda stood from examining the books on the bottom shelf.

"What about a grief book? Maybe there's something in that category about starting over," I suggested as I went around the shelf. And found books on the history of cars. "Or maybe I could find something in my shop tomorrow?"

Amanda smiled as she followed me out of the shop. "Did you have a productive encounter?"

"No, the owner wasn't working." I headed to the next souvenir shop. "But I left my card."

"In my experience, you need to call ahead and see when your target is going to be in the store. It's an old salesman's trick." She shook her head as we window-shopped. "Can we grab something to eat now? I'm beginning to feel a little peckish."

\* \* \* \*

By the time we got home, Greg had already called to tell us he wouldn't be there for dinner. I parked the car in the driveway and turned to Amanda. "Do you want to go out and find something for dinner? There's a lovely seafood restaurant just down the highway. We can drop these packages off, let Emma out, then head out for dinner. Or we could go to Diamond Lille's if you're feeling like comfort food."

"I don't want to be a bother." Amanda looked tired.

I shrugged. "If we eat at home, I have to cook. If we go out, I get a break too. It's up to you, though. If you're too tired, I can grill something."

"I'd love to get some seafood. It's not something we eat a lot at home." She smiled as she grabbed her bags. "Just tell me what's easiest for you. I'm the interloper here."

"No, you're the guest." I grabbed the rest of the bags and went through the gate. A package was sitting on my doorstep. After unlocking the door, I picked it up and put it on the table inside. I'd deal with it later. "Emma, let's go outside for a minute. Then we have to leave again."

The look I got from my dog indicated that she had heard exactly what I'd said and understood it. She just didn't like the idea. When she came back inside, I gave her a treat and rubbed her neck. "We'll be home soon. We just have to go get something to eat."

Emma curled up in her kitchen bed, her back to me. Message received, but not appreciated. Sometimes I thought my dog was just a little too smart for her breed.

We got a table easily since it was Monday. As we walked through the room, I saw Molly sitting with a man near the windows. She didn't look up, so I didn't interrupt. After we ordered, I saw Amanda staring over at the table. I leaned closer. I figured she'd forgotten where she'd seen Molly before. "That's the woman who's looking for her daughter. The one that was at the mission the day Kane died."

Amanda slowly turned her head. "I recognized her. But the man she's sitting with? That's my ex-husband, Vince Penn."

"I didn't realize you remarried after Greg's dad died." I tried not to stare at the man. He was dressed in a black jacket, dark jeans, and what looked like cowboy boots. His hair was salt-and-pepper gray. I couldn't see his eyes, as they were focused on the papers in front of him. Whatever he and Amanda were doing was keeping them focused on the discussion and not on the rest of the restaurant. "Is he a lawyer?"

Amanda huffed. "Not even close. He runs a PI firm out of Los Angeles, or he did the last time he called, asking if I wanted to invest my retirement money in his business. It was, according to him, a sure bet. I'd lost enough money during our marriage. I told him that I didn't plan on losing more. That was our last conversation."

"So, maybe Molly hired him to find Carlie?" I smiled at the waitress as she dropped off our drinks.

"That man couldn't find his way home," Amanda said. "Anyway, let's enjoy our dinner. Hopefully, they'll leave soon and not see us."

I nodded as I sipped my soda. "I used to be a family law attorney. I saw a lot of people taking care of the results of bad decisions. There's just something about love that makes you blind to all the warning signs."

"Is that why you and Greg took so long to marry?"

Her question came out of left field and shocked me. I guess it shouldn't have. She was Greg's mom. I adjusted the silverware, not looking at her as I spoke. "For me, I wanted to make sure Greg was the one. I'd been married before, and it was more of a partnership than a marriage. So when I met Greg, I wasn't sure how to deal with all the feelings."

"And then there was Sherry. Jim said she gave you guys a hard time." Amanda paused as the waitress brought our salads. "I'm sorry about that."

My thoughts went to the letter she carried in her purse from her first daughter-in-law. I wondered if she'd already given it to Greg. I decided it didn't matter. "Sherry was a challenge, but she was Greg's issue, not mine. She wanted the Greg she had in her head. Successful, powerful. Not the man in charge of South Cove's police force. Greg can do anything he wants, but he loves it here. And so do I." As I said that, I wondered if that was why he'd snapped at me about the resume. Had he felt like I was pushing him?

"Sherry did want the best for him. No matter if Greg wanted it or not," Amanda admitted. "When Greg first came to South Cove, he called and told me how happy he was. Of course, Sherry was furious he'd taken this job and not one in LA or with the state police force. She got him to leave South Cove once in a last-ditch effort to save their marriage. Even then she wasn't satisfied, and that's when they divorced. It broke Jim's heart, since he'd just lost his wife."

"Well, we're settled here." I didn't care if Greg took the new job or not. I just wanted him to be happy. I focused on my salad.

Amanda squeezed my hand. "I can see that."

We were almost through with dinner when a shadow appeared on the table. Vince Penn stood in front of Amanda, blocking her exit from the table. "Amanda, what are you doing here? I didn't think you would ever leave Nebraska." Vince reached out to hug her, but something in the look Amanda gave him stopped his movement. "I'm up from LA on a case. Maybe we can get together before I head back. It would be great to catch up."

Amanda shook her head. "Sorry, I'm busy with family events. Greg's getting married this week."

"Oh, I hadn't heard that Sherry left him." Vince glanced at me, then refocused on Amanda. "I bet you were devastated. You adored Sherry."

"I loved my son's wife. Now he'll have a new wife that I can adore." Amanda smiled at me.

I waited for her to introduce me, but she didn't. After a long second, Vince turned and held out his hand. "I'm Vince Penn, private investigator. Molly tells me you're Jill Gardner and you run the local bookstore, as well as being engaged to the police chief here. That must be Greg."

I shook his hand briefly. Deek would say his aura was troublesome. To me, Vince just felt slimy. "All true. Molly is desperate to find Carlie. I hope you're not capitalizing on her fear."

His eyes flickered and he studied me. I guess he thought bookstore owner meant I would be a pushover. A Mary Milquetoast. "Molly is well taken care of, believe me."

I wondered what it cost in Vince's terms to be well taken care of. I'd have to mention this to Greg. Maybe Vince didn't have the right papers to be doing private investigation work in South Cove. A girl could hope. "Well, that's good to hear. It was nice of you to stop by, but we're in the middle of dinner and a private conversation."

This time it was Amanda who stared at me. Finally, she nodded. "Yes, it was nice to see you again, Vince. I probably won't see you again with the wedding being so encompassing. I hope you have a great life."

We went back to eating, and after watching us ignore him for a few seconds, Vince turned on his heel and left. I heard him utter a not-so-nice swear word under his breath, but I didn't worry about it. He was gone and that's all that mattered. Once he was outside the door, I set my fork down. "Sorry if I ran him off sooner than you'd like."

"I would have been happy not to talk to him at all. You made him leave. That was brilliant. You're good at getting your way." Amanda smiled. "Thank you."

"I wasn't always. But I'm learning. Vince seemed—" I wasn't sure how to say smarmy without hurting Amanda's feelings.

"He acts like a used car salesman. And not the good ones." Amanda sighed. "I was lonely. He was so attentive before we got married. Then he quit his job and hung around the house. He said he was planning this new business venture, but he never got it off the ground. At least, not until now."

"Does he know about the last couple years?" I avoided using the word *cancer.*

Amanda shook her head. "I don't want him to know. He'd marry me in a heartbeat to be my beneficiary. But if I ever remarry, it will be for love. Not to have someone to take care of me."

As we headed home, I thought that maybe Amanda had also grown in the last year or so. Facing a life-threatening illness or situation had that effect on people. She was quiet as I drove down the highway. You could still see the ocean, but soon the sun would set and we'd be plunged into darkness until the next morning. Unless it was a full moon.

From what I could see, Amanda was still pulling herself out of the darkness, but at least she could see a light at the end.

I let Emma out as soon as I got home, then turned to Amanda. "I have ice cream or wine or we could do both. Maybe find a reality television show and make fun of the contestants?"

She leaned on the doorway to the kitchen. "That sounds lovely, but I'm tired. I think I'm going to my room to read. Do you have a bottle of water I could have?"

I handed her the water and waited until I heard the door shut upstairs before letting Emma inside. I sat down at the kitchen table with a glass of wine and texted Greg about our dinner.

The response came back fast.

*Vince Penn? Are you sure?*

*He introduced himself. He was with Molly Cordon. Should I be worried about her?*

There was a long pause. Then Greg responded. *Molly's not your concern. We're getting married on Saturday, remember?*

*Vaguely. I just hope my fiancé remembers and shows up for the ceremony. And I remember what he looks like.*

*Believe me, even if I have to ask Lorenzo from Bakerstown to arrest my suspect, I'll be at the altar waiting for you on Saturday. Speaking of that, Jim has a room for me at the Castle for Friday night. Just don't want you to worry if I don't come home.*

*So you can't see me the night before the wedding, right?*

*Exactly. It gives both of us a night to run away if we want, without having to do it at the ceremony.*

*You're silly. It was probably to keep the couple from fighting due to the stress before the wedding. When are you coming home?*

*Probably about ten. Eat without me.*

*We already have, remember? Your mom is upstairs reading. She was tired.*

Again, his response was delayed. I was about to tell him to go work and not worry about me, when he texted.

*I hope she's not talking to Vince. Anyway, I need to go. Love you.*

*Love you too.*

I set down the phone and looked at the ceiling. It wasn't like I could stop her from contacting anyone she wanted to, but I didn't think after what happened this evening that she would reach out to him. But you never knew what was going on in other people's relationships. I'd just have to take her at her word.

Emma was watching me from the corner of the kitchen. "Want to go watch a cooking show?"

She barked her enthusiastic response and we moved the party into the living room, where I had a book to read. We could only control what was in our area of influence and Greg's mom did not fall under mine. She might someday, but not today. Today I was going to watch junk television and eat junk food. And worry about my wedding.

# Chapter 7

Tuesday morning, Greg was already out of the house when I woke up. I knew he'd come home because there were dirty clothes in the laundry basket. And his towel was wet, so he'd showered sometime this morning. I dressed in my running clothes and headed downstairs to sip half a cup of coffee and get Emma ready to run. The door to Amanda's room was closed when I walked by, so I assumed she was still asleep.

We got down to the beach before anyone else was there. Of course, early morning January wasn't a prime beach time, except for people looking for wash ups and shells. I had enough shells to cover the outside of my house. Or at least the garage. Instead, I put the shells I collected in a container for a future mystery project. I didn't know what I was saving them for, but when I found the perfect craft, I'd have more than enough.

I unhooked the leash and let Emma run next to me. She liked running in the waves, getting doused at times and sometimes biting at the wave like she could control its path. Emma was the original law-of-attraction thinker. If she focused enough, I would take her for a run or give her a special treat. Sometimes I failed her positivity test, but Greg never did. He was attached to my dog almost as much as he loved me. Or at least that's what I told myself. I loved seeing them together, but Greg was the better dog parent.

It was a fact of life that I needed to accept. But thinking of her theory of life made me remember the book Kane had given me. I should take it back, but maybe I should read it before I did. Just to see what he thought would bring us closer.

Maybe I'd read Kane's book later.

Refocusing on Greg, I vaguely wondered if he'd be a better human parent as well. Kids. We were just getting married, so why was I already thinking about kids? At least we already had the dog and a house for our perfect life.

I saw someone walking toward me, and for a minute I thought it was Amanda. But instead, it was my friend Esmeralda. She had on her work outfit of capris and a short-sleeved top. The weather this morning was cool, but not cold. She was carrying her sneakers and walking barefoot on the sand. Emma had already run ahead to greet her.

"What are you doing out here?" I snapped Emma's leash on her collar when I met up with them.

"Greg called me to see if you'd gotten up. No one answered at the house when I walked over to check, and I didn't hear Emma barking when I knocked. I took a chance you might be out here. It's a beautiful morning for a run. I should be more disciplined and get out here too." Esmeralda started walking back to the parking lot with me.

"His mom must still be asleep." I took a deep breath, trying to slow my breathing from the run. "When do you have to go in?"

"Not until eight." She glanced up at the sky. "I think the weather's going to be beautiful on Saturday. You lucked out with an outdoor wedding."

"I didn't have much of a choice unless we wanted to wait until spring." I glanced over in the direction of my house. "I wanted to make sure Amanda would be able to make it."

"She's had a bit of a struggle." Esmeralda nodded, then laughed when she saw my face. "Amanda and I chat when she calls to talk to Greg. I know her health was the reason you put off the wedding the first two times."

"You never said anything." I was beginning to respect my friend's sense of loyalty.

Esmeralda shrugged. "Not my story to tell. Anyway, Greg said to get dressed and get down to the diner for breakfast. He's carved out a couple of hours so the three of you can have a meal together."

"Did he tell you he's staying at the Castle Friday night?" We climbed the stairs from the beach to the parking area, Emma walking between us.

"Greg's traditional. He says this is his last wedding, so he hopes you're in it for the long haul." Esmeralda turned toward the road.

"He could replace me in a heartbeat. The tourists are always making comments and asking if he has an available brother." I smiled as we paused by the side of the road, waiting for a car to go past. "Maybe. But he'd have to want to move on. I think you're stuck with him, even beyond the grave."

We crossed the road, and Esmeralda turned to go up her driveway. I hugged her. "Are you telling me that there's an afterlife? That Greg and I are soulmates?"

She hugged me back. "If there is such a thing, then yes, I believe the two of you are soulmates. As far as the afterlife, my entire career is based on that probability. I'm sure you know I wouldn't just make up my visits."

I didn't quite believe in Esmeralda's talents, but then again, there were a lot of things in the world I didn't know about. Her godson, Deek, read auras. And he was pretty accurate on what type of personality you'd have based on your aura. And the main part was that Esmeralda was my friend. There was no way I'd call fraud on a friend, even if I didn't truly believe. "I'm still a nonbeliever, but I believe in you."

"Almost a good save. Go wake up your mother-in-law and have breakfast with your man. He misses you." Esmeralda turned and hurried up the walkway. "I need to finish getting ready for work. I think it's going to be a busy day."

"The voices tell you that?" I smiled at her.

She shrugged. "The calls from yesterday. The frat house is doing a winter rush event and they're looking for garden gnomes."

Amanda wasn't downstairs when I came inside the house. I got Emma her breakfast and checked her water. Then I ran upstairs. I paused at the guest room door and knocked. "Amanda? Greg's taking us to breakfast."

No response. I knocked louder. Still no response from the room. I opened the door and saw a piece of paper on the bed.

Opening it, I read the note. "I'm walking into town to meet Vince for breakfast. Don't worry about me. I'll be back no later than ten."

Greg was going to have a fit, but it wasn't his life. And besides, if they were having breakfast, we knew just where to find her. Diamond Lille's. I wondered if we'd get a separate table or if Greg would want to sit down and break bread with his former stepfather.

As long as Greg didn't break his nose, we'd be good.

After I showered, I texted Greg, letting him know I was leaving the house and walking up. It wasn't my place to tell him that his mom wasn't with me. He'd find out sooner rather than later. My phone rang as soon as I came up the hill.

"Why are you going to work?" Aunt Jackie asked as I came into view. I glanced up at the apartment above The Train Station. She was standing in the living room window, watching me. "I'm not. I'm having breakfast with Greg."

"I hope you didn't leave his mother home alone with Emma." My aunt was always direct and to the point.

"Nope, she's already at the diner. Look, I need to go. Was there a purpose to this call besides finding out if I was working today?"

"No. I just saw you walking into town this early and hoped you hadn't forgotten that you were off this week. It happens."

Now I felt bad that I jumped on her. "Sorry, I'm just a little nervous."

"You're getting married Saturday and Greg's in the middle of a murder investigation. I'd be nervous too. You know how he gets when he's working a case." My aunt said something else, but the phone must have been muted. "Harrold's up and he's making pancakes. I better go. He likes to flip them and if I'm not there to watch, he gets grumpy."

As I walked the rest of the way to Diamond Lille's I wondered how Greg and I would be when we retired. Right now, with his job and mine, sometimes we barely saw each other. Other times, we were under each other's feet. It was feast or famine in our relationship. I expected to run the bookstore forever. Or at least as long as it made sense, but I did want to travel like my aunt and uncle were now. They'd gone on four cruises since she'd retired from the bookstore. I was sure they would have been out of town this weekend, except for my wedding.

Greg was waiting outside when I arrived and frowned when he saw me alone. "Is Mom still asleep?"

"No, she's already here. She left me a note saying she was meeting her ex-husband for breakfast. She should be inside." I hugged him, then stepped into the busy diner. Tiny, Lille's chef, was famous for his breakfast skillets. And it looked like most of the townies were here before they went off to work. I saw his mom at a booth. I pointed them out as we waited to be seated. "Shall we sit with them?"

"Not unless you want me to lose my appetite. I didn't get along with Mom's ex even when they were married. And after, well, she didn't get what she deserved out of the division of assets." He smiled at Lille. "Good morning. A booth for two if you have one."

Lille frowned at him and nodded toward Amanda and Vince. "I take it you want it away from those two?"

"Please." He smiled and glanced out the window. "In fact, you don't have garden seating yet, do you?"

Lille actually laughed, something I'd never seen her do. Lille ran the diner with an iron fist. And she hated me, even though I was now related to one of her favorite customers, Harrold, at least by marriage. "I have a booth available over here by the kitchen."

We followed her and sat, looking at the menus she left. A few seconds later, Lille was back and filling coffee cups for both of us. "Congrats on the wedding. I love your location. The mission fountain has always been at the top of my list of venues."

"Thanks, Greg found it." I smiled at him, knowing that it would make Lille even happier that I didn't find the place.

"Well, aren't you full of surprises?" Lille smiled at Greg. Totally ignoring me. "Carrie will be right with you."

Greg sipped his coffee and waited until she was out of earshot. "I don't get why you don't like her. She's very personable."

"To you. It doesn't matter, I'm used to it." I glanced over the menu. "I'm having a sausage skillet and French toast. What about you?"

He shrugged. "Not sure. I need to fit into my suit this weekend. Maybe I'll have eggs and fruit."

"You're kidding, right?" I looked up from the menu and saw him grinning.

"Of course I am. I'm having the omelet stuffed with biscuits and gravy and hashbrowns." He set the menu down. "You've got to know me better than that by now."

"I'm off my game right now." I leaned forward. "Have you eliminated Molly?"

"Not talking about the case." He turned in his seat. "But it is interesting that Vince is working for her and now is chatting up Mom again. Either he wants something for Molly, or he's pitching her another unique moneymaking opportunity for her to spend her retirement funds on. The guy's a sleaze. I don't know what Mom saw in him in the first place."

"Maybe she was lonely." Now that I knew what Greg was getting, I wanted that too. But I'd stick with my semi healthy order. I set my menu aside and realized he was watching me. "What, did I say something wrong?"

He shook his head and reached out to stroke my cheek. "No. You are always able to say just the right thing. You're right. Mom might have been lonely. And the scam artist over there filled some need. But hopefully, she'll find a nice guy before she takes that kind of leap again. Her financial statement can't take another hit like King Vince."

"Sorry that he brings up bad memories. Were you still at home when they married?"

Greg paused when Carrie came to get their order, then he continued. "No. He came after both Jim and I were out of the house. She met him at a church retreat. I think he was just looking for a good mark. The marriage only lasted a few years, but most of that time he was already gone and they were working on the divorce. She told me everything one night a few years ago. She was so embarrassed."

"Things happen. People lie. And there are a lot of people who live on hope, even after getting their teeth knocked in time after time." I snuck a look at Amanda. She didn't look like she was falling for the lines again. But you never knew. "Just one more reason I left family law. If you buy a bad book, you're out thirty, thirty-five dollars, tops. If you marry the wrong man, it's expensive."

"You're not worried about marrying the wrong man this time, are you?" He took my hand and kissed the top of it. "I'm a workaholic. I snap at you for pushing buttons you don't realize are there. And my family can be challenging."

"You've met my aunt. I own my own business so it's all on me. And I don't know what button I pushed. Unless you're talking about the resume. Greg, if I stepped over a line, I'm sorry." I did love this man.

"You didn't know there was a line, or rather a cliff, there. I'm the one who should be sorry. We'll talk about it later. Mom and her friend are coming to the table." Greg stood and greeted his mom with a kiss on the cheek. "Mom, I thought we were having breakfast. Vince."

Vince reached out a hand. "I guess I was just faster on the invite, sport. How are you? I hear congratulations are in order."

"Vince, this is my fiancée, Jill." He nodded to me. "Jill, this is Vince Penn, Mom's ex."

"We've met before." Vince pulled me into a hug. "But I love welcoming a soon-to-be member of the family."

I saw Greg's eyes flare with anger. But he kept his mouth shut about both the hug and the mention of family.

"Vince is going to walk me over to the bookstore and I'll meet you there when you're done with breakfast. I wanted to get the second book in a series I've been reading." Amanda hugged Greg. "Sorry about missing you this morning."

"No problem. I'm sure I'll be home for dinner." Greg's meaning was clear. They would be chatting about what Vince wanted. And soon.

After they left, our food showed up. I started to say something, then Greg held up his hand. "Just don't. He's another button. It's my mother's decision whether to bring him back into her life or not. I just hope he doesn't hurt her again."

We ate in silence for a few minutes, then we started talking about the logistics of the wedding and the night before. He grinned when he told me about Jim's planned bachelor party. "I told him there can't be any alcohol and I'll be on call. But he still wants to do it. I think we're going axe throwing."

"As long as he doesn't put my picture on the target, I'm fine with that."

As we finished breakfast, I knew he had a lot on his mind, so I told him about my aunt calling as I walked by because she assumed I'd forgotten I wasn't working. And about how nice it was to see Esmeralda on the beach. I didn't ask him who had killed Kane Matthews, even though that was what I wanted to talk about.

It was too early in the investigation for Greg to be desperate enough to ask me for help or a theory. He liked my input. He just didn't want to acknowledge it.

Or at least that was my story. I pushed away the almost-finished skillet and ate the last piece of French toast, dragging it through the warm maple syrup. I kind of regretted not getting the biscuits-and-gravy omelet, but not enough to give up the touch of sweetness with the French toast.

"I took your mom to Solvang yesterday and stopped into the bookstore. The new owner wasn't there, but I left my card." I emptied my coffee cup and put it by the side of the table, hoping Carrie would see I needed a refill.

"You should visit all the local bookstores. Maybe do a business-to-business type meeting with them once a quarter to talk marketing ideas. The business group has done a lot for South Cove." Greg cleaned the leftover gravy off his plate with a spoon and ate it. "I don't know what Tiny does to make this so good, but I have never made sausage gravy that tasted like this."

I pulled out my phone and texted Deek about Greg's idea.

"Did I say something wrong?" He smiled at Carrie as she refilled both our cups. "We'll take our check now. I've got to get back and Jill's having a brainstorm. I can see it growing."

"No bill. Lille says it's her treat and happy wedding." Carrie glanced around and saw that Lille was on the other side of the restaurant. "I've never seen her comp a meal before except for a celebrity."

"Well, please thank her for the meal and remind her that she's more than welcome at the wedding and reception. She knows the location." Greg smiled and held up his cup when Lille turned toward us. I hurried to follow suit, but she'd already turned away.

Today was just not my day.

# Chapter 8

When I got to the bookstore, Amanda was sitting alone at a table, reading. A large coffee in a to-go cup sat in front of her. She waved at me, and I held up a finger. I needed more coffee. How I needed more, I didn't know, but if we were going antique shopping today like we'd discussed yesterday, I needed coffee. Deek was at the counter.

"I thought this was Toby's morning," I said as I ordered my coffee.

"Dude called him in to go with him this morning to the compound, New Hope? I thought you'd already know." He poured me coffee and two pumps of caramel. "Mom's sorry she won't be at the wedding, but she hopes to make it for the reception. She has standing appointments on Saturday mornings that she can't cancel."

"I'm just glad she's coming. I know Esmeralda will love seeing her." I glanced up at Deek. "Are we closing the store like I suggested?"

"Judith and Tilly are going to work Saturday. Judith's sending her present with me. Tilly didn't feel comfortable attending." Deek leaned forward. "I think she needs the hours. She's been having some problems with her boyfriend."

"Okay, as long as they know they can close and come to the reception." I took the cup. "Anything else I should know?"

He shrugged. "The women from New Hope came in yesterday. Bought books. Stayed and drank coffee and ate a treat. Then they were hustled back into a van. They never meet your eyes when you talk to them. Have you noticed?"

I nodded. "It's like they don't want to connect to anyone outside the compound. I hear them laughing and talking between themselves, but not with outsiders. Anyway, with Kane gone, it might just break up."

"Oh, no. They've already picked a new leader. I guess he was the second-in-command before. He came in looking for you. He said he'll be at the next business meeting." Deek leaned down and pulled out a business card. "Here's what he left for you."

I read the card. "Roger Matthews. I wonder if he is related to Kane?"

"It's his brother," Amanda said as she came up from behind. "Vince told me that this morning. Molly was hoping they'd disband, but I guess Kane had a succession plan in place. Just in case. Once I told Vince I wasn't interested in dating again or financing his business, he tried to get me to talk to Greg about Molly. So I got a little information."

"Well, you can tell Greg, but he's not going to just remove Molly from the suspect list because you ask him. He wants to find the killer, not just someone who might be." I was beginning to not like Vince too.

"Which is what I told Vince, but hope springs eternal with that man." She handed Deek her coffee cup. "Can you refill this? I need some caffeine since I didn't get much sleep last night."

"We can just go back to the house," I suggested.

Amanda shook her head. "Let's hit a few antique shops, then take Emma to the beach. I like watching the waves. I guess Greg will be joining us for dinner. Or does he just want to yell at me for seeing Vince?"

"Maybe on the dinner part. He wants to, I know that. But if he gets a break in the case, he'll be gone." I thanked Deek for the coffee. Amanda knew her son well.

"Well, if he doesn't come home, maybe we could order pizza? I never order pizza for dinner at home." Amanda held the door open. "It's too bad the store next door doesn't open until ten. I'd love to see what they have."

Josh was sweeping the front steps as we walked up. "Hey, Josh, do you think we could do a walk-through? This is Greg's mom, Amanda. Amanda, this is my friend, Josh Thomas." I didn't want to remind him that I'd gone with him on some crazy adventures lately. But I would if he said no.

He smiled at Amanda. "So nice to meet you. Greg King is well respected in South Cove. He does a great job. Of course you can come in now. If you find something, Mandy can help you with the purchase. She's inside setting up a new display."

"Josh and Mandy are newlyweds," I added, to his discomfort. If having Amanda here opened doors like this, maybe she should stay around. As we entered Antiques by Thomas, Amanda started talking about her and Vince. How it happened and how it ended. Greg had the story right about the ending, but the beginning had been magical. Vince had been attentive, brought her flowers, and listened when she talked. Everything a woman wanted in a partner. But as soon as the ring was on her finger, he changed. He became controlling. He kept asking about her finances. And he quit looking for work.

"I didn't know what to do. He had good excuses. Great stories. But I knew something was wrong. Now I wish I'd trusted my instincts. I started having doubts just before the wedding, but I went through with it anyway. I thought it was just wedding jitters." She paused at a beautiful dresser, stroking the wood. "Should have, could have, would have. Right?"

"So is this why the questions yesterday about why I waited so long to marry your son?" I was beginning to understand where Amanda was coming from. "That's a beautiful bedroom set. I keep saying we need to replace what we have. Maybe after the wedding."

"Yes. Sorry about the inquisition yesterday. Sometimes I let my insecurities and faults color my view of your relationship. Thank you for humoring me." She glanced at the price tag. "This is a nice set. And it's in great shape."

"Josh has good stock. And he has a helper who can fix anything that needs it." I followed her to the next setting. The antiques were in more focused groupings than the last time I visited. Probably Mandy's influence. "I did have my doubts that I'd ever remarry. But Greg just kept showing up and saying the right things. I can't imagine life without him."

Amanda smiled at me. "Now that's a good reason to get married."

We thanked Mandy for letting us in early, then walked back to the house, where I let Emma out and grabbed a couple of water bottles for us. We took the Jeep to Bakerstown and found several stores to wander through. I bought a garden gnome for the backyard. I thought Greg would get the humor. As we left the last store, we saw three vans in front of a fabric store and men in suits waiting outside.

"The New Hope group must be shopping." I pointed Amanda toward the store. "Do you mind coming in with me?"

"I'd love to go inside. We need to get tulle and ribbon anyway for the shower of good wishes as you walk down the aisle. We need wild bird seed too." Amanda grinned. "Or are your friends handling that tradition?" "No one's mentioned it. Don't people throw rice?" I held the store's door open for her.

"Rice swells up in the birds' tummies. Especially since you're having the wedding outside at the mission, we should do birdseed." Amanda patted my arm. "Don't worry about it. I'll make up a basket for you. How many guests do you expect?"

I wasn't going to be the one who told her that swelling rice was an urban myth. Instead, I gave her the number of guests we were expecting, and we headed over to the right section. I scanned for the women of New Hope and found them in the cotton section. Someone must make their dresses. As Amanda talked about matching different fabrics to my wedding colors, blue and silver, I looked at each woman's face, trying to find Carlie.

When I locked gazes with an older woman, she smiled, dropping the fabric she'd been considering, and walked over to where we were standing. "You're Jill Gardner, owner of that cute bookstore in South Cove, aren't you?"

I smiled and held out my hand. "That's me. I'm sorry, I don't think we've met."

"I'm Maryanne Matthews. Roger's my husband. He just took over the New Hope leadership after the tragic loss of Kane. Our brother was so charismatic. He's always been that way. I met Roger in college, so I've been part of the family for years." Maryanne glanced at the men standing outside by the van. I turned to follow her gaze. They weren't watching her, yet. "Anyway, I don't have a lot of time. They don't like us to converse with nonbelievers. I saw you at the open house talking to Kane. Are you curious about the church?"

"You mean, am I thinking of joining?" I shook my head. "I've got a lot going on right now, with the business, and family…"

Before I could add to the list of excuses, Maryanne nodded. "And the upcoming wedding. I'm so happy for you. Weddings are the best, especially when you're marrying your soulmate. Anyway, I just wanted to meet you formally and extend an open invitation to our services."

Then Maryanne hugged me. I patted her back and saw Amanda watching us. I slightly shrugged my shoulders, indicating that I didn't know anything more than she did.

When Maryanne stood back, she glanced outside again. This time a man was watching her. She smiled and nodded her head. "Remember, you're welcome anytime." Then she hurried over to the other women. "Are we about ready, then?"

Amanda came over with two shades of white tulle for me to consider. "Which one is better?" Then she dropped her voice to ask, "And what the heck was that?"

I pointed to the correct shade, which I was sure she already knew. "I have no idea. But I think I see Carlie Cordon over there by the plaids."

Amanda reached for another roll of tulle. She positioned herself behind me so she could see the section I'd mentioned. "Do you want one of the ribbons to be larger or both the same size?" Then she dropped her voice. "I think you're right."

"Let me take a picture of everything we're considering, and I'll send it to Aunt Jackie so she can match it up. If we wait a few minutes, she should text back." I took out my phone and aimed it at Carlie. Then I asked Amanda to hold the fabric against her shirt for contrast. I changed the focus and got an even better picture of Carlie. Then I texted Greg.

His response came quickly. *Stay out of it. I'm asking Bakerstown to send a car to bring her in for questioning.*

Amanda and I moved to the ribbon section. She glanced at the woman as she looked through the ribbons. "Is Greg sending someone?"

"He's sending a car to pick her up for questioning. We're supposed to stay out of it. But I'd like to see it go down—unless you feel uncomfortable? We can leave."

Amanda shook her head. "I'm fine. Besides, we still need to pick a ribbon color and have everything cut. We'll be here a while."

We were at the cutting table when the trouble started. The men hanging around the van saw the police officers first. One man came in and tried to move all the women out of the fabric store. They glanced at their watches and argued with him. Finally, they moved to the checkout line. He took the fabric out of the youngest girl's arms and pushed her toward the door.

"Everyone but Maryanne, get into the vans. Maryanne, if we have to leave, I'll send someone back to get you. Wait outside when you're done." The man pointed to the register. "Everyone put your stuff there and get into the vans. I'm not telling you again."

Maryanne looked over and saw Amanda and me watching. "Fred, you're making a scene. Ladies, follow Fred out to the vans. I'll get your fabric, don't worry."

Fred turned and glared at us. Then he moved toward the door. He had bigger things to deal with. The cops were at the door.

"Excuse me, ladies, can you hold still," an older officer asked as another one stood blocking the doorway.

I glanced out the window and saw that officers from a second car were blocking the men from New Hope from entering. Right now, it was all civilized. I only hoped it would stay that way. I looked over at Amanda. "If you see a gun pulled, drop to the floor and head to the back room. I'll be right behind you."

The woman who had just finished cutting our fabric whispered, "The backroom door is right behind us. I'll lead you there."

"I'm hoping we'll be fine. But there are a lot of angry men around." I leaned against the counter to watch the officer.

He held up his phone and checked five women against what I suspected was Carlie's photo. Fred was on his cell phone, talking quietly at the side of the room.

"These five are okay to leave." The officer in charge nodded toward the man at the door. When those women had left, he turned to the next five. He struck pay dirt with the second face he checked. "Miss, would you step aside near the register?"

Maryanne waved her over and put her arm around the girl. I heard her murmur words of comfort. They watched as the officer went through the rest of the women, checking something on his phone before stepping to the next one. Was there more than one missing girl?

The officer sent a second girl over to where Maryanne was standing. Then he released the rest and Fred left the store with them. I saw everyone climb into two of the three vans. Fred and one other man stood outside the last van, watching.

The police officers were still watching them.

The officer in charge walked over and nodded to Maryanne. "You can go too, ma'am."

"Not until I finish my business here. What do you want with my sisters?" Maryanne nodded to the clerk, who started running the fabric, notions, and patterns through her register.

The officer glanced out the window to where Fred and his friend were still waiting. "These women are your sisters. By birth?"

"No, not by birth. As you probably already know, we belong to New Hope. The men outside drive us on our errands so we don't have to bother with driving ourselves." Maryanne handed the clerk cash to cover the bill. "You still haven't answered my question. Why are you detaining my sisters?"

"They have been reported missing by their families."

"We are their family. And they are of age. Have you never heard of someone choosing not to be around a toxic family environment? Why do they not have the freedom to worship the way they choose?" Maryanne took the bags of fabric, handing one to each girl. "I take it you're escorting them to your station. Where is it located, so we can send our lawyer to save our sisters from this unlawful detainment?"

This was the most I'd heard any woman living at New Hope say. Apparently, she was part of the leadership. At least for the women.

"We're on Main Street, ma'am. And your attorney is more than welcome to talk to our captain." He frowned at the bags. "They can't take those with them."

"My sisters are helping me carry the fabric for our new dresses to our van. Do you expect me to carry all these heavy bags by myself? If you want, they can set them on the sidewalk and Brother Fred and Brother Keith can load them."

"That would be best. We don't want these women to disappear again." The officer looked over at me and Amanda. "Are you two with these women?"

Amanda put a hand on my arm, stopping me from responding.

"No, sir. We are just shopping for my new daughter-in-law's wedding this weekend. We're making birdseed favors for the guests to throw at the happy couple. It's so much better for the environment than the traditional rice." She held up the ribbon. "And we're using both of her colors on the ribbon. Blue and silver. Won't it be lovely?"

The officer blinked at the information overload. "Well, please stay where you are until we leave the area. I don't expect a problem from a religious organization"—he turned and looked hard at Maryanne before continuing—"but it's better not to put civilians in harm's way."

He turned away and started moving the women toward the door. Once they were outside, I turned toward Amanda as I watched Carlie and the other woman getting into the back of a police car. Maryanne stood with

Fred and watched the car pull away as Keith loaded the bags from the fabric shop into the back. Then they all got into the van and drove away. "You overwhelmed him with information about the wedding so he'd leave us alone." I grinned at her while the clerk finished cutting our ribbon. "He didn't have a wedding ring on so I took a chance that talking about a wedding would make him uncomfortable. And it did. He didn't even ask us our names." Amanda took the ribbon and the receipt the clerk gave us to use to check out. "He's probably going to hear about that from his captain."

"Especially if the lawyer starts talking about overstepping." I was impressed by Amanda's plan. I had used the ploy of giving too much information about unimportant facts before, but not with this level of finesse. I might just learn a few tricks from hanging out with Greg's mom.

We left the fabric store and glanced around the strip mall to see what other stores were there. Amanda took a deep breath. "The air here is so warm. And I'm starving. Any good Tex-Mex places around? I haven't had good Mexican food since my last trip."

We were in the middle of lunch when Greg called me. "We're eating at the Three Tequilas. Do you want me to get you a to-go order?"

"Sounds good, but no. I've already eaten. I thought you were in the fabric store with the New Hope women," Greg said.

"We were. Your mom's doing a birdseed packet to replace the traditional rice."

A second of silence held on the phone. "I'm not sure what that means, but great. Anyway, the report doesn't list your names."

"The officer didn't ask us our names. Or the women who were working in the store, for that matter," I added.

"Sloppy work. Now the attorney will have holes to punch through. Anyway, Toby's running Molly into Bakerstown to talk to Carlie. I suspect Vince will show up at the station too."

I didn't respond, as Amanda was focusing on her food but listening carefully to my side of the conversation. "Okay, well, are you still going to be home for dinner?"

"Probably." He sighed. "I guess they found another missing girl with Carlie. Bakerstown has this facial recognition program that they spent a pretty penny to buy last year. I have to walk around with high school yearbook pictures in my pocket to identify people."

"It's not nice to have tech envy. Especially if it solves another case." I smiled as I dunked a chip into salsa and took a bite.

"It's not solving my case. In fact, now I have another possible suspect— the father of this other girl who sent Kane Matthews death threats last year when Kane wouldn't let him talk to his kid." He sighed again. "Esmeralda just buzzed me. I have a call from Bakerstown PD. I better take it. Where are you headed now?"

"We'll be heading back to go play on the beach after lunch." I smiled at Amanda, who nodded. "Let me know if you're not coming home. I'll grab a couple of pizzas from the winery for dinner."

"Sounds like a plan, either way. Love you."

He ended the call and I put my phone aside.

"Someone's in trouble?" Amanda smiled.

"I think they're going to be once Greg rats us out as being there. I just hope that they don't want to interview us before next week. He did say that the other girl's father had sent death threats to Kane."

"Sounds like there were several people not happy with New Hope's former leader. Maybe that will help Greg solve the case sooner rather than later. I'd hate to think you'd have to delay the honeymoon any longer than you have already." Amanda sipped her strawberry margarita. "This thing is strong. I might just take a nap when we head to the beach. I love the sound of the waves."

# Chapter 9

Darla Taylor showed up at the house around nine on Wednesday morning. She brought coffee from the bookstore as well as a dozen of Sadie's snowflake cookies. I'd already taken Emma running and Amanda was up and making birdseed packets. We'd stopped at a garden supply store and bought the seed on the way home yesterday.

Greg hadn't made it home for dinner, but he'd promised he'd be here tonight since Jim and Beth were coming for family dinner. We were grilling steaks, and I was making mac and cheese to go with it along with a salad. Simple, but filling. I'd put off picking up my dress until tomorrow because Amanda wanted to take Beth to Santa Barbara for the day. We had two more days to fit in all the tourist stops Amanda wanted to hit before the wedding. Friday was busy with the rehearsal dinner and Saturday was all about the wedding. Greg and I had a room in a nearby upscale hotel on the beach for Saturday night and he'd promised we'd have brunch together Sunday morning. Then life would go back to normal, which was actually crazy, until the honeymoon. Maybe Amanda and I would have more time then.

Or whenever Greg found out who killed Kane. The guy was dead and he was still messing with my life. At least he wouldn't be attending any more of the business-to-business meetings. But now I had to deal with his brother, Roger.

"So, Jill, what have you heard about Kane's death? Is it going to affect you having the wedding at the mission?" Darla directed a question to me after opening with a few conversational questions for Amanda. Darla never showed up without an agenda. She was my friend, but she also was the local newspaper reporter. And when Darla was on an assignment, she didn't let go until she found out what she needed to know. "I know the two of you weren't friends."

"I barely knew him. Go interview the mayor. He and Kane were buddy-buddy. Or they were until the mayor found out Kane was filing for a religious exemption on the property." I broke a cookie in half and nibbled on one side. I would eat the whole thing, but maybe this would keep me from eating two. Or more.

"Wouldn't that be a thing? Maybe the mayor killed Kane for failing to add to his tax base." Darla giggled. "Of course, he wouldn't have killed him. It would have been Tina. Tina always does the wet work in that relationship."

"I take it Tina's his wife?" Amanda sipped her coffee, clearly amused by the conversational turn.

"For better or worse. Tina's in it for the long haul. I think she believes that someday Baylor might take her to the top of the California political heap, at least." Darla explained our mayor and his wife's agenda. Then she turned back to me. "So you're telling me you haven't been investigating after finding Kane's body on Sunday?"

"Darla, I've been a little busy," I tried to explain.

Amanda held up her hand. "I'm afraid I'm keeping Jill too busy to get involved with Greg's investigation. Well, me and the wedding. Do you want to help us make birdseed packets while we chat?"

The look on Darla's face was priceless. There was nothing she would more hate to do more when she had on her reporter hat. "Sorry, I need to go check out my next lead. Jill, please just think of me if you hear anything. I need to put this story to bed by Thursday night. Especially since we have the rehearsal on Friday."

I smiled at Amanda. "Darla's one of my bridesmaids."

"Oh, fun. So we'll have lots of time to chat. My other son Jim and his girlfriend are arriving today. I'm sure Beth will be able to help me finish these up in no time."

Darla stood and motioned me to follow her to the front door. "I didn't think you wanted all the trappings of a traditional wedding."

"It makes her happy." I shrugged. "As long as we don't have candlelighters and ten sets of groomsmen and bridesmaids, I'm fine with a little birdseed. Besides, it's outdoors and the birds will appreciate it."

"Just remember, it's your day. Well, yours and Greg's." Darla pulled me into a quick hug. "I can't believe you two are getting married. Finally." "Don't hold your breath until I walk down the aisle on Saturday. Lots could go wrong between now and then." I glanced over at Amanda, who was counting out her packets and making piles of ten. "I don't want to jinx it." Darla stepped out onto the porch. "The one thing I've found out is that Roger Matthews has a bit of a rap sheet. He's not the angel his brother was. Or maybe Roger was always the brawn and Kane was the brain."

"Why would he kill his brother? That would be like killing the golden goose, right?" I thought about the open house. The security the compound had set up was over-the-top. "And if Roger was in charge of security, he could play to his strengths, not pretend to be in touch with some higher power. Kane was off-the-charts charismatic. Is Roger?"

"That's a good question. I don't know. But you can be sure I'll find out." Darla pulled out her phone and texted a note.

"Just be careful," I called as she walked out to her vehicle. "I don't want to have to replace a bridesmaid last minute."

"I love you too," Darla responded as she held a hand above her head to wave at me.

As I closed the door, I realized I was worried about Darla pushing the wrong buttons with the New Hope group. I'd seen firsthand yesterday the power they had over their people. If Darla got in their way, she could be thrown into one of those vans and disappear. Just like Carlie and the other woman taken in by the police, who were now in the local hospital's mental ward on a seventy-two-hour hold. They'd both reacted violently to seeing their family member. The Bakerstown police chief suspected they had some kind of drug in their system, so he had them tested and kept safe until he could be sure he was getting the full story.

Greg had been called to Bakerstown last night to help with Molly. Vince was pushing her to "claim" her daughter and take her out of there. Greg told Molly if she took Carlie now, her daughter would just run back to New Hope. At least with the medical hold, she'd be drug-free when she made her choice. And maybe Molly could help Carlie make the right choice.

Greg had told me all this as we sat and ate warmed-up pizza after he'd finally come home last night. He didn't think Molly was involved in Kane's death, but he hadn't been able to rule her out yet.

When I came back to the kitchen, Amanda looked up. "Anything you want to talk about?"

I shook my head. "Darla's always looking for a story. Even when there isn't one yet. Greg will find out who killed Kane Matthews, not only because he's good at investigating, but because he wants justice to win. Sometimes the press wants quick results when it's really a lot more than a paragraph on page one with a picture."

"And yet, you're friends with her," Amanda said.

I smiled as I moved the cookies out of my reach and grabbed an apple to cut up. "She's a fierce friend and I'm lucky to have her."

Amanda smiled at that description but didn't respond.

After our coffee was gone, I opened my laptop. "So, what else is on your to-see list?"

She shut my laptop. "Let's hang around the house today. I need a break. When Beth and Jim arrive, they're going to be a lot. If you need to do anything for the wedding or go shopping, that's fine. I'll just hang out here with Emma."

I wanted to chat with Amy and see whatever paperwork the New Hope group had put in when they opened their compound. I also wanted to run to the library at the college and see if I could find out anything about Kane, his brother, or the church itself. Then I wanted to stop at the mortuary, where our county coroner lived and worked. Doc Ames loved to chat about his cases and I could pretend that I was there to see if he and Carrie were coming to the wedding.

All things I couldn't do with Amanda. Not without Greg finding out. I tucked my laptop into a tote. "This works out great. I need to check in at the shop, then run to Bakerstown and pick up some things for dinner. I'll be back no later than four. Jim and Beth are due in at six, right?"

"That's what they said. Jim's usually early, so I'd expect them around five," Amanda warned as she moved to the couch. "I'd love to relax with a movie. Seeing Vince the other day, well, he's draining. Even on his best behavior."

Man, I understood that. I'd been in relationships like that, where it was all about the other guy. Walking on eggshells and trying not to cause a scene. "Do you want me to bring you back anything?"

"I wouldn't say no to a bag of peanut M&M's." Amanda turned on the television. "Anything special I need to do for Emma?"

"She'll tell you when she needs to go outside. Just don't leave her out alone. And only in the backyard. We have too much traffic for her to be out front. There are wild animals that like to hunt local pets. Although most of them are smaller than Emma. I just don't want to take a chance with her." "I'm a good babysitter, I promise." She patted the couch and Emma came up to lie beside her. My dog could be bribed with a movie. Or a treat. Or a rub on the head. Basically, any kind of attention.

I grabbed my keys. "I'll see you in a few, then."

I headed to see Amy first. If I ran into Greg, I could explain it away with wedding banter. Just like Amanda had at the fabric store. I just hoped Greg was busy enough to be as gullible as the Bakerstown officers had been.

The mayor's car wasn't parked in his assigned spot, so I thought I might have lucked out. When I went in the front door of city hall, Amy was standing in the hallway, refilling her water bottle. "Hey, friend."

"What are you doing here? I thought you were on tour guide duty all week?" Amy closed her pink bottle and hugged me. "Not that I'm complaining. Do you have time for lunch?"

"Not today, sorry. Greg's brother is showing up for dinner tonight with his girlfriend. Amanda loves this girl, so I need to make sure the food is good to even be in the running for her attention." I followed her into her office. "I wanted to know if you had the New Hope file close by and if I could look at it."

"You're investigating?" Amy shook her head, incredulous. "You are getting married on Saturday, have your in-laws to entertain, and have a store to run. And you want to add in solving a murder? Are you crazy? I would have checked myself into a spa for the week."

"And yet you didn't," I reminded her. "Anyway, I'm not investigating. I just don't understand who Kane was or the structure of New Hope. I know I don't need to know, but when has that ever stopped me?"

"Well, if Greg asks, you found it on my desk. Open." She pulled it out of a drawer. "You're not the first to ask. Esmeralda made a copy of the file yesterday. That's why it's still here. I figured there might be others who wanted to see it. Besides, the mayor doesn't like me to leave the desk unattended. Even for a trip back to the file room."

"I promise I'll keep you out of it." I grabbed the file and sat in Amy's visitor chair, taking a picture of each page as I flipped through. I'd read it later. A name jumped out at me. "Maryanne Matthews? That's right, she said she was married to…" I couldn't remember the guy's name.

"She was Kane's sister-in-law. She's married to Roger. Or at least that's the rumor. I don't think there's a legal marriage license in the bunch." Amy leaned forward. "I hear they found ten girls hidden on the compound."

"Close, but it was only two. And they were at the fabric store when the police stepped in. They didn't look like they wanted to leave anytime soon." I took a picture and turned the page. It was copies of three driver's licenses. Kane, Roger, and Maryanne. I took another picture. Their licenses were from Oregon. "They aren't local."

"They had a compound in Oregon, but they were growing too big and that's why they moved down here. They thought the political climate was more conducive."

I looked up at Amy. "More conducive than Oregon? That a pretty liberal state."

Amy shrugged. "That's what they said. Anyway, that's all I have."

"I guess if you were run out of your old town you wouldn't tell your new town your troubles, right?" I finished taking pictures of the information in the file. Thank goodness Amy was my friend. If not, I'd have had to file actual paperwork to get the information and then Greg would find out. And right now, I'd rather not fight about me sticking my nose in his business. At least before the wedding.

I closed the file and handed it back to her. "Don't you think it's weird that two brothers were at the helm of this church? I can't see both of them being called to serve."

"Sometimes it happens. The church becomes a family business." Amy put the file in her drawer. "Do you believe that either Kane Matthews or his brother were called to lead a church? I'm probably not the best person to talk to about this. Have you talked to Pastor Bill? I know he had some strong feelings about New Hope's addition to our community."

"That's a good idea. I'll go see him." I glanced at my watch. There was no way I would get to Bakerstown and back if I went to see Bill. Besides, I'd see him Friday when he was at our wedding rehearsal. Maybe I could sneak in a conversation then. Or just before the wedding. Didn't he do counseling for people getting married? I could say I wanted to talk about the wedding.

Greg was going to kill me and I was going to hell for using my own wedding as a means to investigate Kane's murder. It was that simple.

As I walked to the door that led outside, Amy called after me. "No one would think anything of it if you just stayed out of this investigation.

You've got a lot going on with your personal life. Like a wedding. No need to be at odds with your groom. Believe me, you'll find plenty to fight about after the wedding."

I knew Amy was right. I should stay out of this. I walked to the Jeep, but instead of getting in and going home, I crossed the street and went to the bookstore. I could still change my mind about going. But I needed at least a dozen cookies. Maybe two. One for the house and my additional visiting in-laws. And a dozen for Doc Ames.

Judith was manning the store this morning. She had her short gray hair dyed purple this month. She grinned as I came into the store. "Hey, boss, I'm glad I saw you before your big day. I told Deek and Evie that I'd work that Saturday since Tilly needed the hours. I'll send my gift over with Deek."

"You don't have to give us a gift." I slid onto a stool and glanced around the bookstore. People were sitting at a few of the tables, some over on the couch, reading. It felt very Zen. "You've got a nice group of people. It's usually dead in here on Wednesdays."

"Most of these people are from my yoga class. I told them I had additional hours this week. They try to get in and support me. It's kind of sweet." She smiled at the younger group in the shop. "And then there's my hiking group, they come in on Saturdays when I work. I think they want to try to talk me into going with them."

"You know you don't have to work full-time if you don't want to." As we talked, I sipped the coffee she'd poured for me.

"I do if I'm going to Italy next year. I'm already trying recipes from an Italian cookbook and I've been taking a language class at the local college on Thursday nights. That's why I can't work then." She lowered her voice. "So, are you here hiding?"

"Hiding?" Now I was confused.

"From your houseguest. I didn't get along with my mother-in-law, but she's gone now. She would have been so happy to hear that her precious son and I divorced a few years ago. But she didn't live long enough to celebrate."

I chuckled. "Actually, I like Amanda. I think she likes me, but who knows. Anyway, I need two boxes of a dozen cookies each. Can you just charge my account?"

"Not marketing?" She grabbed a box from under the counter. When I shook my head, she pointed the tongs toward the case. "Anything specific?"

"Whatever you have the most of. I don't want to leave you short."
While Judith set up my cookies, I checked my email to make sure I wasn't missing anything wedding-related. I had a reminder from the bridal shop for the appointment to pick up my dress tomorrow. Everything else was confirmations of the place and time. I had an email from an author looking for a place to hold a signing. I forwarded that to Deek. He was my author whisperer.

Judith put a bag holding the boxes on the counter in front of me. She glanced at my barely touched coffee. "Are you staying around to drink that or do you want a fresh one in a travel mug?"

"You can put this in a mug, then just add more coffee." I handed her the cup, then put my phone away. "I'll be happy to have everything back to normal next week."

"Then you'll go off on your honeymoon and have to reacclimate again. But traveling is so worth it. Do you know where he's taking you yet?" She finished off the coffee and put a lid on top of it before handing it to me.

I took the coffee and grabbed the bag. "Not a clue, and it's making me a little anxious. I don't know how to pack. Or if I need to go shopping. He's being tight-lipped around the location."

"I'm sure you'll love it, no matter where you wind up. You kids love each other, even a cynic like me can see that." She waved up a new customer who was standing off to the side, not wanting to interrupt our conversation. "Have a wonderful weekend, Jill."

As long as I got my sleuthing done without Greg finding out, I just might have a wonderful weekend.

Jessica Fletcher never had these types of conflicts.

# Chapter 10

I'd checked the Bakerstown Funeral Home's website and saw that they had a funeral scheduled at ten this morning. I figured there were things that Doc needed to do afterward, so I decided to visit the college library first and see if I could find anything on the Matthews brothers or New Hope church. Now that I knew they were from Oregon, the search might be narrow enough to allow me to find relevant news articles on the church.

As I scanned the options that came back, I saw an article about a church burning. It happened over twenty years ago, but the Matthews name was attached so I clicked the link. It gave me a microfilm summary of a church fire that had been suspected to be arson. Joshua and Mary Matthews had died in the fire. Joshua had been the pastor of the church. I glanced at the name of the newspaper. *Newport Free Press.* Opening my photos from the New Hope file, the driver's licenses showed that the Oregon addresses were in Beaverton. I looked up both on a map of Oregon. I thought Newport was on the coast, and that was right. But Beaverton?

I found it, and as I studied the map more, I realized it was near Portland. It might be a coincidence. I lived in California and I didn't know people who lived in Sacramento. We were separated by miles and several thousand people. And yet, it felt like it was important.

I put in a request for a copy of the article, paid the fee, and set it to go to my email account. I could have used Evie's school account and saved a few dollars, but it all went to support the library, so I didn't have a problem with paying a few bucks for a wild goose chase.

By the time I was done at the library, I had a few more pieces of information. Like where all three principals, Kane, Roger, and Maryanne, went to school. It was a small Christian college. Roger and Maryanne had been married in the school's chapel the week after graduation. Maryanne's family was listed in the article from the small town where the school was located, but the only family listed for Roger was his brother, who was also his best man.

Roger had graduated with a bachelor's degree in criminal justice and Kane had a bachelor's in philosophy with a minor in religious studies. His discussion of the context in the interpretation of books including the Bible when I saw him at the open house made sense now.

Maryanne had a business degree.

Between the three of them, they had what they needed to start a church. But why had Kane been their front man? He oozed charisma. Had it been as simple as that?

I printed off what I could and tucked the sheets into the folder I'd packed in my tote. Before I left, I sent the photos of the New Hope business application to the printer as well. Being an alumnus at the school had some privileges. Like cheap copies.

I headed back to my Jeep and hurried over to Bakerstown Funeral Home. As I'd expected, the parking lot that had been full when I drove by on my way to the college was now empty, except for Doc's old blue truck and the newer minivan hearse he used for his business. As well as for any official business.

Carrie's little green MG wasn't in the parking lot. I assumed it was parked in front of Diamond Lille's, where she worked. I didn't know how long her shift would be, but my time to chat alone with Doc Ames was narrowing fast.

I went in the unlocked front doors, turned left, and headed to Doc's office. I'd rather find him here than downstairs doing the nonpaperwork part of his job. Fingers crossed, I knocked on his partially closed door.

"Come in, Jill. What did you bring to bribe me to chat?" He smiled as I pushed the door open. He was sitting at his desk.

"How did you know it was me?" I handed him the box of cookies I'd brought.

After taking the box, he used it to point at his computer. "I put in a security system. I've had a few break-ins recently. Can you believe it? I'd like to think it was just kids daring each other, but some things have gone missing. This way, at least I know who's robbing me. And the cops are alerted if it goes off when I have the system set."

"I'm sorry to hear that." I sat down and put my purse on the other chair. Now I was glad I'd locked my Jeep. Greg had trained me to lock up, no matter where I was and how safe I felt. It made him feel better. Even though no one had tried anything for years. Since I'd moved to South Cove. At least with my car.

"I don't mean to make you uncomfortable. I'm sure it was just random kids. But now with Carrie living here, better safe than sorry." Doc Ames leaned closer. "Do you want some coffee? Or a cookie?"

"I think I'm coffeed out." I smiled as he opened the box, holding it out for me to grab a treat. "And don't tempt me with a cookie. I'm hoping my dress fits tomorrow. Wedding planning is stressful, and we all know I eat my emotions."

He took a snowflake cookie and put the box away. "Carrie will love these. What can I help you with? I'm assuming you're here because of the Matthews boy downstairs."

"I am. What can you tell me about how he was murdered?" I opened my notebook and uncapped a pen.

"Officially, nothing."

When I didn't react, he leaned back and sighed. "You're going to get me disinvited to your wedding and Carrie already bought a new dress."

"Not going to happen. Now, how did Kane die?" I was hoping he would say something like he was killed with someone's bare hands. That would eliminate Molly. Maybe not this new parent that Greg found or even Pastor Bill, but Molly would be off the suspect list. "When Greg's main suspect found him, he looked like he was praying. Then he just fell over. At least according to her story."

"He was posed. From what I could see, he was killed there, on-site, but maybe not in that exact place or position. There was evidence that he was lying on his back when he died. He was strangled with a thin wire, maybe the cord from his headphones. Although why someone would choke him, I don't know. His attacker was either very angry or very strong. And the only reason I'm telling you this is to see what you remember of the scene. I'd like you to walk me through it. Maybe this will make more sense then."

"What's bothering you?"

Doc shook his head. "First tell me about what happened. Tell me what you saw."

I went through why I'd been there and what I saw after leaving the chapel with my mother-in-law's purse. "Soon-to-be mother-in-law," I corrected after I was done.

He shook his head. "So all you saw was the body on the ground? I was hoping you'd seen something that would explain the posing. It's like they were making fun of his position as head of the church."

"Yeah, I kind of got that too. Which makes Molly a good suspect." I sank back in the chair. Maybe I should just sit this one out. If Molly had killed Kane, maybe I was just looking for clues that explained away her being there.

"What does this Molly look like? Her physical shape? Is she tall? Fit?" Doc grabbed a second cookie.

"She's probably in her fifties. Maybe five foot two, if that. She's tiny. I bet she wears a size two or something stupid like that." I hadn't been a size two since high school. And I didn't remember that.

"I don't think she could have posed the victim if she's that small. It's hard to move dead weight. That's why they call it that." He wrote down a note. "I need to get Greg an estimate of what body type the killer would need to have to pose him after death. And if she attacked the guy, he would have had to be sitting down unless he walked past her standing on a stool, waiting for him. I need to check that angle as well. You've given me some things to think about."

"And maybe help to exclude Molly Cordon? I hope so." I glanced at my watch. "I need to go. Greg's brother, Jim, and his girlfriend are coming for dinner."

"The brother who swore he'd never remarry after his wife died. That's an interesting twist I didn't see coming." He stood to walk me out.

"Me neither. I briefly met Beth a few months ago, but I'm looking forward to learning more about her and how she won over the confirmed widower." I gave Doc a quick hug. "Thanks for chatting with me."

"If anyone asks, we were just sharing some cookies and getting caught up before your big day." He leaned closer. "Your fiancé gets a little miffed if he thinks I'm feeding your sleuthing habit."

As I drove to the grocery store, I thought about what Doc had said. If he was right, Molly could be removed from Greg's suspect list. Of course, Pastor Bill couldn't be removed, but he wasn't the only man in town who could have killed Kane. Kane's own brother probably met the same criteria. And he was the new head guy for New Hope. That seemed like more motivation than a disagreement about translations of the Bible. At least in my book.

When I got home, Greg's truck and what looked like a second rental car sat in my driveway. I was busted. I grabbed the cookies, hoping they would give me an excuse. As long as Judith didn't mention what time I left the store. And I had the grocery bags in the back.

I could hear voices, but no one was in the living room. I went to put the cookies in the kitchen and realized everyone was sitting outside on the deck. Greg peeked inside the back door. "Lock the front door, grab a beer, and come out to sit with us. If you're done investigating."

I almost denied it, but it wouldn't do any good. Greg knew me. And probably too many people had seen me. "Give me a second. I need to put the groceries away."

Emma greeted me as I came out on the porch. Then Greg waved me over to the love seat and I leaned down into a kiss. "There's my bride."

"I thought I'd be home before you guys got into town." I sat next to Greg and smiled at Jim and Beth.

"Blame this one. I swear, every time we leave for vacation, he sets his alarm for some ungodly hour and we're on the road with the chickens. So our flight was at the crack of dawn. At least flying, I have a bathroom available. He doesn't like to stop when we're driving."

"You need to stop too many times," Jim grumbled.

"I'm a girl. Deal with it." Beth poked him in the side. In response, he put his arm around her and pulled her closer to him.

"I'm just glad we're out of the car. I can't believe how small a normal car is these days." He sipped his beer. "I take it Bill Doyle is doing the service?"

The quick change of subject surprised me. "Yes. Bill and his girlfriend, Sadie, are friends. Well, I was friends with Sadie first. She supplies the treats for my shop. I brought home some snowflake cookies for dessert."

"I made a chocolate cake while you were gone today. But I'm sure the cookies will disappear fast around these boys. They were always big on sweets growing up." Amanda rubbed Emma's head. She had a glass of iced tea instead of a beer. And, I noticed, so did Beth.

I pushed away the comparison. And the guilt for serving store-bought cookies rather than making my own. But Sadie was a cookie wizard. There was no comparison.

"So, Jill, what were you doing today?" Greg leaned back in his chair, watching my face.

"I stopped by to see Amy, then spent some time at the shop. Judith was there alone, so I wanted to make sure she was doing okay. She's going to keep the store open on Saturday with Tilly." I glanced over at our guests. "Amy's my best friend. And I told my staff they were all welcome to come to the wedding, but Tilly's going through a bit of a rough patch. Anyway, I picked up the cookies then. And since I had a little bit of time, I ran to Bakerstown to drop cookies off with Doc Ames. I haven't seen him in forever and I wanted to make sure he and Carrie, who works at our local diner, were coming to the wedding. Then I grabbed a few groceries on the way home."

I saw Greg processing the stops. The only one I had left off was my trip to the college library, but I wasn't sure I could lie well enough to make that about the upcoming wedding.

Greg leaned forward. "Why don't you tell my family what Doc Ames does?"

Greg was onto me. I could feel the gloat coming. But I *had* talked to him about the wedding. "Doc runs our local funeral home. He used to be single and kind of lonely, but then he and Carrie started dating. He's much happier now."

Greg blinked first. "Doc Ames is also our county coroner. And if I know my Jill, she was probably there talking about Kane Matthews's death."

"I'm glad I don't have to give a report on where I went each time I left the house." Beth smiled at me then changed the subject. "Kane Matthews and his groupies. That's such a strange story. Did you all know that New Hope was a cult? How in the world did they get approval to set up here? They were forced out of Oregon a few years ago."

Jim put a hand on Beth's arm. "Beth's kind of an expert in modern-day cults. She did her thesis on it when she got her master's in religion last year."

"Which gives me almost enough credibility to be a church secretary." Beth laughed and leaned into Jim's arm. "I'm working on turning my thesis into a book about cults in today's world. People are drawn into these groups by the feeling of family and being special. There's a real need for that kind of closeness in today's world. Loneliness is the cult's number one weapon in gaining new followers. By the time the individual realizes what's going on, they're too deep into the situation."

"It's too bad you weren't here last week. Amanda and I went to the open house held at New Hope. It was disturbing." I met Greg's gaze and he shrugged. I guessed the conversation wasn't treading on the investigation. "The women in the church are treated like they're in the Middle Ages. None of the women spoke except to offer us food or drink. Kane was telling me they were turning their bakery into a commercial venture. He wanted Coffee, Books, and More's business, but I explained we were happy with Sadie. He inferred that maybe she wouldn't want to continue her bakery after she married Bill. Well, that's how I took it. Huh, I'd forgotten about that part. Anyway, they have a huge library with all kinds of books."

"Of course, that's what you'd notice," Greg teased. "Any books on devil worship or killing off your spiritual leader with a signed plan from the killer inside?"

"Not a one. But Kane had books from all types of religious practices, positive thinking, and the law of attraction stuff. It was eclectic. He gave me a copy of *The Four Agreements* to read."

Amanda broke in. "That's what the video felt like. I've gone to several seminars on the law of attraction. Don't frown, Jim. I'm a grown woman who can decide what my belief system contains. Anyway, when we were in their great room or chapel and the movie was running, it felt like the third day of one of those seminars. Where you think you can do anything."

"I'm not even touching the fact that you're attending these feel-good growth experiences." Greg grinned at his mom. "But the comparison with that type of organization isn't far off."

"That's how they pull people into the church." Beth elbowed Jim as she talked. "Stop looking like that every time I call it a church. It's just a word. Anyway, they're filling a need that more traditional churches aren't anymore. And with the state of the family so disjointed, well, you've got a lot of people out there looking for something to believe in."

"Which is why Carlie dropped out of school to become a disciple?" I took a sip of my beer. "That has to be some strong mojo to get into someone's mind that quickly."

"She was probably introduced to the organization by a guy who she thought was interested in her," Beth corrected me. "They like to hit college campuses because the kids there are all trying to figure out who they are as an adult. And the cult feels like a safe place to land."

"Who was the other woman Bakerstown found in the fabric store? Do you know?" I met Greg's gaze, wondering if he would talk about her and her family. "Oh, and did Carlie go home with Molly?"

"Sometimes it takes a while for people to leave." Beth leaned forward. "It's like that statistic on abused women. It takes them seven times to leave for good."

"If they live that long," Greg added. "Carlie's safe right now. And I don't have more information on the second woman."

"Well, aren't we a cheery group." Amanda stood and headed to the kitchen. "Let's get dinner started before we attempt to solve the rest of the world's problems. Seriously, please, let's talk about something else for a while. I'm feeling very depressed. And we have a wedding in three days. Let's talk about that."

As I followed Amanda and the others into the kitchen, I wished we hadn't changed the subject quite so fast. I thought that Beth might just have some insight into the workings of New Hope and maybe even why its spiritual leader was killed. I'd have to get her alone to find out.

# Chapter 11

Greg took Thursday morning off from work to hang out with Jim. Sometimes he needed time to process away from the investigation. The girls headed into Santa Barbara to pick up my dress and eat at Amanda's favorite Mexican restaurant. Emma went with the guys, who were hiking the trails at the mission where we'd be married on Saturday. I figured Greg wanted to be close by town in case something broke in the investigation. And by spending the morning hiking, he could clear his mind.

The bridal shop opened at ten, so we had time to stop at the beach when we got into town. Beth slipped off her shoes as soon as we hit the sand. "I'll never get used to this. You're so lucky to live here. I tried to talk Jim into moving after we make it official, but he's tied to his job. Honestly, I think it's his men's church group he'd miss the most. They have weekly meetings and do monthly service projects. And quarterly, they do something over the weekend. They call them spiritual retreats, but I think it's more about the fishing and hiking."

"At least he has hobbies. My sister's first husband didn't leave the house for fifteen years, unless she was with him." Amanda took her shoes off as well, using Beth's arm to stabilize herself. The women had a bond. They were comfortable with each other. I was on the outside. They didn't mean to put me there. It was just that they'd spent a lot of time together during Amanda's illness.

At times like this, I wished I'd had a sister. Someone who knew my history. Who got bad jokes because she'd lived through those times too.

Instead, I had my aunt, who had pulled me out of a bad situation and showed me what it was like to have a home.

"You both are always welcome here." I joined their barefoot club and we walked down the beach. It wasn't crowded yet. The cooler weather was keeping all but the fanatics and tourists off the beach. I wasn't sure which group we fell into.

A few red roses washed up on the shore and Beth pointed them out. "Was there a wedding here earlier?"

I shook my head. "Not a wedding. Probably a burial at sea. They toss the ashes over the side of the boat along with flowers."

"You know, I've thought a lot about death and what I'd want." Amanda held up her hand as Beth started to say something. "Let me finish, dear. Talking about death is part of life, no matter if you're sick or well. I'm not saying anything about my current health status. Anyway, I'm not sure what I want yet. So I guess either I can't die, or I'm leaving the decision up to the four of you. Please don't fight about it."

"You're so thoughtful." I grinned at Beth. "I'm sure the boys will be able to pull themselves out of their grief to make all the decisions for you."

"It's the main reason to have children. To pass on your baggage." Amanda put her arms around both Beth and me. "I'm so glad you two strong women are in the boys' lives. I hope we'll be doing another wedding soon."

Beth blushed and dropped her gaze. There was definitely a story there. "Let's just get through this wedding first before we start talking about another one."

"You said you wanted to make it official," I teased. "You're right. I've never been this close to getting married. The last time I got married was on a whim and such a bad decision, so I had no thinking time. This time, with Greg, the countdown clock hasn't stopped, yet. We've been a month out, but never three days. I'm thinking the world's going to end just before the rehearsal dinner is about to start."

Everyone laughed, but Amanda was quiet as we walked. She took my hand. "I'm sorry you had to put off your ceremony because of me. Twice."

"I'm just glad you're here for this one." I leaned over and kissed her on the cheek. "Let's go get my wedding dress. I hope you like it."

As we walked back to the car I saw a familiar black Hummer pull into the parking lot. Men in suits got out, and then they opened the back door. Roger and Maryanne Matthews looked up at the sky as they left their vehicle. Roger was in shorts and a cotton shirt. Maryanne was in a cute sundress. Not the plain long-sleeved cotton dress that she'd worn during the visit to the fabric store. She was actually showing her legs and neck. They took their shoes off and started walking hand in hand down the beach. One man stayed with the vehicle, the other followed the couple at a discreet distance. In his suit on the beach, the guy looked like he was auditioning for a new *Men in Black* movie.

"Hey, Beth. Look at that couple to our left. That's the new spiritual head of New Hope and his wife. I've never seen them in regular clothes before." I met her gaze in the rearview mirror but didn't start the vehicle. We sat there and watched the two walking down the beach for a while. Then I saw the man near the car turn toward us. He said something into his lapel mic and started walking toward the Jeep. "And it's time to go."

After we'd left the parking lot, Beth looked at her phone. "I think I got a few good pictures of them. So that's Roger and Maryanne Matthews? You're sure?"

"I'm positive. Even if I hadn't recognized them, the black Hummer with the goons gave it away. Kane used to cruise Main Street in that vehicle. Maybe they're considering doing a burial at sea for Kane and wanted to check out the view." I turned onto the highway that would take us downtown.

"I don't know. From what I saw, they looked like any other couple in love on a beach. Maybe Kane's passing didn't cause much grief." Amanda glanced over at me. "It's weird, isn't it?"

"I'll tell Greg tonight when he gets home. He can decide if it's suspicious or if we're just overthinking their grieving process." I focused on driving to get my dress and not thinking about how upset Greg would be if Jim was killed. There would be no way I'd get him to take a walk with me on a beach. And if I did, he wouldn't be smiling like Roger had been.

When we got to the bridal shop, both Amanda and Beth decided to buy new dresses for the ceremony while I tried on my wedding dress one last time. My runs with Emma must have toned me because it was just a little loose. The dressmaker who'd made the alterations pinched it tighter.

"I can take it in another half inch if you want. You'd have to pick it up Friday evening, though." She started to pin it.

"I don't know," Amanda commented. "I like the dress a little loose. It gives you some movement. If you tighten it more, you'd look terrific, but I think you look that way now." Amanda brushed the woman's hands away. "Look in the mirror."

I studied myself. I loved the way the dress made me look soft and perfect. Then Amanda pulled the back and I felt it tighten. I took a breath in. I did look skinnier, but it didn't change who I was. Or who Greg was marrying. "I think it's beautiful the way it is."

The dressmaker was smiling. "I do as well, but most brides, they're so worried about being thin for their wedding day. And you are slender, don't get me wrong. They want to look like children, not mature women. You look beautiful now."

"Okay then. We're good. And I don't have to add a trip to Santa Barbara before my rehearsal on Friday."

Beth giggled. "Which is the real reason you don't want the alterations."

I put my hands on my hips and let the dress swirl around me. "I want to be able to enjoy the reception without changing out of this dress. I only get to wear it for a few hours. I want to be comfortable and enjoy it during the reception."

After my dress was packed up and Beth and Amanda bought their dresses, we took all the packages to the car in the parking garage and walked to the restaurant. After we got settled with virgin margaritas, I turned to Beth. "Tell me everything you know about New Hope. When was it started? Was Kane Matthews the first leader?"

"Jill, this is your celebration lunch. Are you sure you want to talk about that cult?" Amanda put a hand on mine.

"Yes, if it's all right, I'd love to know what Beth knows. I think we're missing something by treating this like any other church. There has to be something that we're not seeing. And it all starts with the beginnings of the church." I turned toward Beth. "Please?"

"Okay, it's your party. Besides, no one ever wants me to talk about this." Beth grinned as she started explaining the history of the Matthews brothers and New Hope. Like I'd suspected, they'd started the church right after getting out of college. The small town had welcomed a new church, especially since it focused on updated music and a mission of serving others. There were no dues to pay to a larger organization, so all of the money stayed with the church. And Kane kept bringing more people into the fold.

Beth lowered her voice. "Then the whispers started. From what I read, there were rumors of improper relationships between Kane and quite a few of the followers. He liked his girls young. And it seemed like he might have crossed the line between legal and felony at least once. The church deacons voted to oust him, and he left—with the church coffers, Roger, Maryanne, and many of the true believers. That's when they moved to California."

"Were there actual charges filed?" Now I understood the creep factor I'd felt when I had been under Kane's gaze. I'd felt stripped down, just by his look.

"None of the women or the parents would talk to the police, so they were able to just leave." Beth took a bite of her shrimp fajitas, which had been brought during the discussion. "Amanda, you were right. This is amazing."

I took a bite of my fish taco and almost groaned. The food here was tasty. But something in Beth's story was bothering me. "I didn't find any of this online. How did you find out?"

Beth set her fork down. "I went to Oregon and interviewed the former church members. The church changed its name after the trio left, of course. But it wasn't hard to find people who would talk to me. They just weren't willing to talk to the police."

"There was an article about a pastor named Matthews who died with his wife in a church fire in Oregon. Any relation to our friends?"

"Their parents, actually. The church had an electrical short and the Matthews couple lived next door. They tried to save the church records and perished. The church paid for the boys to go to college after that. Blood money, was the rumor. Apparently, the pastor had been complaining and asking for an electrician to come and fix some faulty light fixtures. The boys were at a Scouting campout for the weekend. When they came back, they were orphans." Beth took a sip of her drink. "I'm surprised they decided to form a ministry after that. They had to be heartbroken."

I thought about the way Roger had looked when we saw them on the beach. Not heartbroken at all. He'd lost all of his family now except his wife. Wouldn't that have affected him at least a little?

"Now, I'm insisting we change the conversation. I'm feeling sad for those little boys and I don't want to cry while we're welcoming my new daughter into the family." Amanda passed me the empty chip basket. "Shall we get more?"

I signaled to the waitress. "Why not? My dress still fits. Which is a miracle all in itself."

When we got into the car to head home, my tummy was full of yummy food. And my mind was filled with questions. So the people who'd come to California with the brothers were true believers. And judging by Carlie's disappearance into the group, it looked like Kane was still attracted to a younger crowd. Had he stepped wrong again? And had it been his brother who had ended his life?

Or had Molly found out what was happening and killed him to save her daughter? There were too many questions. As we drove back to South Cove, Amanda napped in the back seat and Beth was busy watching the scenery as we drove alongside the ocean.

She glanced back to see if Amanda was still asleep, then turned to me. "Oh, I forgot about the Facebook group."

"New Hope has a Facebook group?" I should have thought about that. But I didn't even try to search the normal outlets. I'd gone straight to the research library and its powerful search engine.

"Not New Hope, but the families of people who have joined and left their lives behind. They're always tracking the group's movements. I hung out there for a while and interviewed people who would talk off the record. They were all so desperate to get a light shined on the community. They thought maybe that might bring their loved one back. It rarely happens. By the time the families find out where they are, the new member has been indoctrinated. They believe the hype."

Instead of dropping Beth off at the Castle, where she and Jim were staying, she waited at my house for Amanda to get ready for dinner. Beth and Jim were taking her out tonight. They'd asked me to come along, but I'd excused myself. The wedding was on Saturday, and I hadn't finished my vows.

Tomorrow night was the rehearsal and dinner. My friends had a party planned for me at South Cove Winery after dinner and I'd invited Beth and Amanda to come along. Amanda had asked to just get a ride back to the house after the dinner. She said she'd babysit Emma.

Jim had set up a bachelor party for Greg at the same time. They'd probably head to Bakerstown. Or maybe just stay at the Castle since Jim had also gotten Greg a room there for Friday night. Tonight would be the last night I'd have alone for a while. I wanted to put on pj's and slippers and watch a sappy movie. All by myself. Well, myself and Emma.

I'd also turned down dinner with Harrold and Aunt Jackie. I knew they thought with Greg working, I'd be alone. But what they didn't know was I kind of liked being alone. I wondered if my aunt was worried that I'd be one of those runaway brides, so she was trying to keep an eye on me.

Amanda came down dressed for dinner, and she and Beth headed out to Beth's rental car. They'd decided to keep both Jim and Beth's rental as well as Amanda's while they were here in California. That way, both Jim and Beth would have access to a vehicle. When I'd asked Beth about the car situation, she'd shrugged. "I like knowing I have a car available, just in case. Being stuck is my worst nightmare."

Pausing at the door, Amanda took my hands. "You can change your mind and come with us. We both know that Greg will be working late. Come and have a good meal. I worry about you."

"Thank you, but I'm looking forward to some quiet time. It's not that I don't love having all of you around, but I've got some business to take care of and some vows to write. I should have asked Deek to write them for me. He's so good with words."

"A local writer?" Amanda asked, trying to stay chill about it. Beth had already gone out to the car and was waiting.

"One of my staff. You met him, right? The one with the neon green cornrows?" I waved at Beth. "Anyway, I didn't ask. Now I have to be elegant and poetic."

Amanda patted my cheek. "Just be honest. Speak from your heart. It's never failed me."

I watched Amanda's shiny blue compact pull out of the driveway with Beth at the wheel and I waved. I hadn't exactly lied to my soon-to-be mother-in-law. I did have to finish my vows. Or at least give them a good edit. But the real reason I stayed home was to research Facebook for a family group. Maybe there was at least one upset parent who looked like he or she could have killed Kane.

I also wanted to write down everything Beth had told me about the church and its history. If there was still time, I'd see what I could find out about the church fire that had killed the boys' parents.

It was official. I was hooked on this amateur sleuthing role.

# Chapter 12

I was upstairs on the bed reading when Greg came home around eleven. Amanda was already home from dinner and asleep. She'd brought me a piece of apple pie from the restaurant. I'd put it in the fridge for later. Emma ran downstairs to greet him, so I didn't worry that it was some random stranger in the house. I heard him going into the office and locking up his gun and then he must have hit the fridge and let Emma outside one last time.

When he came up, he smiled at me. "I thought you'd be asleep."

"With the lights on?" I pointed upward.

He snorted and took off his uniform. "Like that hasn't happened before. I'm going to grab a shower. Is the pie in the fridge claimed?"

"It's mine," I said. "But I'll share. You get showered and I'll go down and get the pie. Do you want a bottle of water or anything?"

"Water would be great. I don't think I'm even going to be able to finish the pie. I'm tired. I drove into Bakerstown to talk to the parent group that swarmed the station. Everyone wants to know if their daughter or son is at the compound."

I'd checked out the information Beth had given me earlier. New Hope Lies was an active Facebook group, and I'd seen the notification that the group was meeting in Bakerstown. One of the members had live-streamed it for others who couldn't get away or weren't located in California. "It must be hard on them."

"Some of them haven't seen their kids in years. One woman said it had been three years for her ex-husband. New Hope isolates the new members and has them cut all ties with their families. New Hope is their new family." He leaned on the wall and stretched out his shoulders as he talked. "Wait, you're too calm about this. How did you know?"

"Beth did her dissertation on cults. She studied New Hope and had mentioned on the ride home that there was a family Facebook group. I found it. They have lots of information about the new compound. And a lot of angry parents saying crazy things." Greg couldn't be mad at me. I didn't go anywhere or put myself in danger. And Beth had been the one to tell me in the first place. He should blame her.

But all I got was a sigh. "Of all the people Jim could have fallen in love with, we get a cult expert just as a cult leader is killed on my watch. If I didn't know better, I'd say she was a plant."

"Jim wouldn't lie about dating someone. Besides, she stayed with your mom during treatment. I think it's kismet. She's nice and smart."

"Did you have fun with Mom and Beth today? Jim called and said you missed dinner."

"He ratted me out? Wow. I wanted some time alone," I admitted. My need for a night to myself shouldn't have been hard to accept, but Jim thought he knew what was best for everyone.

"Well, they missed you." He turned and headed to the adjoining bathroom. "Don't eat all my pie and don't forget the whipped cream."

I used a bookmark and set my book down on the bed. The book was an older one I hadn't read when it was first released. *Pack Up the Moon* by Kristan Higgins probably wasn't the best book to read just before pledging your life to another. The main characters had only been married three years before the wife died of a rare lung disease. It went back and forth between her past POV and his current one. The story's emotions were heavy, but also light. And there were letters. Handwritten letters from the wife to the husband, one a month for a year. To help him cope. I'd laughed and cried while reading it. It was a great book. I just hoped I had time to finish before Saturday. I didn't want to think about anything during our special time on Saturday. Not even the investigation.

Man, I must love this guy.

I ran downstairs and got out the pie, cutting it in half and putting it on plates. Glancing at the box, I saw the New Hope label. I guess they'd found at least one restaurant to supply. I hoped the pie wasn't as good as it looked. I grabbed forks, a bottle of water, and a can of whipped cream. Then I picked up the plates. Emma had followed me downstairs and licked her lips.

"No way. You know you can't do sugar, right?"

The look on my dog's face seemed to deny that fact even existed. We went upstairs and I set the plates on the dresser with the whipped cream and the water.

Then I went back to reading.

"That must be a good book," Greg said. He stood in front of me, dressed in sweats and holding the plates of pie. "I've been talking to you since I got out of the shower, and you've been lost in the book. And you're crying. What's wrong?"

"I just hit another sad part of the book. It's so good." I put the bookmark back inside and closed the book, putting it on my nightstand.

He held out the plates. "And that's why I love you."

"You better. We're getting married in two days." The thought gave me chills. But I couldn't tell if they were good chills or warning ones. Either way, the deed was going to happen. Come hell or high water.

I sat up on the bed, curling my legs underneath me. I took one of the plates. "My wedding dress is in the guest room closet, so don't go digging in there for anything before Saturday."

"I need a suitcase. I guess I need two. One for Friday night and one for Saturday night." He took a bite of the pie. "This is tasty."

"Yeah, I was afraid of that." At Greg's puzzled look, I shrugged. "It's from the New Hope bakery at the compound. I hope they don't put Sadie's bakery out of business. It's hard to compete with free labor. And just leave your Saturday clothes on the dresser. I'll pack them with mine in a suitcase. It's just one night. But don't forget your suit. I'm swimming in that pool on Sunday before we leave. They heat it in the winter."

"Good to know." He finished his pie. "Yeah, I think Sadie might be in trouble if the rest of their products are that tasty. And speaking of our friend, I had to have a chat with her boyfriend about the fight he had with Kane last Sunday at the diner. The guy goaded Bill into taking a swing. I didn't think that was possible."

"From what I heard, Kane made a crack about Sadie. Got to love a man who stands up for the woman he loves."

"Unless he also kills the guy who trash-talked his girlfriend." Greg held up a hand. "Don't kill the messenger. Bill might have an alibi for time of death if he gets permission for me to talk to the man he was counseling at the time."

"And if he doesn't?" Bill felt a strong duty to his parishioners. If the guy didn't want anyone to know he was being counseled, maybe Bill wouldn't have an alibi.

"We'll find another way to verify. Bill didn't do this. We both know that." He stood and reached for my plate. "I'll run these dishes and the cream back down to the kitchen. Do you need anything before I lock up and come to bed?"

I glanced at the book. I could get a few more pages read before he got back.

He chuckled. "Don't worry about it. You can leave the light on so you can read. I don't think a freight train rushing by the house could keep me from falling and staying asleep."

Another reason I loved this man. He got me.

* * * *

I didn't sleep well that night. I blamed the book, but I thought it was more likely the upcoming ceremony this weekend. My first marriage had lasted maybe a year, and mostly that long because neither one of us cared enough to file the divorce papers. He'd been nice, but he wasn't Greg. I'd known from the second time I met Greg that he was the one. Or at least could be the one. I'd thought he was still married when I worked with him to solve Miss Emily's murder. Although I wasn't sure he'd see it like that. We were a match made in heaven from the first case. I wish I'd ordered some sort of sleuthing decorations for his groom's cake. Of course, we were in the middle of a case, so maybe it was a little tacky.

I went over and picked up a framed picture of Miss Emily that I kept on a hallway table. She and her dog, Monet, had been my first friends in South Cove. She'd basically challenged me to change my life for the better by moving here and opening a bookstore and coffeehouse. I'd taken a leap of faith then, and now, years later, I was taking another one.

I heard voices downstairs, so I hurried to get ready. I'd shower closer to the rehearsal time. For now, it was packing for the night away and getting my outfits ready. And my aunt was coming over to chat later today.

The smell of pancakes filled the room, but when I got closer I realized it was waffles. Waffles with hot maple syrup and bacon. Greg was frying eggs at the stove and Amanda was finishing setting the table. She looked up and smiled at me as I came into the kitchen. "I was about to go up and wake you."

"My alarm didn't go off." I'd turned off all my alarms for this week, probably not the wisest thing. I might sleep through my wedding tomorrow. "No worries. I'm just an up-with-the-chickens kind of girl lately." She poured me a coffee and motioned me to sit. "I wanted to thank you for being so nice to Beth yesterday. She was so worried about meeting you."

"Me? Why?" I took my coffee and took a long sip. The cobwebs started to fade immediately. Thank you, coffee.

"She and Jim ran into Sherry a few months ago. I tried to tell her that you were nothing like Greg's first wife, but she worried that you two wouldn't have anything in common." Amanda pulled a baking sheet filled with waffles and bacon out of the oven. "Greg, are the eggs done?"

"Yes, and I don't think it's fair to compare Jill with Sherry. I was young and an idiot when I got married the first time. Then I kept trying to fix the marriage. But I was the only one trying. She just wanted to fix me." He walked over to where I sat and put an egg on my plate. "Good morning, sweetheart. When's your aunt getting here so we can talk about your failed relationships too?"

"Hopefully, not until after you leave for work." I grabbed a waffle and smeared butter on it as the other two sat down at the table. "Which is good for me, since my aunt has a long memory."

"Great, I get all the fun." He grabbed a waffle and several slices of bacon. "So what time am I expected at the mission?"

"Three p.m. sharp. Bill has a men's group meeting at five so he won't be able to come to the dinner, but Sadie's coming." I'd gotten a text message from Sadie this morning on the change in plans.

"I think he's avoiding me." Greg sighed. "It's hard to be the head detective in a town where a lot of your suspects are also your friends."

"You could take that job with the state," I reminded him. "You never did tell me what was wrong with that resume I made for you."

He didn't say anything, and when I looked up, he and his mom were staring at each other. Finally, he sighed and turned toward me. "The resume was fine. The problem is that years ago Sherry got me hired at a station in the city without me knowing that I'd even applied. I thought I was just going in for an interview to see if I'd like the transfer, and they thought I'd already accepted the job."

"Didn't you have to leave South Cove in two weeks?" his mom added. "Sherry had already turned in their notice at the apartment and rented something new. He had no choice."

"Marvin was so mad." Greg ate a piece of bacon. "He'd hired me over the guy he'd wanted. I told Sherry that she got this one. If she ever did it again, we were done. Five years later, I got a call from the head of security at LAX. He'd gotten my resume and wanted to talk to me about the job. I hadn't turned in a resume."

"That's why you were so mad when I made up your resume. I thought you were just dragging your feet. You thought I wanted you at a better job." I grabbed another slice of bacon. "You thought I was being a Sherry."

"Look, we were getting married. I was stressed about that. Then out of the blue, you make me a resume. It felt suspicious."

"I thought I was doing you a favor," I said, then consumed the bacon. "I don't want you to do anything you don't want to do. I thought you were dragging your feet because you didn't want me to have to close the store. I was being thoughtful."

"Now, isn't this nice? You're communicating instead of assuming what the other person thinks or feels." Amanda took another waffle. "It's a *Gift of the Magi* situation. I think you two should do fine as a couple."

Greg went to work shortly after breakfast, and left that conversation with his packed suitcase. He needed to make sure everything was okay at the station before he signed out to be at the rehearsal at three. After that, he was off the clock. If anything big happened in South Cove that couldn't be pushed off until Greg came back, the police chief in Bakerstown would deal with it until nine o'clock on Sunday night when we returned to South Cove. I'd argued for Monday morning, but Greg didn't want to impose on his friend. I might have been able to talk him into it if Kane hadn't gone and got himself killed. I kissed him goodbye and took Emma for a run. We both had nervous energy to get rid of before the rehearsal.

Later that morning, Aunt Jackie parked in front of the house. She brought wrist corsages for all the women in the wedding party. "I called your florist and had these made up for the rehearsal tonight. I thought it might be a nice touch. The Wooden Bench is all confirmed and they will be expecting us at five. Then at eight, you and your girlfriends can go and play at the winery."

"You have it all timed out. Are you coming to the after-party?" I glanced at the flowers. They matched my colors and the flowers for Saturday's festivities.

"No, I'm going home and putting my feet up. I can't be in heels that long anymore." She smiled at Amanda. "Nice to see you again, Amanda. What are you working on over there?"

"Birdseed bundles for the exit from the ceremony. I've got enough for the guests, but I wanted a few extra, just in case." She pushed the large tan basket filled with ribbon-tied bundles of tulle. "What do you think? We need someone to hand them out as the guests enter the area reserved for the ceremony."

"I'm sure Deek and maybe Evie would love to help." I just hoped Toby would be able to make the wedding since he was one of Greg's groomsmen. We had too many friends entwined with our livelihoods. Toby was a deputy for Greg as well as a part-time barista for my coffee shop. Sasha was coming with Olivia, so I knew he'd want to spend some time with them. We still hadn't been told what the chance was of a rekindled relationship between him and Sasha, but at least they would be together for the wedding.

"Jill? Did you hear what I said?" Aunt Jackie asked. She and Amanda were watching me.

I smiled, trying to get them to relax. "No, I was thinking about Toby and wondering if he was going to be off duty. I should have asked Greg, but I guess he's handling it. Sasha's in town for the wedding. I hope the girls invited her to the party tonight."

"Well, Toby is one of Greg's groomsmen, so I'm sure Greg adjusted his work schedule. Besides, Toby let me know that he might bring Sasha and Olivia to the rehearsal." My aunt finished my thoughts. "Why are you worrying about all this? You're getting married tomorrow. You need to be thinking of the ceremony. Do you have your vows written?"

"Yes, I've finished my vows," I grumbled. My aunt could find the one weak point in Hoover Dam. I hadn't finished, but I had a rough draft. I needed to finish them up and print them off so I could have them for tomorrow. I needed to pack for Saturday night. Toby was babysitting Emma, so she needed a go bag in case he decided to take her somewhere. I grabbed a notebook. "But I do have a few things to finish up. Maybe I should call Judith and make sure she's set for Saturday at the bookstore."

"Don't worry about that. I'll stop in before the rehearsal and make sure they have checklists for the shifts." My aunt opened her purse and made a note in a small blue notebook. She glanced at the page. "Oh, and

Harrold wants to make sure you still want him to walk you down the aisle. That you haven't changed your mind."

"Harrold's the only older male role model I have in my life now. I didn't know my father, and Uncle Ted got the joy of raising my cheerful teenage self. And he's gone." I shook my head. "No, please let Harrold know I still want him to do me this favor. I'd appreciate it."

"He just wanted to make sure your day was perfect and you'd chosen him out of love, and not some obligation to me." My aunt squeezed my arm. "I know you don't like to talk about your parents."

"And I'm not going there today." I closed my eyes and imagined the wall in my mind that I'd built around any memories I'd had of my parents. "I'm sorry, Aunt Jackie, I just can't."

She pulled me into a hug. "I'm sorry I brought it up. Harrold just wanted to make sure you had an out if you didn't want him to walk you down the aisle. For any reason."

I finally had some semblance of a normal family. I didn't want to question it now. "I'm thankful to have both of you in my life."

My aunt stepped back and felt my forehead.

"What is that for?"

"Just checking to see if you are sick. You're being very sentimental." My aunt winked at Amanda.

"I learned from the best." I ducked as my aunt playfully tried to swat at me. "Seriously, I'm glad the people I love are going to be here for me this weekend."

# Chapter 13

By the time everyone arrived at the mission for the rehearsal, it was about ten minutes past three. The afternoon had turned warm, and the sundress I'd chosen for the event felt perfect. I'd even taken off the sweater I'd brought just in case. It felt like the nature gods were blessing our wedding. Or at least our practice wedding. Emma rubbed against my hand. I swear she could tell what I was feeling most of the time. Today, it was just pure happiness and joy. It was finally happening. I was going to be Mrs. Greg King. Or Jill Gardner King. Or maybe Jill Gardner-King. Amy used the hyphenated form. It seemed modern. I also needed to make that decision before I signed the marriage license tomorrow. Or did I sign Jill Gardner one more time? I needed to ask my aunt.

We were just about ready to start the first walk-through for tomorrow's ceremony when a scream came from the building behind us. Greg met my gaze and took off from where he, Jim, and Toby were standing by Pastor Bill at the stone arch.

He touched my arm as he ran by. "Get ready to call 911, but stay here until I call you over."

"Okay." I wanted to see who had screamed. I glanced around at the people near me. Aunt Jackie was standing next to Deek, who was serving as an usher. Harrold walked over and led her to a chair, then they sat, waiting. Amy, Darla, and Esmeralda were all standing next to me. Justin followed Greg and Toby toward the building. Jim gathered Beth as he came back to stand with Amanda. Matt followed them from where he'd been sitting.

"What's going on?" Matt put an arm around Darla, looking around the circle.

"I'm not sure. Did everyone hear a scream? It's not like it's a bobcat or a mountain lion, right?" I clicked Emma's leash on her collar. We'd brought her to the rehearsal since she was going to be our flower girl. Maybe we should have chosen Olivia, the human child at the rehearsal, but I hadn't known that Sasha was coming until it was too late to get her a dress.

Evie had come to the rehearsal to hang out with her cousin, Sasha. Now, she sat on one of the white chairs, looking worried.

Maybe this wedding wasn't meant to happen. Wait, where were Sasha and Olivia? They weren't sitting in the chairs by Evie.

Soon, Toby came back up the path with a shaken-looking Sasha and a confused Olivia. Toby carried the little girl. "Stand down, Jill. There's nothing to do."

I put the phone back in my pocket. "Where's Greg?"

"He's walking through the building, just to make sure there's not someone pulling a prank." He handed Olivia to Evie, who took her to a chair. Sasha followed them. Then he came back to me. "Sasha says she was playing hide-and-seek with Olivia and saw a man in a priest's robe dissolve into a wall."

Sasha must have heard him. "I did see him. He even looked at me, made the sign of the cross, then turned and walked right into a wall. I swear. I saw him."

"Okay, honey. I believe you." Toby smiled at Sasha, then pulled me farther away. Emma followed us since I still had her on a leash. "There are rumors about a ghostly priest who hangs out at the chapel. I guess anything's possible."

"But you, and Greg, think that maybe someone was trying to scare her." I glanced back at Sasha, who was telling her story to a small crowd gathered around her. "He's looking for what? A fake wall?"

"Or a spot someone could hide. Sorry to interrupt your rehearsal with this. As soon as Greg gets back, we'll get started." We walked back to where Pastor Bill was now talking to Sasha.

He looked up at me. "Are we ready to get started again?"

"As soon as Greg's back." I reached down and rubbed Sasha's shoulder. "Do you need to go home? Evie can take you back to the house."

She looked up at me, fear still shining in her eyes. "Do you mind? I know I'm being childish, and it is your wedding. But I swear, I saw him. Or I saw something."

I glanced at Evie. She nodded, answering my unanswered question. "We can go hang at my house and make cookies. I bet you need some sugar after that."

"You can still come to dinner if you're feeling better." I hugged her. "Don't worry about us. You do what you need to do. Just know that I'd love to have you at the wedding tomorrow."

The look of fear told me all I needed to know. Sasha and Olivia would be no-shows for the wedding. If someone was pranking her and I found out, I was going to give them a piece of my mind.

Evie pulled Sasha from her chair and Deek grabbed Olivia. He met my gaze. "I'll be right back. Olivia's booster is in my car."

Greg was coming up the walk from the mission. He put his arm around me. "Never a dull moment around here, right? No sign of a prankster. Maybe our Sasha is just tuned into the other side. Where is she? I wanted to ask her if she'd seen ghosts before."

"Evie took her back home. She's wrecked." I leaned onto his shoulder. "Nothing to worry about, then?"

Greg looked behind us and groaned. "I didn't say that. This place is starting to be a problem. Maybe we should have this wedding at Bill's church."

"I'm not letting one ghost chase me out of a wedding venue. You know how hard it was to find a place." I shook my head. "Let's get this practice over with so we can go eat. I'm starving."

"When are you not?" He kissed me on the top of my head. "I'm going to miss you tonight."

"I suppose ditto is the wrong answer?"

He tapped me on the butt as he walked away. "You're a brat, Jill Gardner. Which is probably why I love you. Strong women, we're cursed with loving them."

"Breaking up now wouldn't make me a runaway bride, would it?" I called after him.

He turned, walking backward away from me, and grinned. "You'd never make it out of town."

* * * *

The rest of the rehearsal went off without a hitch and Pastor Bill left for his next appointment. I noticed he kept looking at Greg as the practice went on. I hoped he didn't think Greg was going to arrest him on the spur of the moment. Besides, he wouldn't do that until after the wedding. I could assure our minister of that, at least.

Sadie was one of the first at The Wooden Bench as we gathered for the rehearsal dinner. She hugged me. "Less than twenty-four hours and you'll be Mrs. Greg King."

"Are you taking Bill's name when you get married?" Sadie would know all about this custom. I sat down in the lobby area, where we were waiting for our separate room to open. Greg was off looking for the catering director, who was supposed to have already opened the door. Maybe we'd have a ghost sighting at the dinner too. Things happened on the coast. And I wasn't having the best luck with my wedding events.

"Of course I am. I guess it's an old-fashioned notion, right? 'Wives submit to your own husbands.' I've always dreamed of being a wife and a mother. I've done both now, but I guess I want to jump into the fray again."

"You two will be so happy. You were made for each other." We'd sat down on a bench covered in detailed carvings in a Spanish style. I hoped it was a replica and not an antique. "Honestly, I'm just glad we're finishing this up. When a wedding gets pushed off so many times, it starts to lose its wonder."

Sadie took my hand. "How is Amanda doing? She looks good. Strong."

"A lot better. She's lost a lot of muscle strength, even I can see that, but her tests are all fine." Amanda had chosen to ride to the rehearsal dinner with Jim and Beth. Probably to give Greg and me a minute alone. "It's been nice spending time with her this week."

Sadie shifted in her seat. "So now can we talk about the elephant in the room? Greg has to know Bill would never hurt another soul. Why hasn't he cleared him in the death of that terrible man?"

"Sadie, you know Greg doesn't talk to me about these things. He'll find the killer, and everything will go back to normal."

"The deacons are upset with Bill for letting that man needle him into a response. He's just so protective of the work he does. He truly believes he's doing God's work. That New Hope place is a den of iniquity. Those poor parents. Someone should call in a welfare check on those children." She turned toward me. "You went to that open house, right? Did you see the children?"

I shook my head. "They said they didn't want to commercialize the children in that way." I'd thought it odd that most of the women and all of the children had been kept away from the open house too. But this wasn't the time to talk about it. "Sadie, don't worry so much. Bill is going to be fine."

She leaned her head on my shoulder. "I know I shouldn't bother you about such stuff on your wedding weekend. Bill even told me not to bring it up. I'll be good. I'll promise."

"You're fine. I know you're worried. We've been through cases before that looked different than they turned out. Just trust the system. Greg will figure it out." I hoped that was true, but we didn't have any longer to talk about it as Greg was coming back with a young man in tow hopefully with keys to open the doors.

As I stood, the others came in the large doors from the parking lot and I was surrounded by people wanting to tell me how lovely tomorrow's ceremony was going to be.

"As long as the weather holds." Aunt Jackie pointed out the obvious.

I turned to Esmeralda. "Do you have any contacts who know Mother Nature?"

She laughed and hugged me. "I wish I did, but mythical creatures aren't usually hanging out in the spirit world, no matter what you see on television."

"Well, I'm going to pray for good weather tonight," Sadie offered. "We'll see what He says."

As we got seated, a large floral arrangement was brought into the room. I smiled at my aunt, who was seated next to me. The colors were in my blue-and-silver theme, with white carnations, blue cornflowers, and tulips that looked silver in the light. "You didn't have to do this, but it's stunning."

"I didn't order this." Aunt Jackie stood and rooted through the arrangement and found a card. She read it, then handed it to me. "That's unexpected."

I read the card aloud for Greg. "Blessed nuptials tomorrow. When two become one in the Lord's eyes, nothing can come between them. Your new friends, Roger and Maryanne."

"Roger and Maryanne. Please tell me you know someone else by those names." Greg tucked the card in his jacket pocket.

"No such luck." I stared at the too-perfect floral arrangement on our table. The Matthewses from the New Hope church had sent us a gift.

Somehow, it felt more like a warning or a reminder that they were still here. Watching us.

"Don't worry." Greg turned my head away from the flowers. "I'll deal with it on Monday. This is our weekend. Come hell or high water, remember?"

I smiled at his use of one of my favorite phrases. "We're still getting married tomorrow?"

"I'll be at the mission at eleven o'clock with bells on." He kissed me.

"Bells are going to make quite a racket," I teased as we were served our salad.

The dinner went smoothly, without any more hiccups. I was in the restroom, checking my makeup and hair before I went back out for dessert, when Sasha came into the room.

"Jill, I'm so sorry for the disturbance this afternoon. I don't know why I reacted that way." Sasha gave me a quick hug. "Do you forgive me?"

"If I saw a ghost, I'd freak out too. No worries. I'm just glad it wasn't something serious. I'm so glad you came tonight." I squeezed her forearms. Sasha had worked for me for years while she got ready to go to school. "It's so good to see you and Olivia. I'm so proud of all you've accomplished."

She sighed and looked into the mirror, checking her hair. "Thanks. Honestly, my success has made it impossible for either Toby or I to see a future between us. We're ending whatever this is this weekend. I can't move Olivia back here and keep my job. Toby won't leave South Cove. Not even for us. So we've decided to be just friends."

"Oh, Sasha, I'm so sorry." I watched as she brushed tears off her face. "If being at the wedding tomorrow is too much, I'd understand."

She turned to me. "Oh no, missy. You're not getting off that easily. That ghost isn't going to scare me away and neither is a soon-to-be ex-boyfriend. Both Toby and I are grownups. We want to be here to celebrate with you and Greg. This wedding is long overdue."

"That's what everyone keeps saying." I gave her a quick hug. "I'm so glad you're here. I need to get back before Greg thinks I'm sneaking out and sends someone after me."

Sasha laughed and waved me off. "If Toby's looking for me, I'll be back out in a minute. Men in law enforcement do know how to keep tabs on those they love, don't they?"

As I made my way back to the banquet room, I wondered about Sasha's last line. Had the distance been the only thing that had separated the couple? Or had Toby's need to have control over his life taken over when he thought about the future? The man had spreadsheets for everything. The one thing I did know was that their relationship wasn't my business. I had enough to deal with in my own almost-marriage.

I shivered with excitement. I hadn't felt this giddy in years. I was going to be Mrs. Greg King. And whatever our coupling would bring in the future, I was looking forward to it. Even if I decided to keep my old name. Or hyphenate it. Or take Greg's name.

Those were just details. Our relationship was more than that. Marriage was the joining of souls—one thing the New Hope founders had gotten right on their card. The sentiment was beautiful. Now, if only the source of the flowers didn't give me the willies.

After dessert, Greg stood and pulled me up next to him. Then he addressed the room. "Thank you all for coming tonight and helping me get this one to the altar. It's been a long journey to tomorrow's ceremony and I want my fiancée to know that I've treasured every moment of our lives together so far. Even when we fought because she was wrong."

I kissed him, then turned to add my part of the speech. "You notice he didn't mention the fights where I was right. I'm sure he just wanted to use the word "fiancée" one last time, since tomorrow I'll be his wife. The old ball and chain. I also want to thank my family and friends for being here with us. It means a lot to both of us."

We raised our glasses. Greg looked at me, then at the table full of our closest friends. "Thank you, South Cove, for being our home."

As we were saying good night to everyone, Jim came up to us with Beth and Amanda by his side. "Greg, where are your keys? I'll run and get your bag."

"Maybe Mom can have my room and I'll go home with Jill. I hate leaving her alone with all that's going on." His eyes drifted to the flowers still on the table. We'd decided not to bring them home. The gesture still felt creepy.

"No way, man. She's got Toby just a few steps away in his apartment after we close down the bar." Jim winked at me. "Beth's taking Mom to the house now while we get you to your party."

"I'm going to stay with Amanda until you get home." Beth stepped up and gave me a hug. "I don't want to intrude on you and your friends."

"You're family, it wouldn't be an intrusion," I reminded her, but I could see Amanda was worn out. "If you change your mind later, we'll be at South Cove Winery. Darla got us the back room for the event."

"As tired as I am, she might be there sooner than she thinks." Amanda hugged me. "I'm so excited to have a new daughter, Jill."

Her words made me tear up, but after they'd left us alone, Greg pulled me into the hallway near the exit. "Look, I'm not going to overreact on this, but if you need anything, call. I'm not sure our friends at New Hope have the best intentions. After Toby drops Sasha off at the winery, I'm having him put the flowers in the vault in the station. I want someone to check for bugs."

"Bugs that are not in the insect family?" I snuck a look back at the banquet room, where the floral arrangement still sat.

He tapped my nose. "That's why I'm marrying you. Your quick brain."

"Do you think someone at the church killed Kane?" I whispered, hoping the sound wouldn't carry back into the floral arrangement and its possible microphone. I'd been thinking it was more likely one of the parents from the group on Facebook that focused on bashing New Hope and calling it a cult.

"Let's just say I'm curious." He kissed me. "Have fun with your friends."

I waved at Amy, who was waiting to ride back to my house with me to drop off the Jeep. "You too. I'll see you tomorrow."

"You can count on it. Bells or no bells."

# Chapter 14

Darla had outdone herself. I wore a sash that proclaimed me The Bride and the music was all my favorites. She'd hired a perfect DJ. We were able to chat and dance and drink and eat until my eyes started closing on their own. Pizza, mozzarella sticks, and other appetizers kept coming from the kitchen. Beth had changed her mind and arrived about an hour ago. She was currently out dancing with Amy on the makeshift dance floor. The only time we ran into other people was on the way to the restroom. Everyone I saw wanted an invite to our private party, but it was a girls' night only.

Deek had peeked his head in on his way to Greg's bash. He came and hugged me. "I don't know. Maybe I should stay here. Be the token male for your group."

"Toby already tried that line when he dropped off Sasha," I told him as he grabbed a slice of pizza for the road. "I'll see you tomorrow, right?"

"I wouldn't miss your wedding for the world. Your aura is bright silver right now. Pure happiness." He raised the pizza in a salute and ran when Darla came to chase him out. I loved my friends.

A few hours later, near the end of the party, Darla sat down next to me. "Matt wanted to come party with us too. He texted me and said that Greg's party is tame. Or lame. I couldn't tell from the autocorrect."

"We always know how to have fun." I leaned into her. "How are you? Busy chasing the facts on Kane's murder?"

"I could ask you the same thing, but I hear you've been out sightseeing all week with your new mother-in-law. I'm surprised you're not investigating." She studied my face and must have seen something. "But you are investigating. I knew it. When did you find time?"

"I didn't do much, just some research at the college and chatted with Doc Ames." I glanced around the room, but Beth was still out on the dance floor. "Jim's girlfriend did her thesis on cults, including New Hope. She's been very interesting to talk to. Did you know there is a parents' group against the church on Facebook?"

Darla slapped her forehead. "That's what I've been missing. I've been so focused on Molly and her search, I didn't think of other victims."

"I think they call them converts," I corrected. Just then, the DJ put on the Village People dance standard, "Y.M.C.A." Beth grabbed my hand and started pulling me onto the dance floor. "Forget that until Sunday. Come dance with us, Darla."

Because she was my friend, Darla joined us, and too soon the party ended. Beth took my arm. "I'm sleeping on your couch tonight."

We said our good nights and I hugged Darla tightly. "Thank you so much for the party. It was a blast."

"Anything for you," she said as she wiped her eyes.

Esmeralda hurried over, pulling on her coat. "I'm walking with you."

As we made our way out into the cold night, I looked up and saw the stars shining on us.

Esmeralda followed my gaze. "It's a full moon. You have the blessing from the winter gods for your ceremony tomorrow."

I snuck a sideways look at her. "I didn't think you talked to mythical gods?"

"I don't. I worship them. It's my religion, not my pastime." Esmeralda raised her hands to the sky. "Nature is so cool. All you have to do is look around to see all the blessings."

"And if you believe, like I do, that there is one true God," Beth interrupted, "then you bless Him for all the wonders He provided us on this earth."

"As long as you don't believe that the earth is ours to use and abuse, like some preachers say"—Esmeralda stared at Beth—"then I agree."

"I agree. We've done a horrible job of taking care of what He's given us." Beth took Esmeralda's arm in hers and we started walking again.

"Amen, sister." Esmeralda leaned her head on Beth's.

Now that my almost sister-in-law and my friend the fortune teller had found common ground and avoided a fight, I relaxed and thought about the night. Why had Roger, or more likely Maryanne, sent the flowers? Public relations? An attempt to be part of the community? They had to have asked the florist to match our wedding colors, but how did they find our florist? And was Greg's hunch about the flowers having a bug in them true?

There were too many questions.

I saw the blue flashing lights as we crested the hill. The police car was at our house. I took off at a run, which wasn't easy since I was in dress shoes. Thank goodness I'd switched out of heels when we'd gone to dinner.

I didn't recognize the officer standing at the gate when he stopped me. Then I realized he had a Bakerstown uniform. "Ma'am, you can't go in there."

"I'm Jill Gardner. I own this house. What's going on? Is Amanda all right?" Just then, I saw Amanda come out on the porch with Emma. She waved me over.

"Sorry, ma'am. I didn't know. My partner is checking out the backyard." He moved aside and let us through.

I hurried up the stairs and, putting my hand on Emma's head to try to quiet her, I looked at Amanda. "Are you okay?"

"Oh my, yes. Sorry if I scared you. After Beth left, I took a long bath and was just getting into bed when Emma and I heard someone at the front door. I walked down and peeked out your office window. The man was dressed in black and was trying to open your lock with those tools. I locked myself and Emma in the office and called 911, and they sent out a car."

"But you're all right?" Beth asked again.

Amanda smiled and pulled Beth into a hug. "Oh, my dear. I'm fine. The man didn't get inside. I'm sure he was just looking to rob the place for a quick buck. I'm surprised they didn't get that house across the street first."

Esmeralda turned and hurried over to the officer. She spoke with him and they both went over to her house. When he came back a few minutes later, I met him at the gate. "Her house wasn't broken into, was it?"

"How did you know?" He glanced over at Esmeralda's house, which was now glowing with light.

I glanced back up at my house. "Because they wanted something they thought we had. We were all supposed to be at a rehearsal dinner and party tonight. No one was supposed to be home."

"What a great night to break in." The officer—Officer Manning, based on his name tag—nodded. "I get your point. Where's Detective King?"

"He's at a stag party with his friends, but if I know South Cove, he's already heard about this and should be arriving soon."

As I watched, Toby's truck pulled into the driveway. Jim parked his rental car right behind him. Toby and Deek got out of the truck and joined us, followed quickly by Jim and Greg.

I went to Greg. "Everything's fine. Your mom called the cops before the guy could break in. Nothing happened."

Greg hugged me, then went over to talk to the officers. Toby met my gaze, nodded, then followed him. Deek stayed with me and Jim hurried over to Amanda and Beth. The guys were all here, but there was nothing they could do. Unless the intruder had left prints or dropped something.

The second Bakerstown cop, who had gone out back, came through the back gate into the front yard. He held up a black ski mask and a black jacket. "There's a chance we can trace him from these. But that's all I found. He's long gone."

We gathered in the kitchen, with Toby and Greg staying out and talking to the Bakerstown officers. Deek headed back into town to his apartment over the bookstore. I made a pot of coffee as we waited.

"So, girls, how was your party?" Amanda asked as we sat down around the table.

Beth spoke first. "It was so much fun. We danced and ate and danced more. Darla made these mocktails that were fruity and icy. Everyone wanted to be with us, but Darla kept kicking out the guys."

"Well, that's a relief." Jim put an arm around Beth. "I was worried you might find a new soulmate."

"Not likely." She leaned into him and he kissed the top of her head. "But I did learn the electric slide. We should go line dancing when we get home. I hear they have classes. It would be fun."

I tried to hide my giggle when I saw the look on Jim's face. Thankfully, Greg and Toby came in at that moment. "So what's the conclusion?"

"Officer Manning, Tom, thinks that someone knew we were out at a party to celebrate the wedding and hit our house. Or tried to." Greg poured a cup of coffee and held it out to Toby. He took it and went to lean against the wall where Emma was sitting and waiting.

"Odd coincidence." I tried to read his face. "I guess it could be true."

"I think they waited for Beth's car to leave. If it was a random robbery or one that targeted the people at the party, they would have hit Esmeralda's house first while they were waiting for Beth to leave. No, this has to be something related to the murder investigation. I just don't know what they were looking for." Greg looked at me. "You think so too. Have you taken any candy from strangers lately?"

I thought about the last week and places I'd run up against members of the New Hope organization. Kane had been at the business-to-business meeting. Then I'd met Molly. Then Amanda and I had gone to the open house, where I'd talked to Kane about their library. Then we'd seen the women at the fabric store. I shook my head. "Nothing stands out. I'm sorry."

"Well, I'm hiring security to watch the house tomorrow until we get home on Sunday." Greg looked at Jim. "And I'm not coming back to the Castle with you. I'll reimburse you the cost of the room, but I'm not leaving Jill and Mom here alone."

Jim scowled at his brother. "There's a reason the couple separates before the wedding. It gives them both time to think about what they're doing the next day. It's the last time you'll be an individual. After you take your vows and kiss, you'll be one."

"I'm not leaving them alone." Greg shook his head. "Period."

"What if you sleep on the couch tonight?" I suggested. If something happened in the future to break us apart, I didn't want Jim to be able to rub in Greg's face how he set up the end of our relationship by not staying away from me for this one night. I didn't believe in superstitions, but Jim did. "That way we have the separation, but you're still here."

"Or you can have my bed," Toby offered. "I'll sleep on the couch with my Emma girl. No one's getting past the dynamic duo. And I have clean sheets."

Greg looked at Jim, who nodded. "Fine. I'll sleep at Toby's tonight, then after I check in with him tomorrow, I'll run over to the Castle and get ready there. Will that make you happy, brother?"

"Ecstatic." Jim stood and helped Beth up as well. He kissed Amanda on the cheek. "We're heading back to the hotel. I need my beauty sleep. Mom, don't stay up too late reading. We've got a wedding to celebrate tomorrow."

"I'll run upstairs and grab some clean clothes." Greg leaned down and kissed me. "You're going to be okay, right?"

"Toby will be downstairs. I think if they get past him, you'll hear the commotion out in the shed." I rubbed his face. "I'll see you tomorrow at the mission."

"Just don't be late. The ceremony starts at eleven. You're supposed to be there earlier," he reminded me as he walked over to hug his mom.

"Believe me, I'll have plenty of people making sure I get there on time. We're doing hair and makeup here at the house. Aunt Jackie should be here right at eight. Then Darla, Amy, and Esmeralda will be here shortly after."

Greg groaned. "I'll be out of here before eight, then. I'll take the Jeep and drive it to the mission. That way we have an escape vehicle close by if the reception gets out of hand."

Greg mentioning the Jeep reminded me of something. "Toby, no shaving cream on my paint. You can use soap, but shaving cream hurts the paint."

"That's an old wives' tale. Besides, I'm not sure why you're telling me this," Toby said from the door, where he stood waiting for Greg. When I didn't say anything, he caved. "Fine, I'll make sure no one does anything permanent to the Jeep."

"That's comforting." I watched as Greg met up with him.

"I live to serve," Toby quipped. "I'll be right back, so don't lock the door on me."

"No promises," I called after him.

Amanda and I were alone in the kitchen. Well, alone with Emma. Amanda stood and walked to the stairwell. "You have good friends here. I can see why you and Greg love South Cove. I'm heading to bed."

We did have solid friends. I thought about the dance party Darla had put on for me and the girls to celebrate my wedding. They'd known just what to do. I let Emma out and stared at the night sky. I thought about meeting Maryanne at the fabric store. Did the women at the New Hope compound feel the same way? Supported?

Or did they have an entirely different feeling?

# Chapter 15

Even though the rest of the night was uneventful, I slept poorly, again. I'm sure it had more to do with my upcoming wedding than the attempted break-in or the unsolved murder that occurred at the place I was getting married.

Man, it's hard to find a good wedding venue. At least one that didn't have a history of murder on the grounds. The La Purísima Mission already had a famous murder and ghost story attached to the site. I just hadn't thought there would be another murder so close to my wedding date.

At least we'd gotten the ghost sighting over and done with, since Sasha had seen the unfortunate friar last night. Maybe he'd stay away today. Didn't ghosts have to build up their ectoplasm stuff to be seen by the living? I'd have to check with Esmeralda, who was due at the house any minute. She'd know the rules of the ghost world if anyone did.

True to his word, Greg had disappeared with the Jeep sometime this morning before I woke up. A Bakerstown police cruiser sat on the street outside my house. My backyard was fenced, but that hadn't stopped someone from escaping that way last night when the police showed up after Amanda's call.

I poured another cup of coffee and watched as the hairdresser and makeup artist who had arrived with my aunt rearranged my living room to look like the backstage of a Broadway production. A rack stood in the corner, waiting for the bridesmaids' dresses to be added to my wedding dress, which I'd moved downstairs and onto the rack this morning.

Toby poked his head in the front door and frowned until he saw me over by the kitchen watching the chaos. He nodded at me, then pointed to the kitchen. "Coffee?"

"Coffee, donuts, cookies. Sadie did a treat delivery here this morning. We even have fresh fruit in case you're afraid of not fitting into your tuxedo." Emma and I followed him.

"Cool." He filled a travel mug and grabbed a donut. "Are you ready to go?"

"Me?" I looked down at my sweats and flip-flops. I was clearly not ready. "The wedding isn't for hours."

"Not you. Although you do look lovely, boss." He winked at me as he ate another donut.

"Now you're just sucking up. Why are you still here? Did something happen last night when you were on the couch?" A headache was threatening, so I refilled my coffee. I considered adding a shot of Kahlúa to the mix, but figured there would be too much alcohol floating around today as it was. I didn't want to drink so much that I slurred my vows. Or worse, tripped down the aisle. There's a reason that women traditionally have help getting to the altar.

"I'm here for our girl. Emma has a grooming appointment. She needs her hair all pretty for the event too. I'll have her back before the pictures at ten. The florist is making her a necklace in your colors. I don't think we can get her to drop petals, but she'll look festive." Toby grabbed her leash and a third donut. "See you soon."

"Hey, has Greg heard anything about last night's break-in? Did they find anyone?" I tried to catch him before he stepped into the madhouse that used to be my living room.

"Not talking to you about police business, not today, Jill." He waved and disappeared out the front door with my dog. She didn't even look back.

"Well, isn't that something?" I sat down and looked at the notepad in front of me. According to the schedule my aunt had made, I was already five minutes late for my shower. I grabbed my coffee cup and headed upstairs, letting my aunt deal with the setup questions.

It was probably good that Emma was off-site during this craziness anyway, I thought as I came back downstairs. My hair was still wet but I had on clean shorts and a tank. I wore socks, just in case my feet found any speck of dirt in the living room. My aunt had laid out my clothes when I was in the shower. The wedding dress had its own set of undergarments that I'd bought with the dress.

Yesterday, I'd packed a suitcase for our night at the Madonna Inn, a well-known, pink hotel that catered to honeymooners and romantic weekends. I'd put the suitcase in the Jeep before I'd gone to the rehearsal. If I'd forgotten anything, the hotel wasn't too far from civilization, so we could run to a store.

I kept going over items in my head, making sure I hadn't missed anything. Like getting Emma to the groomer. Someone else had set that up, probably Greg, and I blessed him for the forethought. I packed her a travel bag with a bowl, water, treats, dog waste bags, and a small sack of food, just in case. I set it by the door, hoping I'd remember it as we left.

Aunt Jackie stood by me and pointed back to the hairdresser's chair. "You're late. What's that?"

As we walked over to the chair, I explained it was Emma's overnight bag. Aunt Jackie nodded, then snapped her fingers and Evie appeared. "You're driving over to the mission, correct?"

"Yes, ma'am." Evie reached out and hugged me. "It's your wedding day!"

The hairdresser was already putting product in my hair and held up her hands so Evie wouldn't get stuff on her dress.

"Put this in your car and don't forget to give it to Toby as soon as we get to the venue. You *are* following the limo, right?" Aunt Jackie stared at Evie.

"Of course I am. Sasha and Olivia are coming in her car." Evie smiled at me. "I'll be right back."

My aunt had the power of an army behind her. My army from the bookstore. I leaned back and let the hairdresser do her work. "You know you're not the boss of her anymore."

"Oh, dear, I should think you'd know by now that I'm always the boss." She squeezed my arm. "You're going to be a beautiful bride."

Tears started to threaten to fall, but I blinked them away. It was too soon to be crying. However, since I didn't have makeup on yet, maybe this was the time. "Thank you for everything."

"Oh, this was a joy, dear. A joy." She glanced at the door. "It's just too bad your mother couldn't see this."

Before I could respond, Amy, Darla, and Esmeralda surrounded me. Amy held a tray filled with mimosas. "A glass to celebrate this joyous occasion."

"One glass," I warned her. "I don't want anyone throwing up during pictures."

"We're smarter than that, but no promises after the wedding." Esmeralda waited for everyone, including my aunt, to take a glass. "To our dear Jill. She came to South Cove looking for a new profession and found a home. And we're the better for the addition to our family."

Now tears were imminent. I knew red eyes were almost impossible to cover with makeup and I wasn't looking like a hell-spawned raccoon for my wedding pictures. We drank and I waved them all away. "Go get pretty. I want us all to look so hot we melt the camera."

By some miracle, everyone was dressed, hair done, makeup applied and ready to go when the limo arrived. My aunt handed me a bag with my sparkly silver shoes and had Evie lean down and help me into a pair of white slippers with solid soles.

I felt like a princess. And now I knew why there were ladies-in-waiting with the princess in fairy tales. No one could do anything by themselves in these poofy dresses. We moved out to the limo, and I saw Deek coming up the path. "What are you doing here?"

"Your aunt asked me to make sure the house was locked up after everyone left. Don't worry, I'll be at the wedding with bells on." He pulled out his phone and took a selfie with me. "You look amazing."

"Thanks. And thanks for doing this." I should have thought of it, especially after last night, but apparently my aunt had things in hand.

"No problem. Did someone already take Emma?" He paused at the gate. I nodded. "Toby's bringing her. She's at the groomer."

"You girls and your beauty appointments. You know we love you without all that stuff too." He waved as I got into the limo. Amy and Esmeralda tucked my dress in after me.

"I feel helpless. Is this a normal reaction?" I asked after Amy, Darla, and Esmeralda had gotten into the limo. Aunt Jackie was already in Harrold's car and Evie would be following us.

"Like leading a lamb to slaughter," Esmeralda replied.

Amy slapped her arm. "Stop that. She'll dive out of the car. We need to get these two married before anything else happens."

Realization hit me. "I didn't see Beth or Amanda this morning."

"Your aunt got them through the hair and makeup first, then sent them over to be with Greg and Jim. Don't worry about it. They're fine." Darla checked her makeup. "Last night was crazy, wasn't it?"

"You don't even know what happened after we got home," I responded, and told the group about the attempted break-in. Esmeralda filled in parts I didn't know.

"I was wondering why there was a police cruiser in front of your house this morning," Amy said after we were through explaining. "I thought it was Greg's way of keeping you from running."

"All he had to do was get me in this dress and I would be trapped," I teased, and held up the bag that had my shoes. "Add in these, and I wouldn't get far."

Amy pulled her phone out of her bag. "Time for candid shots. No one talk or laugh so I don't get the ones with crazy mouths on all of you."

Amy's warning didn't work. By the time we reached the mission, we were all laughing. The limo pulled up and my door suddenly opened. "Deek, how did you beat us? Did you get the house locked up?"

"Of course I did. Those people were quick to clear out. I didn't set the living room back in order, though. Should I go back and do that?" Deek looked back toward town.

"Don't worry about it," I said as I took the hand he offered. "Thanks for serving as an usher. I appreciate you."

"I write at night when it's slow in the bookstore. I'm doing this so you'll owe me and you don't claim the book was a work product of the bookstore and steal all my royalties when I make it big." He grinned at me.

"I didn't know I could do that. Thanks for the tip." I leaned in and kissed his cheek, then brushed off the lipstick. "Seriously, thank you for all you do."

He smiled and helped Amy out. "Have you guys been doing shots in the limo? Jill's acting weird. She's all lovey and stuff."

I tapped Deek on his shoulder. "Hey, I'm always like this."

Amy laughed as she took my arm and led me to a golf cart, where she settled me on the back seat, facing the rear. My dress flowed over the entire seat. She climbed in the front and smiled at the driver. "No, no you're not. We're ready to go take pictures. Hold on, Jill."

The day seemed to fly by after that. I kept looking over my shoulder. Would I see an apparition? Would a scream interrupt the ceremony? Would Emma run off barking after a deer or rabbit as she walked down the aisle in her flower collar? My worst fear was I'd fall and break something, causing one more delay in marrying Greg.

"Don't be nervous, dear." My aunt kissed me on the cheek as Deek stood by, waiting to take her to her seat. She was the last to be seated. Then we'd start the ceremony. "You'll look like you're grimacing in your photos. You want to relax your face and smile. This is supposed to be a happy day. Please at least act like you're happy."

"Now, Jackie, you're making it worse. Jill, you're beautiful, and any man in his right mind would be honored to have you as his wife. Greg's lucky to have such an outstanding life partner." My new(ish) Uncle Harrold always knew the right things to say. He pressed a coin into my hand. "It's an antique Greek drachma. My grandfather gave it to my mother on the day of her wedding. I haven't had the opportunity until now to pass this on to a daughter. I hope you'll accept it as a symbol of my confidence that you will have a long and happy marriage. Just like my parents and their parents before them."

"Don't you want to hold on to this for your son?" I felt the weight of the coin as well as the family heritage in my hand.

"No, dear, it doesn't work that way. I have to pass it on to a daughter or someone I consider my daughter. I only have two. You and Lille. And you got married first." He curled my hand around the coin. "Now you need to pass it on to your son, who will pass it again. Generation to generation. It's the way the world works, and traditions keep us human."

Great, one more reason for Lille to hate me if she found out about the family tradition. But that was my issue, not Harrold's. "Thank you for this. It means a lot."

"The coin has a high monetary value as it represents your dowry, but what you bring as a person to your marriage is of even more value. You are priceless, Jill. And hopefully, Greg understands that." He folded my fingers around the coin and kissed my hand.

Amy handed me Emma's leash. "It's time to send her down the aisle to Greg."

I bent down to kiss my dog and aimed her toward Greg. She'd practiced this move several times on Friday. Hopefully, having all the people around wouldn't freak her out. I wrapped her leash around and hooked it so she wouldn't drag the leather. "Go get Greg, Emma. Go find Daddy."

She woofed as I nodded to Greg, who had a treat in his hand. Emma hurried to the altar, and I heard the audience giggling at our unconventional flower girl. Then Darla and Matt walked down the aisle. Esmeralda and Toby were next. And finally, Amy and Justin. Jim was Greg's best man, and he was already at the altar with him. Beth would join my side once Amy arrived and even out the optics. My aunt had insisted.

Finally, it was just me and Harrold standing in the walkway, waiting for the "Bridal Chorus" to sound. He kissed the top of my head, probably trying to not mess up my makeup or the veil. "Thank you for choosing me for this honor."

"Thank you for accepting." I leaned my head toward his and hoped I wasn't crying, yet. I didn't want to test my mascara's waterproof claim. The music started and I whispered, "Just don't let me trip."

The squeeze of my hand and a chuckle let me know he'd heard me. And then the music started and I blacked out.

The next thing I remember was walking back down the aisle getting pelted with birdseed. So I'd said all the right things at the right time. I just wished I could remember the ceremony. As we moved to the reception line that would lead people into the area with the food, an open bar, a dance floor, and lots of tables, I saw him.

A shimmery outline of a padre. The one who guarded the mission and blessed the couples who chose to be married there. The ghost smiled and I gasped. I felt Greg's arm around my waist.

"Are you okay? Too much input today? Did you eat anything?" Greg peppered questions at me as the ghost slowly disappeared. I didn't turn to look at Greg, I didn't want to break the spell.

I smiled as he vanished. Only then did I turn to my new husband. "Did I eat? Do you even know me at all?"

He chuckled and leaned down to kiss me. "It was a dumb question. Sorry."

My feet were killing me by the time the reception line was finished. My high heels were sinking into the grass where we stood. Greg had been informed more than once that he'd finally bought the cow, and I was told that I looked beautiful for a ball and chain.

As the last couple left to find the champagne, I turned to Greg. "After that line, I'm sure you're regretting this whole thing."

He pulled me into a full-blown kiss. One that in cartoon land would have blown off my shoes and made my eyes pop out. In our world, it reminded me that we weren't just best friends. We were soulmates. His eyes were smiling when he let me loose. "I think not."

"Good, because I'm so glad we're finally married." I glanced at the tent where the reception was being held. "Would they notice if we left now?"

Greg put his arm around my waist and pulled me close. "I'm afraid so. Let's go party with our friends for a bit, then we'll head off to the hotel. I hear the Madonna Inn has a unique restroom in the restaurant."

"That's what you're looking forward to? The men's room urinal?" I followed him into the tent. I knew he was teasing me, but still.

He turned and took my hand, leading me to the head table. "Oh, that's just the beginning, dear wife. The beginning of our adventure-filled life."

# Chapter 16

Of course, our adventures couldn't start until after Greg closed the murder investigation on Kane Matthews. As we drove back to South Cove on Sunday afternoon, I could tell his mind was on work. And what had happened in South Cove since we'd been gone. Twenty-four hours away and then we were back in the fray. Life as normal. Except now I wore two rings on my left hand, and I couldn't kick him out of the house without filing all the legal papers around a divorce. Maybe it was too soon to be thinking about an escape plan.

"It was a beautiful wedding. I'm so glad we found that mission. Or more accurately, you found that mission." I leaned back and let the sun shine on my face.

"Everyone seemed to love it, even Mom and Jim." He glanced over at me. "Thanks for including Beth in the wedding party. I know it was last-minute."

"If Jim had mentioned she was coming, it wouldn't have been..." I paused. No use getting mad about something that was done and over with. "Anyway, it was nice getting to know her a little more."

"So you saw the mission ghost, huh?"

The quick change of subject made me sit up and open my eyes. "Why would you ask that?"

"Now I know you did. You always answer a question with a question when you don't want to answer the first question. What did he look like?" Greg slowed down for a squirrel who couldn't decide if he was going to dash out on the road or not.

"Just like the story. He was over by the old chapel and dressed in a friar's robe. He seemed happy about the wedding." I leaned back again. "I guess I should have expected some sort of event like that during our wedding. We're just *those* people."

"I'm sorry we have to go back to normal life so soon. As soon as this case is wrapped up, I've told Marvin I'm gone for two weeks—no questions asked."

"Two weeks?" I opened my eyes again and looked at him. "We're leaving for two weeks?"

Greg laughed. "You didn't expect that, did you?"

No, I hadn't. I still didn't know where we were going on our honeymoon. My aunt knew because Greg had worked with her to set up the arrangements. The only thing she'd said was to make sure I didn't update my driver's license with my new name until after the honeymoon. I'd kind of expected that to be a false trail.

Now I wondered.

"Anyway, I'm sorry about having to work. If this Matthews thing hadn't happened, we'd be on our way."

"On our way where?" I tried to make the question sound casual.

"To bright, beautiful Nunya," he responded quickly. A little too quickly.

"Nunya?" I watched out the window at the rolling hills.

"Nunya business so stop asking." He squeezed my hand. "We have time for an early dinner on the way home. I told Toby we'd be there about five so he could drop off Emma."

"Sounds good."

We pulled into a seafood restaurant just off the highway about thirty minutes later. Since it was Sunday, the parking lot was busier than during the week for an early dinner. Greg found a parking spot near the building, and we headed inside. As we were waiting to be seated, I saw Roger and Maryanne Matthews sitting at a table. He was looking at his phone and she was eating what looked like surf and turf. I wondered what dinner was being served on the compound while the church's leaders ate out and ordered the most expensive item on the restaurant's menu.

The hostess walked us right past their table.

Maryanne looked up as we passed by and smiled. "If it isn't the newlyweds. I figured you two would be off on your honeymoon."

"Work issues," Greg said as he held up a finger to the hostess. "Well, have a nice dinner."

"You too, and congratulations on your wedding," Roger said. He'd set aside his phone, looking like he'd just gotten caught reading or watching a game at the table.

We nodded and turned back to follow the hostess.

As we got seated, Greg glanced over at the Matthewses. "He was trading stock. Justin has the same app on his phone. He showed it to me during the bachelor party."

"On a Sunday? And at dinner with your wife? How romantic." I studied the menu. I didn't want to overeat, but I'd been eating healthily for weeks to make sure I fit into my wedding dress. Now all I needed was to not look like a beached whale, if we were going to the beach.

Greg didn't respond, and when I looked up I saw he was still watching Roger Matthews, who again had his phone in his hand.

"Greg? What's wrong?"

He shook his head, then turned and smiled at me. "Sorry, I'm not being romantic either. But from a quick glance, it looked like that account had over two million in it."

"Dollars?" I set down the menu. "Where does a preacher get two million in a stock account? Do you think it's the church's account?"

"Those are both good questions." He picked up his phone and texted someone. Then he put it back on the side of the table and picked up the menu. "That surf and turf looked good."

"I'm going all seafood," I said, thinking of the money in Roger's stock fund. "Who did you text?"

"Esmeralda. I wanted to know if the financial reports from the church had been received yet." His phone buzzed. He read the text and set it down again.

The waitress came and asked for our order. Greg ordered his meal and a large iced tea. I followed suit. After she left, he took my hand.

"You could have had a drink. You don't even have to work tomorrow." He kissed my knuckles. "The celebration doesn't have to end yet."

"But you're working tonight?" I nodded to the phone. "I guess Esmeralda got the reports."

"She did, the net-worth statements from the church. I need to head into the station and go over everything." He looked over at the other table. "Funny thing is, the church's net worth is way less than two million. Not including the compound. So now we need to look at their private accounts. I need to find a judge who will give me a warrant."

"I also have important work to do tomorrow," I said as I took the iced tea from our server. "I need to do laundry and take the dog for a walk. And maybe drive your mom to another tourist trap."

He sipped his tea, then added sugar. "I'm jealous."

"You are not." I leaned back in my seat. Life was back to normal.

\* \* \* \*

When Monday morning came, I found myself alone in the house. Greg had gone to work early. Amanda was hanging out with Jim and Beth for the next two days before they all left for home. And I'd already run Emma. I'd started the laundry last night before grabbing a book to try to relax. So after I rotated my last load from the washer to the dryer, I was done. Sure, I had a ton of thank you notes to write, but I'd had Toby put the gifts in the office so Greg and I could open them together and write the thank you cards then.

The process had worked when we got engaged. And doing them together forced us to spend time together as a couple. But now, with the investigation ongoing, it wasn't time to add this task to Greg's already full list.

Besides writing the thank you notes and returning any unwanted gifts, most of the wedding stuff that had overwhelmed my life a week ago was gone. I needed to take my wedding dress to the cleaners and get it boxed up for my currently nonexistent daughter. She'd probably hate it anyway. But it was a cute tradition. And take the drachma to my safety deposit box at the bank.

I opened my laptop, planning on updating my status and seeing what was going on with my virtual friends. I saw that New Hope Lies, Friends and Parents of Deceived Members had a new post. Their name might be long, but at least it showed a clear direction for the group. And they'd let me join the group without having to answer any questions.

A man, Tanner O'Dell, had posted an update on his missing wife, Heather. I pulled out my notebook where I'd been writing down ideas and noted the important facts of Heather's case.

She was at the compound. The security cameras at the fabric store showed her buying denim the day Amanda and I watched Carlie being detained by the police. I compared the grainy black-and-white screen shot to the summer picture on the lake he'd also posted of his wife.

At the end of his post, he wrote, "Just wait, I'll have some answers today. That is if the South Cove police aren't on the take, like we believe they are."

I texted the link and the last line to Greg. "What is he planning?"

Greg called instead of responding. "I can't believe they did that. We got an anonymous tip last night asking for a welfare check—someone's kids had gone to the compound with his wife. This must be that Heather. Now the compound knows we're coming, and we'll be the idiots both there and with this group."

"How will the compound know you're coming?" I was confused. Did they have to announce welfare checks?

"You knew. You don't think Roger and Maryanne are smart enough to put a spy into the group? Did they ask you any questions when they let you in?"

I hadn't thought of that. "No. They didn't."

"I've got to go. Toby's probably calling off work for the week at the bookstore until we can get this under control." He paused. "Sorry if it's leaving you shorthanded."

"We'll be fine. I'll split his hours between Deek and me. You get to tell your mom she's lost her personal tour guide."

He chuckled. "I think she's going home with Jim and Beth soon anyway. She's worn out."

"She thinks she's giving us space. She doesn't realize that during an investigation, we have all the space we need." I ended the conversation and opened the Google calendar for the store. Toby had five shifts to cover. I checked my calendar, then emailed the staff and offered to take two and switch for the rest if I could have the early shift.

Then I dug into the links Beth had sent me about the Matthews brothers. I copied my thanks to Greg, so he wouldn't think I was hiding anything.

By noon, I'd read everything and I had an idea. I went into my office and found my old address book. I found the number I was looking for and dialed. I got voice mail, no surprise. Anya Carter was always busy. She worked with Child Protection Services. I also knew she answered her voicemails while she drove to the next appointment.

"Hey, Anya, a blast from the past, it's Jill Gardner. Can you give me a call? I've got some questions about welfare checks." I left her my number and set the phone down. I was at a standstill. At least with the compound. I went back to the Facebook group and looked for any over-the-top threats against the church or Kane himself.

By the time I'd finished, I had ten names. Eight still were members and two had closed out their Facebook page or just stopped posting. I started with these two. I got hits on both with obituaries.

I bookmarked the pages, then looked at the other relatives listed on the obituaries and added them to my list.

If Greg didn't have these names already, I might be adding them to his list of suspects to weed out. Then again, one of these people might just have acted on the threats they'd posted.

As I finished up the list, I went back to the group page and studied the posts that Tanner O'Dell had made. His wife had cleared out their joint bank accounts, cashed in her 401(k), and taken off to join the New Hope church. And she'd taken the younger son, Jimmy, with her.

Mr. O'Dell's post said the older boy had been in school, but when his mom tried to pick him up in the middle of basketball practice he told her he'd get a ride from a friend. Then he'd called his dad to see why Mom had Jimmy in the car with a pile of suitcases. The post had the hashtag #thankgodforafterschoolsports.

Now, the dad wanted his other son back. He'd filed for divorce and gotten full custody, so if Greg did find Tanner's son at the compound, he could return him to his dad.

It all sounded too adversarial for a church, at least to me. Where was "turn the other cheek" and why did the Matthewses pretend to be living a simple life while dining at expensive restaurants? And have two million in stock?

I didn't think I was going to get very far with my internet research. I didn't have anywhere to be until Tuesday morning when I would open the bookstore, so I decided to go shopping and fill our fridge. Maybe I'd get lucky; if I bought a full gallon of milk, Greg would solve the case today. If I didn't buy food on the chance that we might be leaving sooner rather than later, the case would stay open. It just worked that way. I'd buy the stuff to make a pie as well. It would at least keep me busy. I could have my aunt clear out the fridge if we left town. Or Toby. Toby loved getting free food.

I went through the fridge, discarding old stuff as I made my list. The farmers market was closed for the season, so I added fruits and vegetables to the list. I'd figure out which ones when I got to the store. Then I texted Greg and asked if he needed anything.

The reply I got made me curious. *Can't talk. Toby says we're out of dog food.*

I went into the laundry room. Toby was right. We were getting close to being out of Emma's food. I added it and dryer sheets to the list.

I checked the weather and found that it was going to be cool all day. I grabbed Emma's leash. "You can come with me. You'll have to stay in the car when I'm at the grocery store, but we'll go to the dog food place together." Emma wagged her tail. She understood go. And probably dog food. But she'd be so excited when we hit the pet store. I took a couple of ice packs out of the freezer and put them in an insulated bag. I'd put them in the cooler we kept in the back of the Jeep for grocery runs.

But when we got to the car, there was no cooler. Someone had cleaned out the Jeep for the wedding. It took me a few more minutes to find it in the shed. By the time we got going, I was starving. But food would have to wait until we hit Bakerstown since there wasn't a fast-food place nearby.

I'd share my fries with Emma. Neither one of us needed a full sleeve of fries.

I was just finishing up in the grocery store when I saw Molly. She had a couple of TV dinners in her basket as well as cereal, milk, and cookies. When she looked up at me, I saw she had a black eye.

"Molly, who hit you?" I reached up but she turned away.

"I fell." She tried to move past me but I grabbed her cart.

"Did someone from the compound threaten you? I can call Greg right now." I pulled out my phone. "That's not right."

She held up a hand. "Stop. It wasn't anyone from the compound. Let me explain, Jill. Can I call you Jill?"

I nodded and tucked the phone back into the pocket of my sweatshirt. "Yes. I'm Jill Gardner, I mean, Jill King. We just got married. Anyway, that's not important. Who hit you?"

"Vince. The guy who was helping me find Carlie. He was agitated. He wanted to take her from the hospital. I told him this was Carlie's decision. I saw in her eyes that she wanted to come with me, but I also saw confusion. I don't want to push her. She's still at the hospital but voluntarily now. She has an infection. She's so thin."

"Wait, Vince hit you?" Now I was concerned. Especially since this man was Amanda's ex-husband.

"He called me a loser. A wimp. Then he hit me. And then he quit working for me. It saved me from having to fire him. Anyway, that was Sunday morning. I moved to an extended-stay hotel here in Bakerstown. I have a stove now." She glanced at her buzzing phone. "And that's him again. From his voicemails, he's sorry and wants to continue to help me. I think he's just afraid I'll turn him in to the cops."

"You should." I glanced out the large windows in the front of the store. I could see the Jeep and Emma, who was sitting in the driver's seat, grinning. "My dog's out in the car. I need to get going, but I could meet you for coffee in about an hour?"

"I'm fine. I'll come to South Cove tomorrow. Will you be working at the coffee shop?"

"Until eleven." I paused, not wanting to scare her. "Maybe it's better you don't talk to Vince."

"Not planning on it." She snapped her fingers. "I need bread and jam. The room has a toaster and toast is my go-to snack. Especially with blackberry jam."

I watched her walk away and I got in line to check out. I needed to talk to Amanda. Without Greg around. If Vince would hit a woman he was working for, I bet he also hit his wife.

# Chapter 17

Amanda didn't pick up, so I left her a message. I told her that I had some questions about Vince. That might be enough to get her to call and to keep the call private. Neither of her sons needed to know about this old, water-under-the-bridge issue. I didn't even know for sure that Vince had done anything wrong besides hitting Molly.

That was enough for me not to like or trust him.

As I'd expected, Emma was ecstatic to be at the pet store. She had to greet all the checkers and stockers as well as the other two dogs in the store. As we were checking out, I noticed one of the clerks was watching something on his cell phone. He held it out for the other clerk to see.

"I told you, they're raiding the place now. I bet they find all kinds of illegal stuff there. Drugs, guns, and I heard that they're trafficking women and children."

I glanced over as I ran my card through the machine. It was the New Hope compound. Not only was Greg's truck there, but all the South Cove police units as well as several from the county sheriff and a few state police cars. I saw several additional cars parked on the road.

A woman I recognized from having worked with her occasionally, Anya Carter, was escorting children from the meetinghouse into a van parked in front. "They're taking the children."

The checker who handed me my receipt nodded. "South Cove police went in to do a welfare check and all heck broke loose. I hear one officer was shot."

I grabbed my bag and hurried Emma to the car. Then I called Greg. I got his voicemail and left a terse message. Then I called him again. This time he picked up.

"I take it you've heard. I'm fine, but Tim got shot. Shoulder wound. He's at the hospital in Bakerstown. Can you go over and sit with his wife? I can't leave here, and her folks live in Iowa."

"Sure. I have to take the groceries and Emma home, but I'll get there as soon as I can." My breathing started slowing just a bit. "I thought you might have been—"

"Which is why I picked up. Let me talk to you later. I'll call Esmeralda and have her sit with Tim's wife until you get there. She offered but I wanted to see if you had time. You're good at this." I heard a yell from his end of the line. "I've really got to go. I love you, Jill."

"I love you too. Stay safe." I hurried to say both before he hung up. "I will."

Then the call ended. I put my phone in the drink holder next to the bottle of soda I'd bought at the drive-through. It had a screw-on cap.

"Sorry, Emma, but we've got to get you home so Mommy can come back and sit at the hospital. I don't know how long I'll be gone, but I'll find someone to come and let you out in a few hours." I'd ask Esmeralda if she'd stop by on her way home, since she lived across the street. I had a lot of fallback people to help with Emma. I guess that's what made us a community. We were all ready to jump in at a moment's notice.

When I got to the hospital, Tim was in surgery, so they directed me to that floor to find his wife. Dona was maybe twenty-five and, as I looked at her, at least six months pregnant. Had Greg told me they were expecting? I hugged her and met Esmeralda's gaze. "How is he?"

"The doctor says the bullet went straight through. They are repairing a tear in his shoulder or something. I never could listen when doctors talk." Dona rubbed her belly. "Even with this little one. I don't want to know anything I don't have to until it's time."

"How long will he be in there? Have you eaten lunch?" I glanced at my watch. It was almost four.

"I didn't want to leave." She looked up at me. "Is it bad that I'm starving?"

I smiled and rubbed her shoulder. "You're eating for two. Esmeralda, can you take her downstairs, and I'll stay up here and wait for news? If the doctor comes out before you get back, I'll come get you right away."

"If you think it will be okay." Dona looked scared.

Esmeralda pulled her to her feet. "It will be more than fine. Tim needs you to take care of yourself. You don't want to fall and break something because you're hungry. How would you take care of Tim if that happened?" Dona took one last look at the double doors leading to the surgery center. Then she focused on me. "You promise to come get me if there's any news. Even bad news."

The look on her face almost broke my heart. "Dona, I promise. Go take care of yourself and your baby."

As they walked to the elevators to find the cafeteria, Esmeralda turned back and mouthed, "Thank you."

I nodded, then sank into a chair and pulled out one of the three books I'd brought with me to read. Just in case.

My phone buzzed as I settled into one of the plastic-and-metal chairs to wait. I looked at the text. It was from Greg.

*Can you ask Esmeralda to go to Kane's funeral with you tomorrow? I know, don't judge me. I'd go but everyone here is ticked because we pulled three kids out today who were taken from the parent who had custody. Including the guy you sent me earlier. Just watch for anything unusual. Please and thank you, Mrs. King.*

I smiled at the last message and quickly responded *time and place* before he changed his mind.

When Esmeralda and Dona came back, I had good news. I'd been just about to go get them. "The surgeon was just here. Tim's in recovery and doing well. They're keeping him overnight and he'll meet you in room 302 in thirty minutes or so."

"Should I go now?" Dona picked up her bag.

I shook my head. "That nurse, Kathy, she's going to come and tell you when he's out of recovery. They still have to set up his room. Esmeralda and I can't go into his room, just family."

"Okay." Dona set her bag down, then sat in the chair. "He's done with surgery and so that's off my worry list. I need to update my church prayer group and tell them the news."

"We'll be right over here." I took Esmeralda by the arm. When I was sure that Dona was busy on her phone, I turned to Esmeralda. "Greg wants you and I to go to the funeral at the New Hope compound tomorrow."

She listened as I told her what he'd said and why we were going instead of him. Then she glanced at Dona. "One of those so-called guards shot

Tim. I'm not sure I should be going either. At least I don't have to have a gun to hurt someone."

I wanted to laugh, but she was being serious. "I think that's why he's sending you with me. I'll pick you up at eleven?"

"Fine." She glanced at her watch. "I have a client coming tonight. I've called and let him know I might be late, but he said he'd wait. Can you sit with Dona until Tim gets into his room?"

"Of course. That's why I'm here. Thanks for filling in until I could arrive." I leaned closer. "Can you do one more thing, without alerting Greg?"

"You want me to work behind his back?" Esmeralda's face told the story: I'd have to have an excellent explanation.

"Just until we find out if there is fire with this smoke."

Esmeralda stared at me. I guess that wasn't a New Orleans expression.

"Look, can you pull up any records on Vince Penn? I'm mostly looking for domestic abuse charges, but anything would help."

"Amanda's ex-husband?" The unasked question was clear. Esmeralda knew what I was looking for.

"Exactly. I found out earlier that he hit Molly Cordon on Sunday. Before I tell Greg, I want to make sure he didn't hit Amanda when they were married. Or else it's not going to be pretty." I smiled as I saw Dona close her eyes and curl up into the chair. "I'm glad Tim's out of the woods."

"Being in law enforcement is a dangerous position. For both the officer and their spouse." Esmeralda met my gaze and for a second, I froze.

I hadn't even thought about what might happen to Greg. I worried, yes, but over time, his job had started to seem normal to me. At least, normal if you worked all the time and had to deal with crimes and criminals. Had I ever even considered what being Mrs. Greg King would be like, besides the name change and the way it looked on stationery? "I guess this is the for-better-or-worse part of the vows this weekend."

"I wondered if that part of the decision had hit you yet." Esmeralda hugged me. "It wasn't Greg today. Just be thankful for that and be there for Dona. I'll see you tomorrow."

"Oh, one more favor? After your client can you check in on Emma? I might be home by then, but if I'm not?"

Esmeralda hugged me. "Of course. That's not a favor. I love Emma."

I went back to sit with Dona and took out the book I was trying to read. Typically, a book could keep me out of my own head for a while. After I read the same page three times, I tucked it away in my purse. I also put one in Dona's tote. Just in case she needed something to get through the night. Then I sat and thought about my future. About our future.

\* \* \* \*

Greg was home by the time I pulled in the drive. I'd waited with Dona while they moved Tim to his room, then I'd left her with magazines, snacks, and a couple of drinks from the gift shop. I'd even put in a pen and a pretty notebook in case she wanted to write down instructions from the doctor. Hospitals always gave you tons of paperwork when you were discharged, but there was always one thing the doctor said that wasn't on the hundred and thirty-two pages that I then promptly forgot. I'd wake up days later in the middle of the night and realize I hadn't been using a four by six bandage or I'd wrapped the incision wrong after I cleaned it.

But maybe that was just me.

I dropped my keys and tote on the foyer table as I came inside the bright house. I thought the house had never looked so welcoming. Emma ran from the kitchen to greet me, and I sank my face into her soft ruff. I felt the tears before I realized I was crying.

"Hey, what's the matter? I called and talked to his doctor at the hospital. Tim's fine. A little sore but he'll be back to work in a few weeks." Greg had followed Emma out to the living room to greet me, and now pulled me to my feet and into a hug. He wiped my tears away with a kitchen towel that announced it belonged to a farm-to-fork kitchen.

"I don't know. It was just, something Esmeralda said about how dangerous your job is and I got to thinking about it and I'm just glad you're not hurt or worse." I said it all fast, hoping to get it out before I self-edited my words. I rubbed my face. "Sorry, I think this week has just been a bit overwhelming."

He studied me. "Are you sorry we got married?"

I sank into a chair when we reached the kitchen. "No. Not at all. I think I'm just realizing what that means for our future. I knew you were in police work. I just boxed up all the dangerous parts and painted over the seams with South Cove magic. Then when Tim got shot, the box blew wide open. I'm fine. You're fine. We're fine. I'm just being emotional."

"First responders have a higher divorce rate than the national average. It's not just the time away from each other. It's the what-could-happen factor.

I guess I figured we were past that since we've been living together." He put the teakettle on the stove.

"Me too. But something about seeing Dona tonight just kind of broke me. She looked so sad. So fragile." I took his hand. "I'm really glad you're okay."

"Me too." He set out two cups and put tea bags in them. "So I'll break my rule about not talking about open cases and tell you about the welfare check today. The guy you sent me from the Facebook group called in the request for his son. But from his post, I think it was more of a challenge to see if we'd even check up on the kid."

"Yeah, I got that too." I stood and grabbed my notebook and pushed it toward him. "There's a list of all the people who have been posting about New Hope. I've crossed off the ones who are dead now and added any other relatives who might have taken up the cause. Beth has a lot of information about New Hope as an organization. I put in a call to Anya, but I haven't heard back. I saw her on the news report. I guess she's busy with the kids."

"She said to tell you she'd call tomorrow and congrats on the wedding." He turned off the stove when the teakettle began to scream. He poured the hot water over the tea bags and set the cups on the table.

I reached for the honey and added it to my cup. "If my kid was taken away from me, I'd do anything to get him or her back."

"Yeah, I'm thinking the same thing." He glanced at my list. "Have you talked to Molly lately? I called the hotel she was staying at and they said she moved out."

I was backed into a corner. I couldn't ignore a direct question. I think it was in our marriage contract somewhere. Amanda was going to kill me. And Molly. "She's staying in Bakerstown now. She and Vince got into an argument."

Greg's eyes narrowed. "Does she want to press charges?"

"I said an argument. How did you get from that to assault?" I didn't look at him, focusing instead on dunking my tea bag.

"I know why my mom divorced him. Jim and I both know. We were days away from doing an intervention when she called and told me he'd moved out and she was filing the paperwork. I think she wanted to protect herself, just in case he didn't get the point." Greg squeezed the water out of his tea bag and set it on a paper napkin. "Jim and I visited him later that day and explained the facts of life. I didn't hit him. But I've never wanted to smash in someone's face so bad. I know, it's not what you want to hear from the man you just married."

"Actually, I was afraid that if you found out, you'd go after him. We all know the stats on abusers. They don't just stop hitting women. I don't think Molly's going to press charges, but we should watch him just in case he doesn't take the hint."

"He's an idiot." He looked up from his tea. "So Molly's okay?"

"She's shaken up and has a black eye." I sipped my tea. It was nice being home. Telling Greg everything. It had been a crazy day. "Oh, I asked Esmeralda to look into Vince's background. Just in case."

"And she wasn't supposed to tell me, right?"

The tea was working its magic, and I could feel my muscles relaxing. I was home. Greg was here with Emma. All was right in my little world. "Yeah, sorry."

"Honey, there's not much that goes on around here or around those I love without me finding out. But I appreciate the concern." He picked up a pen and started crossing names off my list.

"What are you doing?"

He looked up and smiled. "Removing the people we've already checked for alibis. "Remember, I am a professional investigator. I do know things."

My face warmed and he laughed.

"It's fine. I appreciate your work. Looking at the obituaries for next of kin, that was pretty impressive." He took out his notebook and wrote a few names into it. "I'll have Esmeralda check on these. And I'll have a chat with Vince if he hasn't already skipped town. He's broken ties with Molly, his current golden goose. And Mom's not giving him anything. I've made sure of that."

"Sometimes it's crazy how close these investigations get to the people in our lives." I finished my tea and stood to turn the kettle back on to warm more water. "Have you been able to get our favorite minister off the suspect list yet?"

He groaned as he closed his notebook. "No. Bill took a drive before church on Sunday morning. He was back at the church at ten but the time of death Doc gave me doesn't clear him. It cleared Molly, though. He was dead for at least an hour before the paramedics got to the mission and we have video showing when she came into the parking lot and when she left. And, Mrs. King, the video clears you."

"Wait, I was a suspect?" I turned away from the kettle I was trying to will into whistling.

He shook his head. "We always look at the person who found the body. I thought you'd know that by now."

# Chapter 18

There was a line at the coffee shop when I walked up from the house on Tuesday morning. News vans sat parked around Main Street. I pushed my way through the crowd and ignored the questions being thrown my way as I unlocked the door.

One reporter asked, "Did you know Kane Matthews?"

Another reporter asked, "How has having a cult in your backyard changed South Cove?"

"Any theories on why they used the mission as a murder venue?" a woman standing next to me asked quietly. Then she added, "How was the wedding? Any ghost Kane sightings?"

I stared at her as the lock clicked under my key.

"I have no comment on the murder of, or the life of, Kane Matthews," I said as I turned and stared down the group. "However, if you want to buy coffee or a book, you're welcome to come inside."

When I walked into the shop, most of the group followed me. The woman who'd asked about the wedding stayed outside. I met her gaze and she smiled. I hadn't heard the last from her. I put on an apron, started my coffeepots, and switched on the rest of the lights. Then I turned to the first person in line. "What can I get for you?"

As the line eased, I texted Sadie and asked for an emergency refill on my treat stash before I helped the next person. I thought about calling for help, but things were going well, and most of the reporters got their order and left the shop. If they stopped in again after the funeral on their way back to their home base, the shop would be out of baked goods by one.

With the shop nearly empty, the woman loitering out front came in. She had a disposable cup in her hand that she threw away as she approached the counter. She must have had someone else get her first cup. I tried to ignore what I knew was coming. "Good morning, can I get you another coffee? How would you like it?"

She rattled off her simple order and pointed to the snowflake cookies. "I'll take a dozen of those if you have enough."

"I'll run in the back and check." I didn't wait. I'd already started her coffee and I'd box up the cookies in the back, keeping me out of conversation range. I had two dozen left, so I packed the dozen for her and brought the rest out to put in the case. If I kept busy, maybe she'd leave me alone. I rang up the purchase and gave her the total as I put the box into a large bag, then pushed the coffee toward her. I took her credit card.

"So how *was* the wedding? I would have thought you'd be gone on your honeymoon. I guess marrying a police detective kind of killed off that idea." She took back her card and signed her name on the receipt. Then she left an extremely large tip.

"I was needed at the coffee shop." I nodded to the line. "Work is calling."

The woman's eyes flashed, and I realized she'd thought I'd talk about Kane's death. Even Darla knew better, and she was only a part-time reporter. This woman thought a few dollars in my tip jar would buy my story. Or maybe it was the dozen cookies she'd bought.

She slid a business card my way. "If you ever want to chat, I can pay expenses for a story like this."

I wondered briefly what expenses I might have that she'd offer to cover. She was trying to buy a story from the new wife of the detective in charge of the investigation. She thought I was so self-centered I'd think that Greg's job was interfering with my own happiness and needs. Or maybe I'd be mad about the delayed honeymoon. I bet Sherry would have made the deal in a hot minute. I smiled at her, moved her card to the side, and called out, "I can help the next customer."

After the news vans left, I watched as Molly came into the shop. I'd seen her walking past several times wearing a baseball cap, dark sunglasses, and a huge letterman jacket that seemed to swallow her. When she came into the shop, she headed straight to the counter.

"No one else is here, right?" She glanced back and forth.

"You mean the news people? No. They've gone. I would have thought that you would want to talk to them. To put Carlie in the spotlight." I poured her a coffee. Molly had become a frequent customer in the last few weeks and had been on Deek's list of regulars and their coffee orders. I'd seen her name last week while I was off when I checked the list to see if my regulars still came in without me here to pour their coffee. They had. "Carlie didn't go back to the cult after leaving the hospital. She's staying with me in Bakerstown. We didn't want anyone, including Vince, to know. She's been having a hard time and a local pastor has been helping her reacclimate." Molly glanced at the almost-empty display case and smiled. "He must be from South Cove since he brought her those same cookies on Sunday."

"She's doing good, though?" I refilled my cup and walked around the counter to talk with Molly.

"She misses Kane. He was the draw for her. She thought he was in love with her, but when she got to the compound, she was just one of many." Molly looked around. "That man used the group as his harem. It's horrible. Now that Roger and Maryanne are in charge, Carlie said it's been better. But she believed in Kane. Not New Hope. Thank goodness she got pulled out when she did. I think she's going to be okay."

I'd thought maybe Kane's charisma had drawn people to the cult, but I hadn't imagined he'd been so close to his young, pretty followers. I wondered if Greg knew how Kane had run the church.

"Are you going to the funeral?" I thought I knew the answer.

Molly violently shook her head. "There's no way I'm letting her step foot on the property again. The pastor told her that saying goodbye doesn't require a formal ceremony. And I bless him for that. He's convinced her not to go. Mostly for my safety, but I'll play the victim if it keeps my kid safe."

Molly got up and glanced at her watch. "I've got a counseling session in about ten minutes. Thanks for the coffee and for talking with me. I appreciate everything you've done."

"Molly, about Vince—" I started, but she shook her head.

"Don't worry about him. He left an angry voice mail this morning saying that Detective King had men come to his hotel room and escort him out of town. Of course, he blamed me for telling them that he hit me. But then he said something about his ex-wife's kid, so I don't know who ratted him out for being a bad guy. I just know he's gone."

I couldn't help but glance out the windows to the street. I hoped Molly's words were true. "Just be careful."

She put the hat back on and slipped on the glasses. "You think anyone will recognize me in this getup?"

I let the statement stand. I'd recognized her the first time she walked past the window, but maybe Vince was out of town.

I focused on getting the shop ready for Deek to take over at eleven. I needed to change into clean black pants, a silk tee, and a blazer, my go-to funeral outfit along with black slides. I wouldn't be invisible at the funeral, but maybe I'd fit in enough to not stand out.

\* \* \* \*

As soon as Esmeralda and I walked into the foyer of the meetinghouse, I realized I'd chosen the wrong outfit to blend in. Besides the local community members, like Esmeralda and me, who'd come out of curiosity, everyone was dressed in colors. Bright colors, florals, and celebration clothes. The men were in tan khakis and brightly colored polo shirts, which made them look like they worked on a golf course.

As Esmeralda moved to the chapel area, I paused. "I need to go to the restroom first."

"Do you want me to wait?" Esmeralda glanced at the men standing and watching the group mill around. They weren't carrying guns today since no one had on a jacket to hide them, but they were the security guards.

"I'll find you. Save me a seat." I turned toward the library, where I knew the restrooms were located, except I went down the hallway and tried the door to Kane's office.

It was unlocked. I pushed open the door and slipped inside. The doorway was hidden from the watchful guards in the foyer, but I knew I wouldn't have much time. Maybe he had a journal somewhere. Or a letter from the killer. Of course, Greg would have found that. I wasn't sure what I was looking for, but I'd never have this opportunity again.

I scanned his desk and found his calendar. It was still open to the week he'd died. There was no note about meeting Molly on that Sunday. It noted his sermons, which he called talks, and the times. I used a pen from my tote and turned the page. On the next Tuesday, he'd written my name and Coffee, Books, and More.

Had Kane planned to come see me the next week? And if so, why? Maybe he thought I was the weak link in getting Greg to leave New Hope alone and not support the detractors. I turned to the next week and the pages were blank. I guessed Kane didn't plan too far ahead. I scanned the room again. Nothing screamed at me.

I felt the clock ticking. I was out of time. Whatever Kane had wanted to talk to me about must have died with him.

I listened at the door. Music was starting. I needed to find my seat before it was obvious I wasn't coming from the bathroom. I looked back once again and saw Kane's bookshelf. Had I missed the opportunity to learn more about his life? And maybe his death?

I slipped out of the office and realized the guards were standing near the front door with their backs to the chapel area. I walked over to the restroom, then came out of that door like I'd used the facilities.

No one was watching me as I went into the chapel and spotted Esmeralda.

As I sat down, the jumbo screen at the front of the room was playing a selection of Kane's favorite talks.

"You are made to be happy. To explode onto this world. Not hide your talents under a bushel. And by talents, I mean your intelligence. Your beauty. Your strength. Find what makes you special and capitalize on it. That's what you're made for. For me, it's my height. Everyone loves me because I'm tall, right?"

The audience on the screen and in the meetinghouse laughed along with Kane.

"No. They love me because, for some reason, God gave me the ability to connect with others. To bring you into the fold. To love you and this entire family. To give you a New Hope."

Esmeralda leaned in. "I've been to duller tent revivals with live snakes. The man had the power of words."

The screen froze on a picture of Kane holding up a baby and looking to the ceiling, his words posted on the screen. "Welcome to our family. We've been waiting for you."

"I think we're going to get a time-share pitch presentation." I looked around at the women who were standing now, their hands raised in the air.

"Welcome to New Hope and our celebration of the life of my brother, Kane Matthews." Roger Matthews came on the stage and the picture changed from Kane with the baby to a pair of boys, arms around each other, grinning at the camera. Roger turned to stare at the picture. "That photo was taken three weeks before our parents were taken from us in a fire in their church. They gave their lives to serve. Was there any question what Kane and I would grow up to do?"

The next thirty minutes were all about the story of Kane and Roger. And I could sense an underlying thread. The story of why Roger was the perfect choice to be the new leader of New Hope, no questions asked. I watched Maryanne, who sat on a chair to the left of the stage. She had a notebook and pen in front of her and she was either taking notes or writing down reactions. She saw me watching her and smiled at me. My presence had been noticed.

I couldn't help but compare Kane's uplifting and commanding presentation to the boring one presented by Roger. They'd picked well when they'd chosen Kane as the face of the church. Now Roger had to up his game. If it was even possible.

Maryanne met us in the foyer after the service, as we were getting ready to leave. She put a hand on my arm. "Thank you so much for coming to support us in our grief."

I glanced around the room. There were no weeping parishioners. Just a group of people serving coffee and treats to the gathered group. I felt Esmeralda's hand on my other arm, bringing me back to the present. "I'm so sorry for your loss. If there's anything I can do, please let me know."

"Oh, we'll survive. Roger is already stepping in for Kane in an amazing way, don't you think? He's so good on stage."

Esmeralda stepped in. "Oh yes. The brothers made their parents proud, that's for sure. I'm sorry to bring it up, but Jill's mother-in-law is expecting us for a late lunch. She's leaving town soon since the wedding is over."

"Oh yes." I glanced at my watch while I spoke. "We are behind schedule."

"I was hoping to give you a private tour of the facility. Kane said you were very interested in our book collection. We have several other libraries on the property." Maryanne reached over and plucked a book from a shelf.

I'd been drawn to the library in the foyer as we watched the circus happening around us. A group of men were watching us now. Especially since Maryanne had come to chat with us. "Well, maybe another time."

Maryanne pressed the book into my hand. Kane's face was on the cover. "Please take this with my love. It explains all about New Hope and what we're trying to accomplish. I'd love for New Hope to have someone who understands us to represent us in the local community. I know change can be hard."

The men seemed to relax and stopped watching us. Had they expected Maryanne to blurt out some secret to me?

I tucked the book under my arm. "Thank you for your hospitality. I'll let you get back to your other guests."

Esmeralda and I didn't talk until we drove off the compound and were back on the highway toward South Cove. She turned to me, picking up the book from where I'd set it between us. "That was intense."

"I felt overdressed and uncomfortable." I rolled down the window in the Jeep. "And why give me the book? They've been here for over six months. Now they think they need a contact in South Cove?"

"I have a feeling that changes are coming to New Hope. I also get the feeling that Roger isn't the one in charge."

I met Esmeralda's gaze. "You think Maryanne's making a play for the role of leader, don't you?"

"Politics inside organizations are often more cutthroat than those in the public eye. I think Greg needs to find out where Maryanne Matthews was on that Sunday morning."

I laughed as we turned off the highway and back onto the road that would lead us to city hall and the police station. "The last thing Greg needs is more suspects. I just gave him a list last night."

"If I know your husband, Maryanne's probably already on his list, even if it wasn't written down. The woman is crafty." She went to toss the book on the back seat. "I'd trash that if I were you."

"I have a feeling there's a clue in that book. I might give it to Beth to read, but there's going to be a clue. We just have to find it."

By the time Greg got home that night, I'd read most of the book. I was a fast reader and the writing wasn't very dense for being a religious tome for the church. It read more like a *People* article. He came in with bags of food from Diamond Lille's. "Hello, dear husband. I guess I should have had a pot roast on."

"Esmeralda told me you were given homework at the funeral." He set the bags in the kitchen. "Besides, Jim, Beth, and Mom are coming over for dinner. They're leaving tomorrow morning."

"Already?" I set the book down on the table and watched him head to the office to put his gun in the safe.

"I thought maybe you'd make some headway on these gifts," he called from the other room. When he came out, he kissed me on the head. "Thank you notes must be sent promptly. Your aunt mentioned that to me a few times at the reception."

"I'm waiting for you to find a killer. Don't think that something like murder is going to get you out of thank you note duty." I rubbed his cheek. "You look tired."

"I am. Marvin thinks I should have caught this fiend by now, even with the wedding." He rubbed under his eye, which had started twitching. "Mom was going to stay around another week, but with the investigation and me pulling Toby from your staff, she understands. Besides, we'll see them in June when we go out."

A vacation I wasn't looking forward to. A week in Nebraska. In June.

"I'll be right down." He ignored my unspoken comment. "And they will be here in just a few minutes. Do you mind setting the table?"

"It is my wifely duty, kind sir." I stood and curtseyed.

He grinned at me. "I know you're kidding, but I'm kind of digging all the wifely housework references."

"Don't get used to it. I'm just trying it on to make sure it itches as much as I'd expected." I snapped my fingers at Emma. "Come on, girl. You need to check the yard barriers for any unexpected rabbits or wolves."

"We all have our roles," Greg called down the stairs.

Both Greg and I knew that Emma was more likely to play with any animal she found than chase it away. But I liked telling her she was an accomplished hunter. It made her feel good as well as gave her confidence.

Something that the women in New Hope needed. For the first time since Molly had shown up that Tuesday morning, I realized I didn't know who Carlie's new counselor was. Was it someone in the brain business, like a medical counselor? Or someone in the heart business, like a minister?

And was it any of my business, either way?

# Chapter 19

Sadie showed up at the shop first thing Wednesday morning with another order of treats. My regulars were almost gone when I saw her van pull up. She brought in the first tray and I glanced at the three people still in line. "Sorry, I'll be out to help as soon as I can."

"No worries, you have customers. Besides, I need to burn off some energy." Sadie paused at the door to the back room. "Tell me that being married is worth the hassle. Because right now, I'm ready to give him this engagement ring back."

I laughed as Sadie disappeared into the back and handed the coffee I'd just created to my customer. "She's getting married soon."

"Heaven help her." The woman at the front of the line ran her card through the machine. When she finished, she turned to follow Sadie out of the shop as she went to get more treats from the van. "Honey, marriage isn't all roses and bonbons. You probably should expect the worst, and if you think you can deal with that, you'll be golden when he's charming."

I smiled at the wisdom Sadie was getting from a stranger. I'd been a divorce attorney for years before I decided to sell coffee instead. I had been in family law, but most of my work was divorces and child custody cases after the breakup. The job was grueling.

By the time I'd served the last few customers in line, Sadie had finished bringing in the extra pastry order. She left the last tray out front and started to refill my dessert case as she waited for me.

"Thank you for this. The news vans swarmed in here yesterday for the funeral. You would have thought Kane Matthews was a celebrity." I held up an empty to-go cup. "You need some caffeine?"

"Please. My women's group at church is talking about the evils of caffeine this month. I only have two vices, coffee and sweets. I don't think I should have to give up either." She finished plating the last of the cookies and put them in the display case. "So, did you go to the funeral?"

I poured Sadie's favorite, then refilled my cup. "I did. Do you want to sit and chat?"

"No time. I'm supposed to be giving a talk at noon to a Bakerstown women's group about my life as a self-employed woman. They want to hear all the dirt on how I had to start my business to raise my child when I became a widow. Now, after almost twenty years, I'm a success." She held out her arms. "I think I need to warn them about how much work it is to raise a child on your own and build a business. I don't think I slept a full eight hours until Nick got into high school and didn't need me to drive him somewhere after school."

"Maybe one of your helpful hints could be to live on a community bus route instead of out in the boonies like South Cove." I leaned on the counter. "How's Bill?"

"Stubborn. He has an actual alibi, but he won't tell Greg the name of the person he was meeting with that Sunday morning. He feels like he'd be betraying a confidence." Sadie rubbed her forehead. "The man would go to jail for something he didn't do rather than break trust. I asked him where his convictions left me? What am I supposed to do, wait for him to get out of prison so we can have a life together? He thinks I'm being selfish."

"He does not." I knew Pastor Bill. He took his job seriously and didn't think the church deacons were his boss as much as the big guy upstairs. "Did he say that?"

Sadie sipped her coffee, then set the cup on the counter. "No. I'm just feeling that way. I'm finally at a point where I can enjoy my life a little. Nick's out of the house and working in London. He's fine. Now, I fall in love and he's going to take the blame for killing someone because he got in a fight with the guy at the diner? It's not fair."

"And it's not going to happen. You know Greg. He never takes the easy way out when he's investigating. But Bill needs to help. Isn't that in the Bible too—God helps those who help themselves?"

"I think it's more implied than an actual commandment." Sadie smiled. "You always know how to make me feel better. Thank you. Now I need to get out of these baker scrubs and into something that doesn't have flour all over it."

I hugged Sadie, wished her well with her talk, then started cleaning up the dining room after she left. Kane Matthews had made an impact on South Cove during his short time as a resident. I wondered how long New Hope would continue after losing their charismatic leader. Roger just didn't have his brother's pizzazz when speaking. I could see the restlessness of the flock even during the funeral.

What happens when the leader is taken too soon? And—the thought chilled me—what if the reason Kane was murdered was to break up the New Hope family? If that was the motive, there were several possible suspects, including Pastor Bill.

A few minutes later, Greg brought Amanda, Jim, and Beth into the coffee shop. I had wondered when the group would be leaving for the airport. I'd sent text messages to Amanda and Beth before leaving for work but hadn't heard back. "This is a welcome surprise. I figured you all were on the way home by now."

"We had to stop by and grab Greg from the station, then come to say goodbye." Amanda pulled me into a hug. "Family doesn't just leave. I wanted to thank you for spending so much time with me before the wedding. It was so nice getting to know you better."

"I enjoyed hitting the tourist spots and spending time with you as well. It's funny, we live within driving distance of these places and we never take advantage of all the fun around us." I turned and Beth hugged me as well. "It was nice of you to come along, Beth."

"I loved every moment. The wedding was beautiful. And living here, you're so lucky. I'd be on the beach every day." Beth repeated her words from the Santa Barbara visit.

I smiled, remembering my own introduction to the magic that was South Cove. "I need to do that. Emma and I run most days, but I need to just go and sit more often."

"Sitting there, listening to the waves, I feel like I'm hearing God's voice." Beth smiled at Jim, who stood near Greg.

"God talks everywhere," Jim reminded her. "Even Nebraska."

Beth laughed and shook her head. "He's got more of a surfer dude vibe here on the coast."

"Beth," Jim started, but then he smiled too. "You always see things through your own filters. One of the reasons I love you."

Greg slapped Jim on the back. "Maybe Beth should have caught the bouquet at the wedding, then."

Jim's face turned beet red, and we all laughed. For a second, I felt like maybe I could be friends with this new Jim, who was softer when he was with Beth. He was so different than the one I'd met years ago when Greg and I had started dating.

"Hey, can I get you guys some coffee and treats for the drive?" I pointed to the display case. "Or maybe a book for the flight? There's got to be some perks I bring to the family."

Beth's face brightened. "I'd love to look around. And just a plain coffee. I need to get back on the no-sugar plan."

"That sounds horrible." Amanda walked with her to the shelves. "Jill, dear, I'll have a mocha with whipped cream, hot. I'm on the live-life-to-the-fullest plan."

I giggled as I went over to start the coffee. "Jim? Greg? I might as well make two more."

"I'll take a large black coffee. I think I'm going to be working late tonight." Greg walked toward the counter. Jim followed, keeping his gaze on Beth.

"I'll just have a black coffee." He glanced at Greg. "Thanks, Jill."

I wondered how hard it had been for him to even say my name. But I let it go. "Sadie confirmed that Bill was counseling someone on Sunday morning."

"Yes, I know that, Jill." Greg glanced at the treat display. "The only problem with that is he won't tell me who."

"If he was acting as a representative of the church, you can't ask." Jim stared at his brother. "You know that."

"It's not an alibi without someone verifying it. Besides his fiancée. Or a receipt from a coffee shop miles away from the mission. God should give his subordinates a better travel plan, so he'd have something to prove where he was if he won't tell me who he was with." Greg held up his hand when he saw Jim ready to speak. "Stop, I was just kidding about the travel plan. And I don't want to talk about an open investigation."

The last sentence was aimed at me. I put three of the cups into a carrying tray, then boxed up several cookies and tucked a plastic bag into the box as well, in case there were cookies left over when they arrived at the airport. "Okay, noted. You won't be home for dinner. I guess I'll just have to find a boyfriend to eat with me."

Jim's eyes widened and Greg laughed. "She's talking about a book boyfriend. She'll be reading on the couch when I get home."

"They're very good company, and they don't mind if I'm in my sweats without makeup." I smiled at Beth and Amanda as they came up with their books. "Oh, these are both really good. I read them a couple of months ago."

"You're so lucky. Owning a bookstore would be like owning a candy store, but it wouldn't make me fat." Beth grinned as I rang up the books and charged them off to my account. "Oh, I sent you my dissertation. You'll probably want to skip a few sections, but I did a chapter on New Hope and have several citations in my research. I think you'll find it interesting."

"I also tucked in the book Maryanne gave me that Kane wrote on New Hope. It's a lot of woo-woo and rah-rah stuff, but you might get something out of it." I liked Beth. "I'm looking forward to reading your dissertation."

Greg and Jim stared at each other. Greg finally said, "They're two of a kind."

"You boys always did think alike. And you always wanted the same toy." Amanda came around and gave me another hug. "We better get out of here and let you two get on with your lives together. I'm so glad you're my new daughter."

I hugged her back and didn't think about the letter from Sherry to Greg in my new mother-in-law's purse. Maybe she'd decided not to give it to him. Either way, it wasn't my business. I just wished I didn't know about it.

* * * *

When I got home, I felt the absence of people in the house. It felt weird. Amanda, Beth, and even Jim hadn't been here long, but they'd carved a spot into my idea of home. I looked at Emma and realized she also was feeling the lack of the buzz we'd gotten from the wedding preparations and then the actual ceremony. We'd already run this morning before I'd gone to work, but I grabbed her leash anyway. "Let's go sit on the beach. We can send your new almost–Aunt Beth some pictures."

I glanced at the office, filled with wedding gifts, as we walked by. "And when we get home, we'll open ten gifts, take pictures, and write thank you notes. The way Greg's investigation is going, I might have to do all of them."

Emma looked up at me and barked. I'd forgotten how many conversations I'd had with my dog, since at times she was the only one around. I was sure this was normal, but I decided I'd look it up on the internet when we got back from our beach time. The web would tell me I wasn't crazy. Or, if I was, it would give me a name for my disorder.

I texted Amy. *Lunch tomorrow?*

I watched as the bubbles bounced on my phone. Please have lunch with me since I'm lonely now. I didn't text that since it looked a little needy.

I blew out my breath when I read her response. *Sure, eleven?*

*Perfect.*

At least I had one appointment that wasn't just work. Now that my degree was finished, the wedding was over, and I'd figured out what was happening with the coffee shop, my to-do list looked a little bare. Maybe I needed to get a hobby or take some classes. Amy was busy remodeling her house with Justin, but maybe Darla or Esmeralda would take something with me. I'd put it on my list to see what was available, then throw out an invite to everyone I knew.

Okay, maybe not everyone. Like not Josh Thomas, but I might see if his new wife, Mandy, was ready to do something without her husband.

Or maybe I'd find new friends when I figured out what my new hobby was going to be. As we went down the stairs to the beach, I saw Molly walking with a young woman. As she flipped her hair out of her eyes, I realized it was Carlie. Molly had reunited with her daughter.

I didn't want to interrupt their conversation, but Molly waved me over to where they had sat down on a blanket on the beach. Emma and I joined them. We were the only ones on the beach. Emma watched the seagulls playing in the waves. I unfastened her leash and she ran to the edge. "Don't go far," I called after her.

The girl laughed as Molly hugged her. "Jill, this is Carlie. We're hanging out in the area until she goes back to school next week."

Carlie stood and held out her hand. "Hi, I'm a recovering member of the New Hope cult. I read a lot of books that came from your store in the last few months. You have quite the collection."

"I don't remember seeing you in the store." I shook her hand. "And we're all recovering from something, right?"

"I like your attitude." Carlie grinned at her mom. "Mom and I went to your store last night. It was my first time there. Maryanne used to bring me the books I wanted. Kane didn't like me to leave the compound. He knew Mom was looking for me. A fact he never shared with me."

Molly grimaced at the mention of Kane. "Well, I was out there. Crying in the wilderness."

Carlie squeezed her mom's shoulder. "I'm so sorry. I wrote you letters, but I guess they never left the compound. Kane used them to get deeper into my head."

I felt horrible for her. "I'm so sorry for what you went through."

Carlie shrugged. "Mostly, it was fine. I just missed my mom at times. I got swept into Kane's world and didn't even realize what was going on. I'd make a horrible interviewee for one of those talk shows. *They kept me in the dark, but it wasn't a bad life.* I'm ready to get back to school, though, and figure out what I want to do with my life."

Emma barked at a stubborn seagull that wasn't moving. I started to get up, but Carlie reached for the leash. "I'll get her, if you don't mind. We weren't allowed to have pets at the compound."

I handed her the leash and watched as she went up to play with Emma and distract her from the seagulls. "She seems good."

"She's a lot better since she spent some time with the local minister, Pastor Bill." Molly watched her daughter carefully. "She thought leaving the compound meant she was turning her back on God. Kane had convinced her that New Hope was the only way. And that the end of the world was coming soon."

"She talked to Bill Doyle?" Now my spidey senses were tingling.

"That's one of the reasons we're still here. If I had my way, we'd be in Maine or somewhere farther away from New Hope. Bill seems to calm her. I guess you must know that about him, since he performed your wedding ceremony. He's also been helping me talk through my jumbled thoughts since I came to town. About Carlie, and then the entire Vince thing. I wish I could thank him."

"Did you meet with him Sunday morning before last? Before you came to see Kane at the mission?"

Molly nodded. "I wasn't sure if I should go. I was worried about putting Carlie in danger. He convinced me to go and at least see what he wanted to talk about."

"Molly, did you tell Greg about this?"

She shook her head. "I don't think so. I was so upset after finding Kane like that. I think it just slipped my mind. And no one asked. They just wanted to know when I got there and why I agreed to meet Kane. Why?"

"I think I have a way for you to thank Bill. Can you tell Greg what you just told me? About meeting with Bill?" I dialed Greg's number and after he answered, I asked him to hold on while I handed her the phone.

# Chapter 20

Greg came home early Wednesday night. I hadn't started dinner because he'd said he would be late, but I'd kept my promise to Emma and we'd gone through ten wedding gifts. The thank you notes I'd written were sitting on the coffee table. I thought it would make it look like we'd done them together if he at least signed the card.

"I thought you were working late." I muted the cooking show I'd had on for company as I read with Emma. Well, I'd read while she'd cuddled and watched them cook food on the television. It worked for both of us.

He leaned down and kissed me. "Someone took my best suspect off the list. And thank you, by the way. I don't think Sadie would ever have forgiven me if I'd arrested her fiancé."

"I was just trying to fill my day by visiting the beach. I can't help it if people interrupt my relaxing." I rubbed his arm. "Thank you for saving Bill."

"I'm sorry I had to have him on the list to begin with. Do you know how many calls I got telling me what a good guy he is and conversely what a butt I was for even questioning him?" He held out a bag he'd been hiding behind his back. "Fish and chips, stuffed meatloaf, and a mini cake from Tiny. He called me just before I left the station and asked if we'd eaten. I said no. I hope I wasn't wrong."

"I hadn't planned anything, so this is amazing. And we can do ten more wedding gifts and thank you cards." I reached for the bag and stood. "Go get out of your uniform and meet me in the kitchen. I'll be the newlywed standing by the home-cooked meal she slaved over all day."

"You've been reading too much fiction. It's starting to seep into your everyday world." He laughed as I threw a couch pillow at him. He reached down and threw it back. "You know playing with them gets Emma interested again. She hasn't eaten a pillow in what, six weeks?"

It was more like three, but she had been better. I grabbed the pillow before she could and tucked it on the couch. I shook my finger at her. "No pillows. Come in the kitchen with me."

When Greg came back into the kitchen, I had dinner all set up, with the food on our fancy china plates. "What do you want to drink? Soda? Tea? Coffee?"

"I'll just have a glass of water." He let Emma outside as he walked past the back door. "I called Bill to let him know that Molly came in on her own, and he broke down and cried. I felt like a bully."

"You're doing your job. Good or bad, you have to go where the evidence leads. I'm just glad I took a beach moment. You know, when I first moved here, I promised myself I wouldn't let my workaholic habits follow me. I don't think I've been very good at fixing that tendency. I was all anxious because I didn't have school or the wedding planning to keep me busy. I need to take a breath on a daily basis." I filled a water glass for him and put the kettle on for hot tea for me.

"Well, one other good thing happened today. Vince's alibi went away with Molly's confession. I guess she didn't know he used her as his alibi for Sunday morning. I get to chat with him tomorrow morning. He's coming in with an attorney." Greg let Emma inside before sitting down to eat. "And he asked if Mom was still in town."

"What did you say?" I worried that tomorrow's interview might not be very cordial.

Greg shrugged. "I told him we weren't talking about her. But that I did have some questions about how Molly got a black eye."

"He probably won't show up." I sat down to eat. I didn't want the food to get cold.

Greg took a bite of his meatloaf. "If he doesn't, I might just throw a warrant out there."

"Do you think he killed Kane?"

He focused on his meal, pausing to respond. "No. I wish I could charge him for that. But I'd love to get him to admit on the record that he hit Mom or Molly. It might keep him from doing it again, knowing he confessed to doing it once. Sometimes a little fear goes a long way."

"Speaking of your mom, did they get home yet?" I thought changing the subject might be a smart idea.

"Jim called on my way home. They'd just landed." He finished off his meatloaf. "It was a good visit with them."

"It was." We ate in silence until the teakettle started shrieking, causing Emma to run for her bed. I wasn't sure why we were so quiet with each other, but maybe he was just trying to keep from talking about the case. I stood and poured the water for my tea. "So you interview Vince tomorrow. Is anything else planned? I've got lunch with Amy. Should I make dinner?"

He nodded. "Until I get ahold of another suspect and motive, I'll probably be home early. I'm still waiting for the lawyers to release the full financial records of the church and the Matthewses. They're being a little less than forthcoming."

"I think New Hope is going to lose a few parishioners with Kane gone. He was very charismatic." I thought about the clip they had shown at the funeral.

"You're saying Roger isn't?" Greg's gaze landed on me.

"Not even close. They showed a collage of Kane's sermons at the funeral before Roger spoke. It was night and day. I watched Maryanne watching the group and making notes." I realized I still had Beth's thesis to read. "After lunch tomorrow, I'll scan what Beth sent me and see if there's anything you need to know."

"Send it to me if there is." He stood and rinsed his plate. "I'll go sign those cards and get us another load of gifts to open. Might as well get something done today."

\* \* \* \*

Greg was gone the next morning when I got up for work. Emma and I went to the beach and ran, then I got ready to open the store. My thoughts were on Kane and his effect on the world. Maybe it was something easy. He'd angered the wrong parent or spouse of one of his followers and that had gotten him killed. But why now? From reading the Facebook posts, they'd been angering people since they opened New Hope. There had to be a different reason.

There was a lull after all my commuters left. I opened the laptop we kept at the shop and opened Beth's thesis. It had chapters, so I went right to the one on New Hope and the Matthews brothers.

Beth had a lot of information about their early lives. For years, their parents had dragged them from town to town setting up tent revivals, until they found the abandoned church in Oregon. When their parents died, they were fostered by a member of the church. Then the church provided scholarships to the missionary college. Kane had never married. Roger and Maryanne married as soon as they graduated. Beth had found the same article about the wedding that I'd found online.

Then, Beth wrote, the rumors started. Kane was a popular minister, but the three kept moving from town to town. Money, women, power. It seemed to be a pattern. But as the three moved, so did many of their parishioners. Finally, when they left Oregon to start over in South Cove, they had over a hundred full-time disciples. And what appeared to be a big war chest. Beth had searched the property records and found the land had been donated to New Hope by the former owner, a widow in her eighties. The church was also named in several will-probate cases.

A whole lot of smoke, but no fire I could pin Kane's murder to. Had someone gotten tired of Kane's money-making process? I went back to Facebook to see what Maryanne's page looked like, but she didn't have one. New Hope had a Facebook page, but none of the women's faces were shown in the posts—until last week, when Roger and Maryanne made a joint post. Arms around each other, they smiled into the camera. It was tagged, "A new day at New Hope in honor of our fallen brother."

Change was afoot. Had that been the plan?

Amy was waiting for me when I arrived at Diamond Lille's. She had milkshakes already on the table for us. "How is the first week of marriage going?"

"Fine, I guess. We had dinner together last night. He's been busy with the investigation since the day after the wedding. The only thing I've got on my planning calendar is getting the thank you notes done." I tucked my tote next to me.

"And the upcoming honeymoon," Amy reminded me.

"If we ever get to go." I glanced at the menu, then pushed it away. I was going with my favorite, even though I had it last night. I needed to refocus my eating before that had to go on my to-do list as well. "Wow, I'm a Debby Downer today."

"You're on the opposite side of a big high. You did the same thing when you got your degree. Big events lead to a letdown when they're over. And it's January. Deaths always go up in January." Amy set her menu down. "It's a statistical fact."

"Is it? Or did you read it online?" Amy could always make me feel better. "Anyway, I'm thinking of taking up a hobby. Do you want to learn a craft or something?"

Amy spit out some of her milkshake onto the table. She grabbed a napkin to wipe it up. When she stopped laughing, she looked at me. "You? Crafting? Have you even looked at the baby blanket you didn't finish for the hospital babies?"

"I finished one." It hadn't been pretty, but it had been done. "I guess I could pull out that stuff and work on the other two blankets."

"Sure. That's a goal. What about the shop?"

I shrugged. "Everything is going well. Deek is dealing with the author visits. Evie's handling the accounting and most of the business stuff. It's running like clockwork."

Carrie stopped at our table. "Tiny wants to know how you liked the cake."

"It was amazing. Thank him for me." I looked over at the window to the kitchen and waved at him. He smiled and waved back. I ducked my head. "I should have stopped there as soon as I arrived. I'm so bad at this."

"You're not bad at being grateful." Carrie pulled out her notepad and pen. "Some people are just not very patient. I overheard you talking about getting a hobby. What about leading a book club? There's one at the Bakerstown library, but it's usually during the day when I'm working. I love sitting and chatting about a book we all read."

"Carrie, that's not a bad idea. Deek's been having writer nights. I'll have to see what nights are open and we'll get one set up." I made a note on my phone for later that day. I could build a book club. Easy. And I wouldn't have to learn to cook or quilt. Or find where I stuck the yarn for those baby blankets.

We ordered lunch and as we were eating, a man came in with two boys. Amy kicked my foot to get my attention and nodded toward them as Lille sat them at a window booth. "The smaller boy is one of the kids they took from New Hope. That's his dad. I helped Esmeralda keep the parents busy in the conference room with coffee and treats until the child protection people brought the kids to the station."

"That's Tanner O'Dell and his son Jimmy," I said as I watched the three study the menus.

"Yeah, how did you know?" Amy turned away from watching the family and focused on me. "Did Greg tell you?"

I shook my head, trying not to stare in their direction. "I was doing some Facebook research. His wife cashed in her 401(k) and their joint accounts and gave the money to Kane."

"Well, the money might be gone, but at least the kid's home." Amy leaned back as Carrie delivered our food. "You can always make more money."

"I wonder why they're still in town?" I texted Greg and asked if he had an interview with Mr. O'Dell today.

He called me rather than texting. "Who told you? Amy or Esmeralda. I swear, I'm going to fire them both."

"Calm down, Greg. No one told me. Tanner's here at the diner eating lunch with his kids. I wouldn't be here if I was him after all that happened, so I figured he must be talking to you." I rolled my eyes at Amy, who was laughing at my side of the conversation. "Oh, and I think you should look at Beth's stuff. The brothers had an interesting childhood and career."

"No smoking guns, though?"

I twisted my lips. There was something I was missing but I couldn't put my finger on it. "I think there's more going on with the church and the brothers. Especially after we saw Roger and Maryanne out spending money. I guess they could be celebrating their anniversary, but not according to this thesis of Beth's. It's in the summer sometime."

"You've got a feeling, though."

I sipped my milkshake. "Stop teasing me. I'll see you tonight."

"Sounds good. I love you, Mrs. King."

Before he hung up, I responded, "I love you too."

Amy glanced at the family. "Greg brought him back for more questions?"

"Yeah, I think it's weird too." I focused on my fish and changed the subject. "So, what's going on with the house?"

Amy got me all caught up on her life, which had been going on around the wedding and festivities. They'd finished a guest bedroom in their new-to-them house and were making plans to update the kitchen.

We spent the last of our lunch just talking, and Amy took the check when Carrie brought it. "Wedding celebrations should be longer than just a few days."

I hugged her as we left. She was going back to city hall to answer phones and deal with the mayor's tasks. I was heading home to go sit on the beach again with Emma. I'd take my notebook with me and work on an idea for a book club. I felt like they did better with a theme. Maybe books written in or about California? That seemed a little limiting. Maybe I'd do a suggestion box for two weeks at the shop.

*Suggest a theme for a new book club.*

If there were two front-runners, we could do two. And one of my employees could run the second one.

I hurried home to get Emma and my notebook. This was going to be fun.

As I doodled on my page, I realized Deek was walking across the sand to where I had set up my beach chair. Emma lay next to me, watching the waves. I think she was learning how to relax with me.

"Sorry to bother you, boss." Deek came over and sat across from me, where he could still see the ocean. "I stopped by the house, then took a chance that you might be out here."

"Not a bother. What's going on?"

"I just had a feeling you needed me. And I've got a favor to ask." He leaned back on his hands, his face tilted up to the sun.

His arrival didn't surprise me. Not after working with him for a few years. Deek had a bit of psychic in him. His mom was a fortune teller, and his godmother was Esmeralda. The sight was in his blood. And he was a true believer. "I did have a question. What do you think about us starting a book club? One for adults?"

"Wow. I hadn't thought about anything like that. I should have. I guess with us being a tourist town, I didn't think about the people who live close by. We could do bestsellers. Or maybe books that should have been bestsellers." He leaned forward, excited about the idea.

"I was thinking about a contest." I told him about my idea of putting a jar on the counter. "Maybe we give out a gift card for the shop for the winning idea. Or raffle it off if more than one person suggests the same idea."

"I'm working tonight, and I'll get something set up. This will be really fun. And maybe this summer, we could do a kids' club. Maybe on Thursdays. We'd have to let the rooming houses know. Maybe they could have a copy of the weekly book on hand to sell, then the kids could get reading early. Especially since we're closed on Mondays." Deek kept brainstorming and pulled a small notebook out of his pocket to write down the ideas. He'd told me before that he always had something to write on just in case inspiration hit him. He'd gotten the idea from Greg. "I'll bring it up at the next staff meeting and see if there's anything else they can add."

As we stood to walk back to my house, I paused as we climbed the stairs. "Wait, you had a question for me?"

He grinned, the smile covering his face. "I just need some time off in a couple of years. Most likely spring."

I knew I was missing something from what he was saying, but I couldn't put it together. "Sure. Are you traveling?"

He nodded, and if anything, his smile grew. "I'll be on tour with my first book. I got a call from my agent. She sold my manuscript!"

# Chapter 21

Greg decided to grill the pork chops I'd taken out for dinner. I'd made a pasta salad to go with the chops and we had frozen corn I'd warm up as well. As we sat outside, watching the chops, I told him about Deek's news.

"So do we throw him a party now? Or when the book publishes?" He sat and took a drink from his iced tea.

"I think then, but I think we'll do something at the next staff meeting. Maybe have Sadie do a cake?" Now I was grinning. "I can't believe he's already being published. It takes some authors years to get their first book out."

"Our little boy's a savant." Greg rubbed Emma's head.

"And to think, you didn't like Deek when he showed up," I reminded him. "Now you're claiming him as a son."

"He grows on you." Greg stood to turn the chops. "Sorry I was grumpy about you figuring out that I was interviewing O'Dell."

"No problem. Did you learn anything new?"

Greg shook his head. "He was at the Castle with his older kid that morning. He'd been staying there since before the open house trying to catch his wife or Jimmy out in the community. His older kid, Tyler, said that he saw his dad sleeping before he went out for a run that morning."

"Wait, so Tanner didn't have an alibi?"

Greg frowned. "The kid said he saw him before he left. And when he got back from the run, Tanner was in the shower."

"So how long does this kid run? He was on the basketball team. Maybe he runs long distance." I could see I was pushing Greg's buttons. "It's not a big thing. Mrs. O'Dell just gave away her half of their retirement savings to Kane."

"This has to be about the money, right?" Greg asked as he rubbed his hair. "I need a haircut. All this hair is blocking my brain cells."

"I think it's cute when it's a little longer." I knew he didn't want to talk about the case, but I wanted to know one more thing. "Did you read Beth's paper?"

He nodded. "I think Jim's in trouble. Beth's really smart. He's not going to be able to get away with anything with her around."

"Yes, Beth's smart. But I was wondering what you thought about the brothers and their history."

He didn't answer immediately. Then he looked at me. "I need to see the financials. I had the city attorney reach out to their lawyers this afternoon. If we don't get the paperwork, we're going to ask for a subpoena. I don't think they want us digging directly in their files."

"Well, at least I get to see you for a few nights. And we'll get more of the thank you notes done."

He grabbed a platter. "Lucky me. Let's get dinner done and get working. Maybe we can finish up tonight. I have a feeling this investigation is about to heat up."

\* \* \* \*

When the stream of commuters slowed down the next morning, I thought about the book club. We'd already had several suggestions put in the jar, and because I'm that girl who can't wait for Christmas morning, I pulled them out and sorted through the slips.

I got out a notebook and wrote down all the ideas. Several were the same—bestsellers or women's fiction. One was a vote for Southern fiction. And one, historical nonfiction about California—bonus if the books focused on the central coast. Josh had been in to get coffee and treats. Antiques by Thomas must have had a staff meeting this morning. I'd seen him scribbling on one of the entry papers for the book club. This had to be his suggestion.

It wasn't a bad idea, I just didn't think it would appeal to a lot of people. Maybe I needed to ask Josh to suggest more local-charm books I could put in that section. He knew a lot about the history of South Cove. Probably more than anyone in town.

I paper-clipped the ideas together and put them back into the jar. Then I drew a line under the last idea and wrote the date and time on the top of the page. Putting the notebook under the counter, I added "review book club ideas" to the daily closing list. If it didn't get done, I could do it in the morning, but I'd love to get my staff involved in the fun.

A man walked into the bookstore, and I realized it was Tanner O'Dell. He walked straight up to the counter. "I have a favor to ask. You don't have to say yes, but I didn't want to just drop them off, just in case."

"I'm sorry, what can I help you with?" He looked nervous. Today, he was dressed in a suit. He introduced himself. "I just got one of my sons back from their mom. She lives at the New Hope property. I've been asked back to the police station for another interview and I don't want them hanging out there. And I don't want to leave my kids at the hotel. Can they stay here while I straighten this out? I've told Tyler, he's my oldest, that they can't leave with anyone and to keep an eye on Jimmy. They'll have my credit card for drinks, treats, and books. I don't care what they buy. I just need a second set of eyes on them while I'm at the police station. It's just down the street and if you need me, I'll come right back."

"We're not a babysitting service and I'm off at eleven. They're more than welcome to hang out, but I'm not stopping them if they leave on their own. I will text you if they do, or if anyone from New Hope approaches them." I understood Mr. O'Dell's worries, but on the other hand, they weren't my children. I didn't have the right to stop them or keep their mother from trying to collect them. "I'll also call the police if someone is trying to take them using force and try to stop that."

He studied me, then nodded. "Thanks. I just didn't know what to do, and I didn't want to take them back to the police station. Jimmy's confused enough, and I thought being around books might calm him about being alone with his brother."

"Books can do that." I nodded. "Look, I'll do my best with them. We have kids that hang here most Saturdays. And if you're not back by eleven, I'll let my coworker know what's going on. Just try to be back before lunch. I'd hate for them to starve."

He grinned. "They eat like starving wolves most of the time. I'm not sure you'd notice a difference. I'll go get them. And thank you, Mrs. King."

So he'd known who I was when he came into the store. That wasn't unusual, but it made me feel a little bit better about his request. He was leaving the kids with the police detective's wife.

When he came back in with the kids, he brought them straight up to the counter. "You're going to wait here at the bookstore for me and hopefully find something to read. You can have something to eat if you get hungry and one coffee drink. Otherwise, it's herbal tea, water, or cocoa."

"Cocoa has caffeine too, Dad," said the younger kid, Jimmy, as he turned toward Tanner. When he didn't get a response, he turned to me. "I'll have a mocha, please, with whipped cream."

I smiled at him and looked at his brother. "And for you?"

He rolled his eyes at his father. "A mocha will be fine. You have flavored waters?"

I pointed to the menu board. "We do our own in the above flavors."

"I'm going to go look for a book. Where's your horror section?" The older kid, Tyler, glanced over at the shelves. "I hope I haven't read everything."

"We just got in the new Grady Hendrix, if you haven't read that." I pointed toward the section.

"I'm coming too." Jimmy followed his brother.

I made the mochas, then looked at Mr. O'Dell. "Do you want anything?"

"I'm coffeed out. I drank a pot at the hotel. I probably should have put a caffeine limit on myself." He handed me a credit card, then stuffed a hundred-dollar bill in the tip jar. "This is for your time. I know it's above and beyond what you do here."

"I get it. If I'd just got him back, I'd be a little protective too." I ran his card and tried to hand it back.

He shook his head, signing the receipt. "Hold it for their tab. I just hope I get back before they get antsy. Thank you again."

"No problem." I put the card into the cash register and closed the drawer. I wanted to tell him good luck, but if Greg thought he might have killed Kane, he might need more than just good luck to get out of the charge. And if that happened, who would take care of the kids? I guessed they'd go back to their mother and the compound.

I hoped that Tanner O'Dell hadn't acted on his Facebook threat and killed the cult leader. I worried about the kids.

By the time Deek came downstairs from his apartment to take over the shop, the kids had bought four books and ordered six more drinks and a dozen cookies. I was beginning to worry about their sugar content more than the caffeine limit their dad had set. I had a running tab going and just kept adding to it as they came to get something else.

I explained the book club vote-tallying system I'd set up, then told him about Tyler and Jimmy. "I hope that Greg will be finishing up the interview soon."

As I said that, Anya Carter walked into the shop with another woman. I saw Jimmy's reaction before I realized what he'd already figured out. His dad wasn't coming back from his errand anytime soon. She smiled at the kids, then came up to the counter. "Jill, I'm so sorry I missed your call. Things have been a little busy."

"Please tell me you aren't here to take the kids." I pulled out the credit card and began to ring up the charges but then I stopped. "Maybe we should have them get a couple more books."

"That's not a bad idea. I take it you have permission from their dad?" Anya asked, looking at the credit card.

I nodded to Deek. "Why don't you go over and help them get another book or two? Anya and I will figure out what's next."

Deek walked over and knelt next to the table. Tyler looked up at Anya, who smiled, then sank back into his chair. He didn't take long to adjust. He pulled his brother into a hug, then they walked over to the bookshelves with Deek.

"Has Tanner been arrested?" I kept my voice low.

Anya shook her head. "Greg's words were that he's being held for questioning. I got a call from the lawyer. They want to make sure the kids aren't in range of the compound, so I'm taking them up to their aunt's place north of here. Jimmy's still on our books because of the removal from the mom, but I got an order from the judge just now and we'll get them someplace safe. I guess the aunt has a cabin she bought just after Mrs. O'Dell disappeared with Jimmy."

Deek brought over four more books and an order for half a dozen cookies. "Tyler's getting their backpacks set up and ready to go. He says they're going to Aunt Kathy's. Is he right?"

Anya nodded. "Tanner called me last night and we started the paperwork. All I needed was a call from his attorney to put it in process. Jimmy doesn't need to go back to that place. They do a crazy brainwashing thing and separate the kids from the parents. He's going to need a lot of therapy without adding to it."

I rang up everything and charged it to the card. Holding it up, I asked, "Can I give this to Tyler?"

"Please. The attorney mentioned it when he called. I guess Tyler's authorized on the card, so he can sign your receipt."

We walked over and I handed the receipt and a pen to Tyler, who signed it and handed it back. Then I gave him the card. "Thanks for hanging out with me this morning. I appreciate having someone here to make the place look busy."

"Dad's got to help the police find Reverend Matthews's killer. He was killed last week because he spoke God's word," Jimmy told me as he tucked the new books into his bag. "We're going to Aunt Kathy's for a while."

"Yep. Spending some quality time with Aunt Kathy," Tyler repeated. "Thanks for letting us hang, Mrs. King. It's a great bookstore."

As the kids left with the social workers, I leaned against the wall and watched them. I felt bad that they had to have another upheaval in their lives, but at least they had an aunt to take them in. I'd been in the same situation when I'd gone to live with Aunt Jackie. And no matter how much better life was at the new place, a part of you still yearned for the old life. For Tyler, that was before their mom had blown up their lives by joining New Hope. Was it the same for Jimmy? Or did he miss the structured life that he'd been living the last six months at New Hope? I guess only time would tell.

I was still talking to Deek about what had happened when two black SUVs pulled up in front of the shop. Five suited men got out, and two of them opened the back door on both cars. Two women got out, and one of the men and the woman from the first car hurried into the shop, looking around at the tables.

Maryanne Matthews was the other woman, and she followed them inside. She glanced around, then walked up to me. "Good morning, Jill. I was told that Jimmy O'Dell was hanging out with you. His mom wanted to see him. She's had no contact since he was jerked from her care last week."

"I'm sorry, there're no kids here." I felt Deek step closer to me.

Maryanne smiled at me and the look chilled my blood. "Now. There are no kids here now. We were told he was here by one of our members. I take it his father asked you to watch him?"

"We're not a babysitting service." I repeated the words I'd told Tanner O'Dell. "We're a bookstore."

I wasn't lying, but there was no way I was going to give Maryanne any information on Tanner O'Dell or his family. Especially not Jimmy.

"Well, I guess that's all we need. If Jimmy isn't here."
Maryanne didn't move.

"Can we get you coffee or a cookie?" I waved my hand toward the
dessert case. "I know you have your own bakery, but you might want to
taste your competition's products. Pies on the Fly produces amazing treats."

Fire flashed in her eyes, but she smiled and shook her head. "Sorry
to have bothered you. I need to go comfort my sister, as she's grieving
the loss of her son."

After they left, Deek turned to me. "Dude! That was intense. She
knew you were lying and you didn't even bat an eyelash."

"I wasn't putting Jimmy in any danger. The question is, who was
in here when the kids were and called New Hope? Or maybe someone
walked by and saw them through the window. Who knew a babysitting
job deserved combat pay?" I grabbed my tote and handed off the shop
to Deek. "I'm going home to take Emma to the beach and soak up some
South Cove magic. I need some positive rays flowing in."

"Best place to get it," Deek called after me.

As I walked home, I got a call from Greg. "Let me guess, you're not
coming home for dinner."

"You're going to have to open a competing shop with Esmeralda.
You're getting good at this." Greg laughed. "Anya told me she picked up
the kids. Thanks for being there for them."

"It wasn't a problem. By the way, we had a visit from Maryanne and
the New Hope goons after Anya left with the kids. Someone called and
told them the kids were at my shop."

The silence on the other end told me the rest of the story. Greg was
worried about the kids. "What did you tell her?"

"That I was running a bookstore, not a babysitting service. But it
worries me that someone is reporting on us to New Hope."

"So you lied."

I laughed as I started down the hill to the house. "Like a fish. I never
understood that saying, by the way. Or maybe that's not the saying. Anyway,
Deek about swallowed his tongue."

"I feel bad for the kids," Greg admitted.

"Are you sure he killed Kane?"

He paused before answering. "He has motive and opportunity. If
someone took my kid, I'd be hot too."

"That doesn't answer my question."

"Let's just say I'm working on an answer." He groaned. "I've got to go. Love you, Mrs. King."

I tucked the phone away in my pocket and headed home to get my dog. I prayed Deek and I were right about the South Cove beach hit. I needed to feel better.

# Chapter 22

The waves hadn't worked all their magic on me yet when my phone rang. "Hey, Beth, how did you know I was sitting on the beach soaking up some rays for you?"

"I must have felt the power," she responded, laughing. "I wanted to wait until we'd dropped Amanda off, but then I got distracted. Then I knew you were working, so I'm sorry I didn't call earlier."

Now I was confused. Had I asked her to call when they got back? "It's fine. I really didn't expect a call. I'm glad you're home safe, though."

"Oh, I'm not calling about that. Something was bothering me about the whole Vince thing. I mean, Amanda told me that she'd divorced him, but I don't think she ever called him by his full name. And she goes by King, so it didn't register until I started thinking about my dissertation. Maryanne's maiden name was Penn."

"Like Vince?" It could be just a coincidence. But maybe it was a connection.

"It could be just a coincidence," Beth said, repeating my thought. "Amanda said Vince said he grew up in Oregon. You don't think Vince Penn is related to Maryanne Matthews, do you?"

"If he is, he needs to repay Molly all that investigation money he charged her for looking for Carlie." Especially if he could have just called his sister and asked if Carlie was at the compound. I stood and brushed the sand off my capris. Maybe Vince was still in town and had seen the kids this morning.

"Well, I just wanted to tell you that. I mean, it might not mean anything, but it's weird, right?"

"I'm going to run to the college and see what I can find out about Vince and Maryanne." I hoped that maybe this would give Greg another person with motive and maybe an opportunity. He was in town when Kane was killed. Molly probably told him about her planned meeting with Kane.

"Thanks for calling. I'll let you know what I find out."

"I'd appreciate it. I know I don't have to add to it now that it's been accepted for my degree, but I feel like I need to add a new chapter to my thesis. Maybe this will make it publishable and get me that position I've been looking for in academia." Beth sounded giddy. "Anyway, be careful and make sure you send Greg to do anything dangerous. I'd like to think you'll be around if Jim ever pops the question."

"I'll be there, I promise." I hung up the phone and gathered the blanket, water bottles, and Emma's water bowl and tucked them into my beach tote. "Let's go home, Emma."

I would have taken her with me to Bakerstown, but I didn't want to leave her in the Jeep when I went into the library to track down Maryanne's or Vince's history. I might wind up empty-handed. And if I did, I'd give Beth's tip to my brilliant husband and not mention that I tried to find out more. Besides, he was busy tonight.

I hurried home, made sure Emma was set for a few hours, then wrote Greg a note. *Heading to Bakerstown. Stopping by the store and the library.*

I grabbed my shopping list just in case.

I paused as I looked around the house. This was the point where Greg would say I stepped over the line and went investigating. However, Beth knew what I was thinking. The library wasn't dangerous. I wasn't heading to a remote cave or searching the ocean or mountain valleys for a friend. I was just visiting the university library to see what I could find on a couple of names.

That was my justification and I was standing by it. Besides, if he got mad, now he had to divorce me rather than just move out. I thought that gave me a bit more leeway. At least that was my hope.

I hadn't eaten lunch and I'd had cookies for breakfast, so my first stop in Bakerstown was the drive-in I loved. Bennie's Bop had incredible fish sandwiches with just the right amount of tartar sauce, soft buns, and perfectly fried cod. And the fries weren't bad. I usually ordered a large so I could share them with Emma, but since she wasn't here, I just got a small order with a large iced tea.

I ate my fries as I drove to the university parking lot, then demolished the sandwich. I guess I was hungrier than I'd thought. As I ate, I thought about Vince and Maryanne. Now that I suspected a connection, it made sense that Vince might have been the one to see the O'Dell kids in my shop this morning. Thank goodness Anya had arrived before I had to fight off the New Hope goons. Would they have resorted to violence? I was glad I didn't have to find out. I knew they carried sidearms because I'd seen them and Greg had been involved in approving the guards' concealed carry licenses. Roger had claimed that most of their guards never left the premises with a gun so they had only licensed a few of the members.

Was it because the others couldn't pass a background check?

All I knew was that both of the men who had come in with Maryanne and Mrs. O'Dell had been carrying. I'd seen the holsters on their belts.

Walking into the library, I felt nostalgic for classes. I'd finished up my MBA last year but I was a lifelong learner. I loved taking on new challenges. Now I understood the feeling that had kept Deek in school long after he'd gotten his degrees. He loved the energy.

Now, he got his learning fix by writing. He was always ordering and devouring new books on writing craft and marketing ideas. And the bookstore hosted not one but two evening writer groups.

I just needed to find my groove to fill my need to learn. Without going back to school for another degree. With the three I held now, I thought there might be enough letters behind my name.

I grabbed a spring-term calendar from the checkout desk, just in case. Maybe there were some community classes I could take. Or at least one. Learning new things made me happy. Which was probably why I was always sticking my nose in Greg's investigations.

Like today.

I made my way over to the periodicals section and logged onto a computer. I'd bought a community membership for access to the library after my student card expired, charging it to the business. I did a lot of reading about new books to order and marketing ideas for the bookstore. Most of those I forwarded to Darla for her to consider for the town festivals she loved to plan.

I looked up Vince's name and it came up with several links. In several states and for several reasons. Most were about investigations. He'd published several magazine articles on when and how to hire a private investigator. My phone buzzed with a text. It was from Esmeralda. *Not sure if you still want this, but I sent you a list of the closed cases involving Amanda's ex. I'm really glad she saw through him fast. A lot of women filed small claims on money he owed them. It's in your email.* I sent a quick *thanks* in reply and logged into my email on the server.

As I scanned the cases, I wondered if there was anything I could use to tie him to Maryanne. I'd print this out at home and go through them one by one, then see if I could get the final court records.

If nothing else, Amanda needed to be aware of the full extent of Vince's issues just in case he tracked her down again. He didn't seem ready to walk away from her. I'd say it was love, but I think he felt she was an untapped mark. Or maybe a challenge, since her son was in law enforcement.

There had to be some kind of thrill that came with lying to all these people. Making them feel something, then taking advantage of that connection.

All I knew was I wanted my new mother-in-law to be aware. What she did with that information wasn't my problem. Even though Amanda was smart, sometimes love got in the way of making the right decision.

I guess I had a new project now. Two, actually. Setting up the book club and finding out as much as possible about Vince Penn.

And I'd thought I was going to be bored.

Besides the articles he'd written extolling his amazing investigative skills, there wasn't much online about Vince Penn. He wasn't on Facebook or any other social media channels, so I decided to see what I could find on Maryanne.

Her online footprint was even more sparse. I already knew she didn't have a Facebook presence. If she wasn't listed in an article about the Matthews boys, she didn't exist. I went back to their wedding announcement. There were two pictures in the small-town paper. A shot of her and Roger, and one of their wedding party. Four attendants. The women weren't anyone I knew by name or by sight. Kane was Roger's best man. I could tell it was him even in the grainy picture, though obviously younger. The other man looked familiar. I glanced down at the article below the photos. The other groomsman was Vincent M. Penn. The bride's brother.

I'd found the connection. I sent the article to my email as well as Greg's and Beth's. Then I packed up my notebook and left the library. I still had time to stop by the store and get groceries before it started getting dark.

\* \* \* \*

I was putting the groceries away and wondering what to have for dinner when Greg came in the front door. I had just come downstairs from dropping things off in our bathroom. "Hey, I thought you were working tonight."

"Why aren't you answering your phone?" He opened the door to the office and glanced inside, then went to the small downstairs bathroom and did the same. When he came out, he headed to the laundry room.

"Did you lose something?" I called after him.

"Your phone?" he called back.

For a second, I couldn't remember where I'd last had my cell. In the library. I'd read Esmeralda's text. "It's probably in my tote. I left you a note that I was going to Bakerstown. I probably forgot to turn the ringer back on after I left the library."

I headed into the kitchen and pulled my cell out of my tote. I had five calls from Esmeralda, two from Toby, and three from Greg. I held it up for him to see. "I found it. Wow. I didn't think I was this popular. What's going on? Did you see the email I sent you?"

"About Vince? Yes. That's why I was trying to reach you. Roger Matthews came in today and told me he was concerned for his safety. That his wife had been acting strange and he didn't trust his brother-in-law." Greg got a soda from the fridge, then checked the lock on the back door. "Did you lock the doors when you went to Bakerstown? Was anything disturbed?"

"No, the house was fine." Now I was beginning to freak out. I put the ice cream away in the freezer.

"Everything okay upstairs?" He still had his hand near his gun.

"I just went into our bathroom to drop off soap and toilet paper. Why?"

He didn't answer. I watched as he went upstairs. I heard doors opening and closing and the squeak of the attic door. He was checking the entire house. When he came back, I'd put the kettle on to heat and sat at the table. "Do you want to tell me why you're searching the house like I have a boyfriend tucked away?"

He chuckled as he sat down. "That option was never on my mind. Anyway, Vince didn't leave town when we thought. Molly got a call from him earlier today. She called the station, worried that he was trying to track her down."

"Why all the focus on Vince? Your mom's home. I talked to Beth this morning. That's what sent me to the library. I wanted to find proof that Vince is Maryanne's brother." I'd already told him about the visit from the New Hope crew. "When the group descended on the shop this morning, it felt really creepy. They were trying to take those kids. Thank goodness Anya was on the ball."

"You said you were worried someone was reporting what he saw in South Cove to New Hope. Do you think that was Vince?"

I nodded. "I didn't see him outside, but then again, I wasn't looking. The kids were sitting by the window reading for most of the morning."

He finished his soda. "I'm heading back to the station. Esmeralda's looking up some of those cases she sent you. I'm interviewing the staff who were working at the Castle that Sunday morning. Maybe someone saw Tanner at the hotel during the time Kane was killed. And now I want to find out where Vince was at that time. It might just be Tanner O'Dell's lucky day."

Greg had good reason not to trust Vince Penn, but he didn't have any direct evidence that the guy had done more than beat up Molly. And maybe Amanda. Murder was a far cry from beating someone up.

Except Roger was now afraid of Vince. I wished there was some excuse I could use to go talk to him and Maryanne. But as I thought of the walls around the compound and all the men with guns walking around, I didn't really want to go inside all that for a social call.

After Greg left, I pulled up Esmeralda's email of court cases involving Vince and sorted them by date and place. Once I was done, I consulted my notes from the articles on the Matthews brothers and their ministry.

The comparison didn't match up perfectly, but more than 75 percent of the cases were in towns where the Matthewses had set up a church. Amanda was an outlier in Nebraska. What had led Vince there?

I put a potpie in the oven for dinner, then got my phone. I turned on the ringer, just in case Greg called again, then called my mother-in-law.

"Jill! I was just thinking about you." Amanda muted the television. "How is married life?"

"Just like it was before the wedding. Greg's working hard to get this investigation closed and I'm back at the shop since he took one of my baristas out of commission."

"Toby's such a nice guy. He loves both jobs." Amanda changed the subject. "So, what's got you up so late?"

I glanced at the clock. It was just seven here. "Oh, sorry, I forgot about the time change. It's not that late here."

She laughed. "You're right. I guess I'm still on West Coast time because I couldn't get to sleep tonight. I'm sitting in my bed watching a home improvement show. I want to redo my bathroom now. Make it more of a spa experience. Anyway, how can I help? Or are you just lonely after having us descend on you last week?"

"I was wondering. Where did you meet Vince?" I heard the effect of the question in her pause. "I know, it's hard to talk about, but it might be important. Was he living in Omaha when you met?"

"No. I'd gone to a women's church retreat on the Oregon coast. We were there for two weeks. It was lovely. One day I walked into town and got caught in a coffee shop by a rainstorm. I was just about to call for a ride when Vince offered to take me back to the compound. I'd seen him at the compound earlier. His church's men's group was helping with some landscaping that the retreat was having done. We started talking. Then he asked me out."

Amanda paused for a minute before starting again. "I hadn't dated since the boys' dad died. Vince seemed nice, like he had the same values as me. So when he asked for my number when it was time to leave, I gave it to him. Two weeks later, I got a call that he'd moved to Omaha."

"He followed you home."

Amanda sighed. "I thought it was romantic, not creepy. I should have told one of the boys, but I wanted to hold it close to see if there was something between us. We got married on a whim. And then he changed."

I could hear the pain in her voice as she told the story. "One more question and I'll let you get back to your remodeling show. Where was the retreat held?"

"Oh, it was a beautiful place. Right on the ocean. I heard they sold the property for a subdivision a few years ago. What was the name of the town that had that cute coffee shop?"

I held my breath as Amanda thought.

Finally, the name came to her. "It was Newport. Newport, Oregon."

I thanked her and told her that if she saw Vince, she shouldn't talk to him. And she needed to tell Jim or Greg if he called.

"Believe me, I've already closed that door." Amanda laughed. "I might be an old dog, but I can learn."

I took a picture of my Vince timeline and texted it to Greg. Then I ate my chicken potpie in front of the television as I watched a cooking show.

# Chapter 23

Vince was still in the wind the next morning. When I came downstairs, Greg had already made us breakfast. Then he told me that he was driving me to work. And he asked me to skip my beach runs unless I had another companion besides Emma.

I knew being careful wasn't a bad thing, but I hated telling my dog that we were staying home.

"Can you ask Deek to work the morning shift with you?" Greg asked as he followed me into the shop while I opened. I'd thought he was just dropping me off, but he'd turned off the truck and followed me inside. While I was making coffee he wandered through the bookshelves, checked the bathroom, and went into the back. I heard him going upstairs to check the hallway to Deek's apartment. Now, he was sitting at the counter, checking his email on his phone while I made him coffee.

"Maybe if it gets slow. I'll have commuters soon. It's Friday. Everyone wants a specialty coffee on Friday." As I handed him a travel mug, two of my regulars came into the shop. "See?"

"If it gets slow, please have Deek come down early. I'm concerned about Vince hanging around town yesterday." He pointed to the chocolate chip cookies. "One of those, please."

"Of course. And we don't know if Vince is even in town. We're assuming he was the one who called the compound. We don't know he did." I wrapped up the cookie, then leaned in to kiss him. "Go to work. I'm busy."

"Look at the lovebirds," a commuter named Selena said, grinning as she came up with a copy of a new release that had come out that week. "You make me hopeful for love."

"You'll find your perfect soulmate soon." I held up a cup. "A mocha this morning?"

She clapped her hands together and nodded. "I think you're my soulmate, since you know just what I want."

Greg laughed and headed out of the shop. He held the door open for several more customers as he left.

I hoped that having people in the store would make him feel better about my safety. I didn't want to face Vince. I'd end up saying what I thought of him and that wouldn't be good. I didn't control my tongue very well when I was mad. He'd used Amanda's love and vulnerability and tricked her into taking care of him. Love was hard enough when it was real. Sifting through all the frogs was a chore.

The door behind me opened about nine and I almost hit Deek with the pan I'd just emptied into the display case.

"Whoa, you're jumpy today." He pulled on the pan I was holding like a weapon. "I guess I should have announced myself."

"Sorry, Greg's got me seeing things." I released my grip on the pan and closed the display case. "You're not scheduled until eleven."

"Your dude called and asked if I could write down here." He glanced around the empty shop. "Something going on that I don't know about?"

"He's at the stage of the investigation into Kane's death where he sees zebras all over," I responded. When Deek stared at me, I added, "He's paranoid about everyone."

"And you tend to fall into finding the culprit. I get it." He held up his laptop. "I'll be over at my favorite table if you need me. I need words today. I've been slacking."

"I'm sorry he called. You don't have to write down here." I didn't want Deek to feel obligated to watch out for me.

Deek shook his head. "Sorry. The dude asked me for a favor. I'm becoming one of his favorites. I can't mess that up."

"You know he's not your boss, I am," I reminded him as he poured a cup of coffee to take to his table.

"Sure. Keep telling yourself that." He made his way to the table and got set up.

Honestly, I didn't mind the company. I kept looking out the window to see if Vince was staring in at me. I was as jumpy as Greg today.

When the morning stayed slow, I went to a table with my laptop and worked on next month's schedule. I didn't schedule myself, instead putting Toby into my usual slots. If he was still on the investigation and not able to work here, I'd fill in. If the investigation was still ongoing, there'd be no honeymoon. Except maybe Greg was doing the same thing with Toby's hours. I probably needed to warn my aunt that we might need help. Or Tilly was needing more hours. I'd talk to her.

As I played with the schedule, I thought about the two-week honeymoon. I was hoping that Greg had made reservations someplace warm where I could lie out in the sun and read. With great food. But with our need for flexibility, we were probably going to Nebraska to stay in his mom's spare room for two weeks. I loved Amanda, but I seriously wanted some sun.

I left the shop at eleven. Greg hadn't called or dropped in to take me home, so I started walking toward the house. A truck was parked in front of Antiques by Thomas. As I walked by, the truck's side door opened and someone jumped out.

A small scream slipped from my lips before I realized it was Josh Thomas. "You almost gave me a heart attack."

"Sorry, we've been waiting for you. Get in." He held his arm out.

"Did we have an appointment today?" I asked. Josh was an odd duck, but he'd been getting less odd since he got married. Maybe he'd left me a message that I'd missed. "Is this about the Winter Wonderland Festival next weekend? I told Darla to just bill us for our share of the costs. With the wedding, I couldn't commit any time to the project."

"It's not about the festival. Get in." He waved me into the truck. I looked inside and saw Kyle, Josh's store assistant.

"Hey, Miss Gardner, I mean, Mrs. King. Congrats, by the way." Kyle started up the truck. "Climb in."

"Don't tell me that Greg asked you to drive me home." Now I was annoyed. Greg was going to get a call from me when I got home. First, he'd chaperoned me to work, then called Deek, and now this?

"Kind of. I stopped by your house yesterday afternoon, but you were gone. So when I saw Greg this morning, he said to pick you up right after your shift. Should I have come inside the shop to gather you?" Josh held his hand out and helped me up into the front of the truck. "I thought this would be more efficient."

"Why were you at my house yesterday?" Now I was curious.

Josh and Kyle exchanged a look. Neither one of them answered my question.

"Why are the two of you grinning like that?" Had the world gone crazy?

Josh leaned out the window. "You'll find out soon enough. It's a pretty day for January, isn't it?"

"Josh Thomas, you owe me." I didn't want to get into specifics in front of Kyle, but he did owe me.

Josh ignored my threat.

"I should back the truck in, right?" Kyle asked Josh as we approached my house. My Jeep was the only vehicle in my driveway.

"That will work." After Kyle parked, the men jumped out and opened the back door. I walked over to see what they were looking at. The bedroom set Amanda and I had seen at the antique store was in the back, along with a new mattress set.

"What is going on? Did Greg buy this?" The bed was beautiful and reminded me of the furniture at the Castle.

Josh handed me an envelope. "Not Greg. He came over and approved it, but someone else bought the set. We would have had it set up Saturday night, but we had a delay on the mattress delivery. I thought you'd want all of it together. Can you open the door and move Emma to the backyard so we can get this set up? I told Mandy we'd be fast."

"Give me a second." I wasn't sure my bedroom was ready for visitors. I hurried and unlocked the door and sent Emma outside. Then I grabbed a basket and cleared out the drawers in the nightstands and anything sitting on the surfaces and put it in my closet. Then I grabbed another basket and emptied the clothes from the dresser.

We had another bedroom to put the extra furniture in, but it was filled with boxes. I ran over there as I heard someone coming upstairs. Maybe we could squeeze in the furniture. I swung open the door to find the room totally cleared of boxes and junk. "What the heck?"

"Surprise," a voice said from behind me.

I turned with my hands up in a defensive boxing stance. When I saw it was Greg, I let my hands fall. "What happened here?"

"Mom bought us that bedroom set you loved, so I cleaned out this bedroom to make room for the old stuff." He studied me. "You're okay with that, right?"

"I'm over the moon. It's just a shock." I hugged him.

"Well, tell Toby, Josh, and Kyle to get up here and we'll move out all the furniture. Then we'll bring up the new, or old, stuff." He glanced inside our bedroom. "Do we need to clean up anything?"

"No, I already cleared out the dressers and nightstands. I can't believe you set all this up without me knowing." I kissed him before heading for the stairs.

"I'm glad to know I can still surprise you with some things," he called after me.

As the furniture got moved and the new bedroom set up, I had a few minutes to read Amanda's note. I took it to the back porch so I could watch Emma as she supervised the activity by the fences.

*Dear Jill,*

*I'd address this to you and Greg, but he's already in on the secret, so I guess this is your gift. I saw how much you loved the bedroom set so I hope I didn't overstep. And if I did, Josh Thomas has told me he will take the furniture back and give you a credit in his store. Minus the mattress set. I hope you like it. If not, the mattress store has a 30-day return policy too. I've enclosed the paperwork.*

*I've also enclosed a letter that I found in my purse a few days ago when you brought it back from the mission. It's from Sherry to Greg. I haven't read it. I didn't know the letter was in there. I should have realized that she didn't come to Nebraska just to visit me one last time. I feel like those women who are used to carry drugs through customs. An emotional mule, right?*

*You can shred it or give it to Greg. It's probably a plea for him not to marry you, which has already happened. She didn't want Greg. She wanted Sherry's version of a new and improved Greg. I can see that you are in love with Greg just as he is, which is all I can ask from a daughter-in-law.*

*Thanks for being you. And enjoy the new furniture.*

*Amanda*

I tucked the note back into the envelope with the receipts and pulled out Sherry's letter. Now that I knew Amanda hadn't been aware of it, I felt better about our future together. I set it aside. I'd give it to Greg. I didn't need to know all it said, but he should have the choice to read it. In case it was an apology or maybe a check for his half of the money in a long-lost joint account that she'd closed.

I saw the book Kane had given me during the open house, *The Four Agreements*. He might have understood the power of positive thinking, but it hadn't saved him from being killed. I opened the book. I'd never read it. I wasn't much for rah-rah cheerleading, positive-thinking, self-help books. Deek handled those types of advance reader copies when we got them at the bookstore. I lived in California; I should be more open to magical thinking. I think it was pumped into the air vents of all the public buildings.

An envelope fell out as I opened the book. I frowned, checking to see if I'd grabbed Sherry's letter with the book. Her letter was still on the table.

I took the letter out of the envelope and read the first line.

*If you're reading this, I'm probably dead.*

I finished reading the letter that Kane had written to me, then smuggled out with his gift of the book. Kane hadn't been in charge of the large security team. Neither had Roger. Maryanne was running the show over at New Hope. Kane had become a liability. He wanted out.

I held the letter up and hurried into the kitchen. The men were gathered in the living room, talking.

"Jill, the bed's ready for sheets and stuff, but I've got to get back to the station." Greg pulled me into a hug. "Thanks, Josh, Kyle, and Toby, for helping get that installed."

Josh's phone beeped with a text. He started walking to the door as he read it. He turned at the doorway and waved to Kyle. "Sorry, it's Mandy. We need to get back to the shop. We've got a guy with a truckload to sell."

Toby must have ridden to the house with Greg because he didn't leave with Josh and Kyle.

"Greg, you need to read this. I think Maryanne and Vince killed Kane." I handed him the two envelopes. "And there's a letter from Sherry that she gave your mom."

* * * *

Darla got the exclusive for her newspaper, but Beth came back to town to help with background information. Kane and Roger were both being manipulated by Maryanne and Vince. Kane told them he was changing some of the covenants of the church. He wanted to become more mainstream in their mission. That Sunday, Kane had thought he was meeting with Pastor Bill at the mission, not Molly. Vince had redirected Bill to talk to Molly. And then he'd met Kane and killed him.

When Greg got back to the station, he'd found Roger there, asking for protection. Vince was at the compound.

It took a while to get people prepped to take the compound from its security guards. The actual takedown had required several local law enforcement agencies as well as Anya and child protective services, so it was the next week before the actual arrest. We almost had a Waco-like standoff in our little town. Beth called as soon as the news cycle started reporting the full story.

The security team was already nervous since no one knew where Roger had gone. Losing a second prophet after one had been killed was one coincidence too far. They weren't willing to die for the cause. They could see the writing on the wall.

When Greg came home that night, he sank next to me on the couch. "It's over."

"Did you call your mom?" I turned off the television even though Emma was still watching the cooking show. We could start again it later. The joy of streaming.

"Beth said she'd call her. Beth thinks she has enough for an epilogue. And she's planning on sending out some feelers to publishing agents. So, fingers crossed for her. I'd love for this mess to turn into good for someone."

"I know one more person who's going to be excited for this to be over."

He looked at me, his eyes almost closed. He'd been up since four, coordinating the arrest. "Who's that?"

"Me. After you sleep for a week and get your prisoners to wherever, we're going on our honeymoon. So where are we going?"

He closed his eyes. He was beat, I could tell. I needed to leave him alone so he could sleep.

"Greg? Maybe you should go up to bed." Our couch was comfortable, but that new mattress was incredible.

"I never told you what was in Sherry's letter." He didn't open his eyes as he talked to me. "Aren't you curious?"

"A little. But you're still here. I assumed the letter didn't sway you to run back to her." I brushed his sandy hair away from his eyes. He did need a haircut.

"First she listed all the ways I'd messed up our relationship, then said she'd forgive me if I came back. I guess she dumped the new husband." He opened his eyes. "I'm so glad you're not a drama queen."

"Is this your way of telling me we're going to Nebraska?" My stomach dropped a little. I'd looked up the temperature and it had been zero degrees for the past week. With a foot of snow coming next week. "Why on earth would we go to Nebraska?" He stood and stretched. "I'm heading to bed. Plan on being out of town starting Saturday. Let Toby know he better not lose Emma."

I watched him walk upstairs. He still hadn't told me where we were going. But it wasn't Nebraska.

# Chapter 24

The white sand was hot on my bare feet, so I slipped into flip-flops before making my way down to the ocean. Emma would have loved running here, but I hadn't run all week. Instead, I'd been hanging out with Greg on the chaise lounges and walking. A lot of walking. Tonight, we were staying at the resort for an authentic luau. Yes, we were in Hawaii. Not the most original of honeymoon destinations, but I loved it. And Greg had known I would. Amy was going to be so jealous.

I walked into the water to cool myself off. We were on the resort's private beach, so I recognized some people from seeing them in the lobby. We'd been friendly, but we'd kept our distance. If there was a mystery hanging around our resort, we didn't want to know about it.

When I got back to the cabana, Greg looked up from his book. "I thought you were swimming?"

"Nope, I just wanted to cool off." I held up my book. "I'm just a few chapters from the end. I need to find out what happens."

"You didn't read ahead?" He held my gaze.

Smiling, I settled on my chair. "I'll never tell."

"Hey, I don't want to disturb you, but I got a call from the DA. Roger turned on Maryanne. He turned over surveillance that clearly showed Maryanne and Vince plotting against Kane and himself. He'd been next on the list for the brother-sister hit team." He leaned his head back and closed his eyes. "I can't believe Mom was married to the guy. Vince is a psycho and Maryanne's worse. Beth says their parents were strict and probably abusive, from what she can piece together from her research."

"Two sets of kids who found a home in their mutual dysfunction. It could be a Lifetime movie."

Greg opened his book. "Beth's getting some interest in her book about New Hope. It might just happen."

"She should call Deek and talk to him about his agent." I pulled out my phone and texted her a message, including Deek's cell.

After Greg went back to reading, I held my book open, but instead of focusing on the page, I thought about Kane and New Hope. He hadn't been the nicest person, but he'd had a vision of a better future. And he was a terrific salesman. Except he couldn't sell his family on changing their ways.

A man is never a prophet in his own backyard. Or something like that. Kane had been trying to change his ways, and that's what got him killed. Like with most murders, life wasn't fair, it was just life. Or, I guess, I should say death.

Not like the situations in the books I loved. I started reading again. Good conquers evil and that's the way it's supposed to be. A hard-earned happy ending for our fictional heroes and heroines. That's why I read. And as a bonus, tonight I got to go to a luau.

Greg and I had finally tied the knot. We had a home in a town we loved. And we had Emma. And friends.

Life was good.

# Banana Blueberry Bread

Dear reader,
When others were making sourdough during the pandemic, I made banana bread. Mostly because I hate wasting the bananas that I buy for smoothies. (And then forget about.)
I love making different versions of this bread for snowy winter days (like today, as I'm writing). Cutting thick slices of this to have with a cup of coffee is the perfect morning treat.
Lynn

Banana Blueberry Bread
Preheat oven to 350 degrees. Butter a loaf pan. You can use the paper from your stick of butter or spray with oil. I just like using butter because it makes the crust taste better.

In a large bowl (or stand mixer), cream together:
1 stick of butter
1 cup sugar
After scraping the bowl, add one at a time:
2 eggs
1 tsp vanilla
Scrape bowl. Then add:
At least two ripe bananas (I usually have three.)
Whisk together in a separate bowl:
1¼ cups flour
½ tsp salt
¾ tsp baking soda
½ cup oatmeal

Then add to wet mixture.
When mixed, add and fold into the batter:
1 cup fresh blueberries
1 cup halved walnuts (sliced almonds would also work)

Pour into prepared loaf pan and bake for 1 hour. Test the top center with a knife or toothpick. If the knife or toothpick has batter stuck to it, bake an additional 10 minutes and check again until knife or toothpick comes out clean.

# Acknowledgments

This is my seventeenth full-length book in the Tourist Trap series, and it all started with *All That Glitters Isn't Gold*. If you don't recognize the title, it's because that was my original title for *Guidebook to Murder*. I'd written the first book, then went on the agent hunt. I didn't find one. So when my first editor, Esi Sogah, then at Kensington, responded to my last-ditch effort to sell the book, I was over the moon. And scared to death.

The road to this book has been twelve years long. And since that first email exchange, I've worked with a lot of people on Jill's adventures. In many cases I don't even know their names. So I'll thank the ones I do know and send out lots of gratitude to my silent angels. Big thanks to Michaela Hamilton for taking on this long-running series when it and I were orphaned. As always, thanks to Jill Marsal for keeping the business side clean and running. And thanks to my husband for always supporting and believing in my dream. I wouldn't have leaped without you letting me vent and explore this life.

Are you over the moon about Lynn Cahoon?
Don't miss her popular Survivors' Book Club series!
Turn the page to enjoy the opening chapter of DYING TO READ, a
Survivors' Book Club mystery—coming soon from Lyrical Press, an
imprint of Kensington Publishing Corp.

# Chapter 1

Rarity Cole sat on the edge of her swimming pool and stretched from side to side. The weather had been perfect all weekend. She'd gone on hikes with her boyfriend, Archer, every day since Friday. Now the normal weekend was over and it was Monday morning. She had the entire day off. Her employees, Shirley Prescott and Katie Dickenson, had been taking turns running the store on Mondays since the first of March. Rarity had a two-day weekend now. She felt like she was back working in corporate marketing. She started making a mental list of to-dos but then realized nothing else would happen if she didn't swim.

"Workout first," she muttered. It had been her motto since January and one of her resolutions. She felt better when she moved first thing in the morning. She believed in the power of goals. They'd gotten her through her treatments for breast cancer and the complete overhaul of her life afterward. She'd moved from St. Louis to Sedona. She'd quit her corporate job and bought a bookstore. And broken up with Kevin. The man who was supposed to be her future husband thought she wasn't fun enough when she was fighting for her life.

Okay, truthfully, Kevin had broken up with her, but either way, it had been a big life change.

Now she lived in a three-bedroom cottage in Arizona with a pool she could use year-round. She loved running the bookstore and hadn't worn a suit to work in months. She had a new boyfriend, Archer Enders, who was planning on moving in with her next month. And she had a baby.

Oh, not a human baby. She had Killer, a tiny Yorkie who had a huge attitude. And an even bigger heart.

Killer was sitting next to her watching the water and the yellow ducky float that also served to disperse some of the chemicals in the pool. Rarity leaned down, kissed the pup, then dove into the water.

When she got out, her phone was ringing. She hurried over to answer the cell phone that she'd left on the deck table. Looking at the display, she smiled. "Hey, baby, how are you?"

"Baby, huh?" Archer sounded amused.

"I figured I needed to up my sweet talk since we are moving our relationship to a new level." Rarity wrapped a towel around her and sat at the table. Killer followed her up on the deck and lay near the French door that led to the kitchen.

"Okay, I guess it works. I called to let you know I got a late afternoon hike today, so dinner's out. Sorry."

"Do you just want to move it to later?" Rarity asked.

A pause on the other end of the line made her think she'd lost him.

"Archer? Are you there?"

"I'm here. Sorry, I'm slammed. I can't make it later either. Look, I'll see you Tuesday night after your book club. We'll talk then." Archer ended the call.

Rarity set down the phone and looked at Killer. "Your friend Archer is being weird."

Killer stood and barked at the door.

"Ready to go in?" Rarity asked, standing.

Killer barked again and ran in a circle.

"I've got a lot of things to do anyway." Rarity wished she'd said that to Archer, but she wasn't used to playing games with him. If he was too busy to see her, there was a good reason. She just had to believe him. He wasn't Kevin.

\* \* \* \*

Later that afternoon, she'd just come back from a run to Flagstaff when a knock sounded at her door. "Come in."

Terrance Oldman, her neighbor, poked his head in the door. "Hey, Rarity. I saw you pull in. Did you get me some of those sausages from the store?" She held up a package. "Two pounds, just like you asked. I could have brought them over."

"I thought I'd come over and see if I can be helpful." He tucked the sausages into an empty bag, then grabbed the milk and juice and put them away in her refrigerator. They worked together in silence until all the groceries were put away.

Rarity held up a packet of salmon. "I'm planning on grilling this tonight if you don't have dinner plans."

"I thought Mondays were date nights with your guy." Terrance sat down at the table. He'd pulled out sodas, one for him and one for her.

"Archer's busy." She hoped the snark wasn't obvious in her voice. "So I decided to cook. I'm doing a risotto with it."

"Sorry, my dance card's full tonight. The guys down at the vet hall have a standing poker game. We do it on Mondays so Drew can come. If you have a police officer sitting down with you, you're less likely to be busted for illegal gambling."

"You're bad." Rarity smiled despite herself. "Hey, can you watch Killer tomorrow? It's book club night."

"Of course. We'll go over to my house and watch a movie. He's partial to Marvel superheroes and you only have channels that show DC superheroes." Terrance leaned down and picked up Killer with one hand. "You can retrieve him whenever your club's over."

"As long as I'm not interrupting your bonding time," Rarity clarified. "So, I haven't seen a lot of you these last few weeks. Staying inside?"

"I have a job." Terrance rubbed Killer's neck and the little dog melted into him.

"Really. The neighborhood watch wasn't keeping you busy enough?" Terrance patrolled the neighborhood with a bunch of retirees who called themselves the Gray Patrol. Break-ins had dropped to almost zero in the neighborhood. Drew Anderson was using the group as an example to other neighborhoods on how to lower crime. It didn't hurt that most of the guys in Terrance's patrol team were ex-military who had come to Sedona to rest when they'd retired. Then they'd gotten bored.

"I wanted a little more. I'm a handyman over at Sedona Memory Care. They've been having trouble keeping their security system online. Someone keeps turning it off, so I'm there to stop it." He didn't look up at her.

"Sedona Memory Care. Where George lives?" George Prescott was Shirley's husband and a patient. He'd forgotten most of their time together now, but Shirley still visited almost daily. "Are you crazy?"

"Rarity, I swear this isn't because of Shirley. Or if it is, it's for her. If George gets out and hurts himself or others, she'll be devastated. I can't turn my back on this. They need me." Now he did look up and meet her eyes. "Besides, he's fighting with the assistant director. George seems to respond to me. We're friends."

Rarity stared at Terrance. "You realize that's all kinds of messed up."

Terrance was in love with Shirley. They'd started hanging out last fall, but she'd ended their friendship when Terrance made it clear he wanted more. Still being married to George, who was alive but not really there, Shirley couldn't deal with the feelings she was having for Terrance. It felt like cheating. Even though they hadn't done anything, even a good-night kiss. In Shirley's mind, she was married. And that was that.

Now, Terrance was not only working at the nursing home where George lived, he'd developed a friendship with the man.

"I know, but I can't step away now. The nursing home needs me to find out why their system isn't working before someone winds up missing or worse." Terrance sighed. "And when he remembers me, George is kind of a cool guy. I can see why Shirley loves him."

"Oh, Terrance. That's so sad." Rarity squeezed his hand. "Do you want a cup of tea?"

He laughed and stood. "Nope, I've got laundry to finish before I head out to the game. Having a real job again keeps me busy. And I'm going to grill a couple of these bad boys"—he held up the sausages—"for dinner before I go. Sorry I couldn't fill in for your guy tonight."

"No worries. I haven't finished the book club selection yet anyway. I need to at least skim the rest of it before tomorrow. Shirley's caught me too many times not having read the book." Rarity walked him to the door and watched out the window as he crossed the lawn between the two houses. Terrance Oldman was a good man, but he was playing with fire with his new job. Hopefully, he'd get the security system fixed before Shirley caught him at the home. Otherwise, Rarity thought, he was going to get an earful.

Shirley could be opinionated.

Rarity glanced at the to-do list she'd made this morning. She'd already crossed off shopping and a swim. Her finger stopped at cleaning the house, then she looked at the next item, finishing the book. She sighed and went to the bedroom to strip the sheets so she could get them in the laundry. Cleaning needed to be done. She was in a bad mood anyway. She might as well make the best of it.

\* \* \* \*

The next morning, she arrived at the bookstore just a few minutes before nine. Without Killer walking with her, she was able to leave the house a little later. The dog always had to stop for a smell, or a hundred, as they walked. The two businesses on either side of her, Madam Zelda's Fortune Telling and Sam's crystal shop, were still closed. They opened later. Drop-in traffic didn't start until late morning, sometimes after lunch. Especially during the beginning of the week.

Katie Dickenson hurried down the path and followed her into the bookstore. Katie was working on her master's at Northern Arizona in Flagstaff, but a lot of her classes were in the evenings, so she had time to work at the bookstore. "Hey, I was hoping to get here first. The store was slammed yesterday. I didn't get all the closing tasks done before I had to leave for class. I hope you're not mad."

"You should have called me." Rarity held the door open for her. "You would have saved me from housecleaning."

"I figured you were out with Archer. I saw his truck go by the shop about three yesterday. Didn't you guys go hiking?"

Rarity started turning on lights. "We went Friday, Saturday, and Sunday. My calves are still killing me. But I was home on Monday. Next time you get swamped, just call. If I can't come in, I'll tell you."

"Sounds reasonable. Anyway, the kids must have been out of school because I had several families who showed up just after lunch. We seriously need to restock the kids' section. I think they might have emptied it out." Katie tucked her bag under the counter and opened an energy drink. "Where do you want me first? Unpacking boxes that came in? Or starting a book order?"

"Let's get everything out and then we can do the book order." Rarity looked around the bookstore. It looked normal, but she knew Katie was a little OCD, just like her. She liked things to look perfect. Rarity only stressed about the back door being locked when she left. She'd put the store's temperature gauge on a timer so that was automatic. "How are the bathrooms?"

"Honestly, I didn't check." Katie brought out a box of books. "Do you want me to go clean first?"

"No, I'll do it. Watch the register while you're checking these in. I doubt we'll get any walk-ins this early, but you never know." Rarity went to the back room and pulled out the cleaning supplies, including a mop bucket that she filled with hot, soapy water from the sink. She moved to the men's first and quickly got that done. She propped the door open and taped a WET FLOOR sign on the doorjamb.

When she went into the women's, she found a book on the sink counter. She grumbled at the long-gone reader. "Clearly you couldn't see the PLEASE DON'T BRING BOOKS INTO THE LAVATORY sign."

She walked out to set the book on a table while she finished cleaning. She didn't recognize the title. And it looked older than what she sold. Maybe someone forgot their personal copy.

Rarity finished cleaning. After she'd taken the trash outside to the dumpster and drained, rinsed, and put away the mop and other cleaning tools, she went back to the front.

Katie was standing at the counter reading the book Rarity had found.

"So, what is that?" Rarity logged into her system.

"The book? It was on the table. There's an inscription in the front. 'To my best friend, I hope you enjoy Alice's adventures as much as I have over the years.'" Katie held the book open and showed it to Rarity. "I think this is a first edition *Alice in Wonderland*."

"That someone just left in the bathroom at a bookstore? I doubt it." Rarity reached for the book and checked the copyright page. 1865. "If this is right, the book is worth a lot."

"Like thousands?" Katie asked.

Rarity checked the binding and the outside of the book. "Maybe even more. Let's set this aside and see if anyone comes to claim it. They should know the inscription if they own the book."

"This is so exciting. I've never held a rare book before." Katie grabbed a pile of books that needed to be shelved.

Rarity went about her day, but the book kept nagging at her. Maybe she had another mystery for the sleuthing group to solve. And for the first time, it wouldn't involve a dead body.

That night at the book club, they discussed the selection they had read, *The Spy Coast* by Tess Gerritsen. Holly Harper had suggested it, and the conversation was getting interesting.

"I don't think it portrays old people in a bad light," Holly responded to a statement that Shirley had just made. "The main character is almost in a relationship with her farmer neighbor. Or she would be if she'd get over losing her husband."

"Sometimes, people don't just get over those things," Shirley countered. "But I guess I wondered why a bunch of spies would settle in a small Maine community. It didn't seem realistic."

"Did you read the author's notes in the back? She lived in a town where that happened. I guess if Thanos can have a retirement plan, so can James Bond." Malia Overstreet jumped into the discussion. "I really liked it, but it was hard to follow why the one woman was running in the first place."

"I think the author added that character to give you more than one person to focus on." Rarity hadn't liked that the opening scene was not focused on the main character either. "What did you think of the local police chief?"

"I would have solved the murder before I let that jerk from the state police take over," Sam said.

"Sometimes that's not an option." Jonathon Anderson was in town and had called to see what we'd be reading. He was an ex-cop who had started his career in Sedona, then moved to NYC to work when his kids got out of high school. Now he and his wife, Edith, lived in Tucson near their daughter and only grandchild. His other child was a detective here in Sedona and was dating Rarity's friend Sam. Again. "When a different agency with jurisdiction over a crime comes in, you have to step back and let them work. And that character was a jerk."

Sam smiled sweetly at Jonathon. "I'm so glad you agree."

Rarity held up a hand. "Okay, let's take a short break, then we'll finish this up and choose next week's book."

Sam bolted for the ladies' room and Jonathon moved toward Rarity. "Maybe I shouldn't have come. It seems like Sam's still mad at me."

"She'll get over it. She was the one who wasn't sure if she wanted to continue her relationship with Drew. The fact that Edith set him up on a blind date when he visited you guys in Tucson wasn't your fault. I know she just wants the best for him."

Jonathon chuckled. "I have to disagree. Edith wants more grandchildren. If she'd known Sam and Drew had started seeing each other again, she wouldn't have invited Heather to dinner. Drew keeps his relationship status close to his chest. I need to go say hi to Shirley and see how George is doing."

Rarity watched as he made his way over to the treat table, where Shirley was getting more cookies out of her carrier. The woman could bake. She thought about going to talk to Sam, but she decided to stay out of it. Drew and Sam were dating again. She didn't want to jinx it.

They ended the club and everyone but Shirley had left the bookstore by the time Archer arrived. He helped Shirley carry things out to her car, and when he came back inside, Rarity was ready to lock up. She had put the rare book into her safe since no one had come by to claim it. Maybe she'd put up a sign on the community bulletin board.

She came out of the back room after checking the lock and gave Archer a kiss. "I thought they'd never leave."

He pushed her hair out of her eyes and took her keys. "Are you ready to go?"

"Killer's at Terrance's, so we need to stop and get him. Are you staying for supper? I have some clam chowder in the fridge." Rarity hoisted her tote over her shoulder and followed him outside.

"I'm not sure. Look, we need to talk." Archer locked the door and handed her back the keys. "I'm not sure that I should move in with you."

# About the Author

*Photo by Angela Brewer Armstrong at Todd Studios*

*New York Times* and *USA Today* best-selling author **Lynn Cahoon** writes the Tourist Trap, Cat Latimer, Kitchen Witch, Farm-to-Fork, and Survivors' Book Club mystery series. No matter where the mystery is set, readers can expect a fun ride. Sign up for her newsletter at www. lynncahoon.com.

# The Tourist Trap Series

## Read where all began...

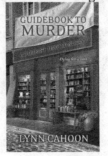

## Enjoy the complete series!

Guidebook to Murder * Mission to Murder * If the Shoe Kills * Dressed to Kill * Killer Run * Murder on Wheels * Tea Cups and Carnage * Hospitality and Homicide * Killer Party * Memories and Murder * Murder in Waiting * Picture Perfect Frame * Wedding Bell Blues * A Vacation to Die For * Songs of Wine and Murder * Olive You to Death * Murder in a Tourist Town * Rockets' Dead Glare * A Deadly Brew * Santa Puppy * Corned Beef and Casualties * Mother's Day Mayhem * A Very Mummy Holiday

Kensington Publishing Corp.
Joyce Kaplan
900 Third Avenue, 26th Floor
US-NY, 10022
US
jkaplan@kensingtonbooks.com
212-407-1515


The authorized representative in the EU for product safety and compliance is

eucomply OÜ
Marko Novkovic
Pärnu mnt 139b-14
ECZ, 11317
EE
https://www.eucompliancepartner.com
hello@eucompliancepartner.com
+372 536 865 02


ISBN: 9781516111756
Release ID: 150189379

Printed in the United States
by Baker & Taylor Publisher Services